# TAKING WING

## Dragonsigns – Book Three

## Ken Hughes

Windward Road Press

LOS ANGELES, CA

Windward Road Press
11923 NE Sumner St Ste 879426
Portland, OR 97250-9601

Publisher's Note: This is a work of fiction. Names, characters, places, and incidents are a product of the author's imagination. Locales and public names are sometimes used for atmospheric purposes. Any resemblance to actual people, living or dead, or to businesses, companies, events, institutions, or locales is completely coincidental.

ISBN paperback: 978-1-7350002-7-5

Book Layout © 2017 BookDesignTemplates.com
Cover © 2021 by Sleepy Fox Studio

Taking Wing/ Ken Hughes -- 1st ed.

To Taguhi
— own that voice!

# CONTENTS

# CHAPTER ONE

# DIGGING

Each blind step clattered in the mine's darkness, catching and shifting to save his balance again and again from the tricks of the rugged footing. Only the sheath of skein over Colin's body blocked out the impacts and let his guiding fingers scrape along the side to keep him moving.

Eric's footsteps had dwindled in the blackness ahead—*getting away!* But those sounds were swallowed by Colin's own steps, and the harsh shouts of the police behind him.

Even with Bea staying behind to explain. But Eric's latest victim was lying back there too, and the police blamed them for one murder already.

A muffled moan sounded in the darkness ahead. Colin risked flicking Bea's flashlight on.

The two homeless women and a man still lay in the tunnel. Their threadbare clothes looked as worn as the rocks now, where they showed through the heavy chains around them... and the smears of silver-green skein Eric had laid over them. Two were still straining in gagged agony, as the stuff slowly consumed more of their flesh to feed itself and grow. Sweat and fear hung thick over them.

Then Colin was crouching down beside those two, saying "Help's coming" and laying his hands on their skein before he wondered if he could control it. Bea had already saved the third of them.

*Let them go, stop, rest, now...* His thoughts pounded against the greenness with all the strength he could throw at it—it *had* to work.

Or the hunger in that skein could spread to his own.

But somehow their muffled grunts softened. They breathed easier, as the skein's feeding ended.

Colin forced himself to turn away and step past them—removing the skein now could start them bleeding. And Eric would do this or worse if he'd found where Colin's mother and sister were hiding, and Terri was too weak already. No, he could only leave these three to Bea and her fellow cops. He pulled away with his feet dragging.

Ten steps deeper in, the tunnel began branching. Left and right, but which side had he come up through? Nothing looked the same from this direction.

Light moved behind him. The police closing in.

Colin plunged into the left path. He switched his flashlight off and willed his skein to flow over it too, to *twist* at light and wrap him in cooling invisibility. But in the narrow shaft, the cops wouldn't miss the faint mirage-outline he'd still leave... and the infrared scopes they carried would pick him out easily. With those scopes to let them move in the dark, they'd be more invisible than him.

He pushed on, trying to keep his breathing steady. He still had enough focus to work the skein's stealth, but he was too worn out to rouse the better-than-human strength it could move itself with, that could have made it carry him. *But I still think I can fight Eric and all the skein magic he's wrapped in?*

Every step ground away more doubt, more of his excuses. No, the next time they met, he'd have to use the spell Eric had used on his prisoners, that would turn his skein to feed on him—*and rouse any skein I'm wearing too. Or else I take my own protection off, and try to survive getting close enough to land the spell's touch.*

It was one more reason he needed Bea, to let her strike with the spell while he grabbed Eric. And instead Bea was stuck back with the police explaining the corpse of Gardner Development's CEO, when their own Lieutenant Hoyle had ordered them to leave Gardner and the tunnels alone.

Eric's footsteps were long gone. He might be all the way through to the mine's other end by now, and heading for Terri.

The voices of the police behind Colin had gone still too. He tried not to think how IR-sighted cops could close in and get a glimpse of him at any moment, all hidden in the blackness.

A quick flash of his light ahead caught the tunnel giving way to broader shadows.

He stopped at the rim of the strange cave basin, that this shaft and the opposite tunnel both reached into. Down at the bottom lay the pile of rocks and the new stones he and Bea had dislodged when they came through here.

And under that...

He needed an edge against Eric, and here it was. They'd left it there before to keep its secret, and Eric must have been too busy with his "experiments" to follow up his suspicions about the mine. But now Colin was alone and Terri needed him stronger...

Or Eric could be watching right now. Colin played the light around the cave, but he saw no glimpse of his enemy. Even a near-invisible figure would have shown up as a halo-outline to him, with the skein over his eyes. And he was losing time.

Colin trotted and slid down the basin's side. It was still hard to believe, that under those rocks was the source of their fight with Eric, and incidents going generations back—maybe why the doomed mine had been dug at all.

He slid a rock aside, and another. Until he saw it.

Glinting in his light, a hint of green. All clinging to what they'd seen were long, winged bones of a dead thing that had to be a dragon.

Colin reached into the rocks. *Bea had apologized to the remains of the beast when she'd taken a fragment...* Now he strained and pulled at a whole armful of the dragonskin they'd known as "skein."

It lay still. He pulled and willed it to come loose and join him, and the great fleshy mass of it never stirred.

Colin clenched his fingers, focused his need. Disturbing this creature wasn't right, but he needed its strength or Eric would only keep killing...

*I'm worn out. I can't even make my own thin sheathe carry me, and I want to make this mountain of it respond?*

*Focus.* He dug into his need and forced the doubts and the aches from his mind. There was only clear, cold purpose, and every moment he'd spent controlling the skein and facing down Eric... and he needed it now, his strength had to be enough... but the skein only clung in place...

Footsteps. Quick, guarded footsteps spilled through his concentration, coming from what had to be the tunnel behind him. The police.

Colin let the skein go, defeated. All he could do was fall back and protect his family, and not let the cops slow him down. Softly he set rocks back in place to cover the gaps in the cairn.

Two quick flashes of his light let him pick his way up the far slope, to the opposite tunnel. His feet on the stones were too loud.

He scrambled into the shaft, part of him bracing for some crushing punch out of the darkness—it would be just like Eric to hang back and catch him at a secret again. Instead he heard a low *come on* back where the cops closed in. Colin flicked his light on and headed away, anything to draw them on past the rocks.

One step after another, he rushed on through the cramped tunnel. There'd be so many more steps ahead just to get back to town. And Eric would only be pulling farther ahead.

Colin jogged on. *Think of Terri—my sister's broken body survived for years in Eric's captivity, while he tried using skein to heal her.* She'd never lost her defiance, and now Eric could be on his way to take her back.

And Zara—*my mother's turned all of her tireless inspiration that's held the neighborhood together, into getting help for Terri.* And they were both alone with the corrupt Lieutenant Hoyle, them and Terri's nurse, and even she'd been part of Josh Gardner's conspiracy to control Eric.

Now Eric had killed Gardner, and he sounded more unpredictable than ever.

More footsteps echoed behind him, farther back now. Had Bea's explanations and the skein-mangled prisoners slowed the cops down at all?

The shaft pinched in ahead, the narrow stretch he remembered. He wiggled and scraped through it, the skein saving him from losing skin. *Skein, skin—how could we not guess that was what it always meant?*

Then he stepped out into the open air.

A cooling breeze flowed over the high hillside, with the sound of birds drifting within it somewhere. Still evening, still the long summer evening, even though his time in the mine had felt like years.

And down the hill stretched the whole long, dusty way back to the roads and then the town of Rayo Hill. Colin's feet dug into the earth, one well-braced step down at a time.

Then he paused to glance back. Around the broad, rugged side of the hill's crest would be the other mine entrance. He could still come around behind those cops and keep an eye on Bea...

That *kiss,* in the mine, after everything they'd been through together. *How can I leave her back there now?*

But, it was her choice to stay and explain to them, cop to cop. And if those IR scopes got a glimpse of him lurking around, he'd only make it worse for her.

He looked at the slope down again. There were aches in his muscles that wanted nothing more than to turn and watch, argue, fight, anything but begin the long way back. And either Eric already knew where Terri was and he was closing in, or they were still safe—did this choice even matter?

"...*careful* with..."

A distant shout, not quite swallowed by the tunnels. Bea's voice. And that warning sounded more concerned, angry, than in danger herself—probably watching the cops handle Eric's victims.

Bea was fine, for now.

He started down the hill. He'd messed up Bea's life in so many ways... but right now his family needed him first, and Eric was still out there.

* * *

The Bacara Hotel looked *mockingly* still, in the deepening night. A single police car sat out front—too few to mean Eric had rampaged through here. And yet, more neighborhood cars clustered in its parking than Colin had seen since they'd made it their safe house.

He tightened his will's grip on the *pull*, the magic shifting that the skein could exert on the light around him to blur him from sight. He crept in the familiar back door.

So, Gardner and Hoyle *hadn't* told Eric where to find Terri? The relieved thought pushed through the exhaustion in his head. Terri might either be back at the hospital or else their drugs hadn't put her at risk at all, and that could leave this place quiet—

Then he heard the voices. A murmur of sounds together, half a dozen or more, and then he turned the corner and saw them.

"Just let us see Zara!"

"Is Terri alright?"

Clarence, Dr. Maza, the del Toro brothers... not quite a crowd, but his mother must have called some of her most loyal and influential friends down here. The two uniformed cops needed their fiercest glares to keep them away from the doors of the suite.

Colin grinned. Did Hoyle really think he could keep Zara da Costa a prisoner here?

A plump woman stood behind the police, and they kept one eye on her as she cringed back against the wall. Nurse Setter's fingers were twisting a necklace that peeped out from under her coat, more frightened than ever—she should be, when she was the one Gardner had used to drug Terri for his threats.

All of them stood on the far side of the suite's doors, except one cop stood watching Colin's side. That left the space around the doors the eye of the storm.

Colin edged toward them, sidestepping beside the wall. He'd be just a faint glint of light to them, some odd reflection that barely moved. The cop he passed never even glanced over.

The taller officer ahead looked at his partner. "You think they really got Simms?"

*Bea?* Colin twisted toward them.

"Maybe. The thing is, will Hoyle get her out of it this time?"

Colin leaned closer.

The second cop's head turned, moved to follow his motion.

Colin froze. The officer blinked, turned back to the people ahead.

There it was, the same problem. Hoyle had refused to tell his men about skein and actual invisible intruders, so the police kept looking past what could be glimpses of real danger. And yet if word did get out, how many other people would swarm in to abuse the skein's power?

Colin moved back to the suite door, and sank down to huddle on the floor, down below eye level. With his ear pressed against the door he could just catch the low, sharp voice inside:

"Prisoner. Ms. da Costa, you told half the town my lieutenant was holding you *prisoner?*" That gruff voice was Commissioner Walters, a model of half-leashed anger.

"For days it was protective custody, but then Lieutenant Hoyle called it reviewing our knowledge of the case here. He turned out to have his own agenda."

The calmer voice of Colin's mother was swallowed by a ripple of the crowd outside. Colin tried to think; if Zara was there, it meant Terri was still there too, and safely recovering from whatever drugs they'd slipped her. Everyone was safe.

"You may have misunderstood," added another, smoother voice. *Hoyle.* Colin's fists squeezed—Walters let the traitor in there, still?

"Tony Hoyle is an honest, valued member of this department," Walters said.

*Liar! This afternoon you ordered Hoyle to come see you, and he defied you, all to keep squeezing us for Gardner's schemes.* But now the commissioner was just closing ranks to protect his own.

"I'm afraid it's not so simple as that." Again Zara's voice was the quietest in there, and Colin lost it in another murmur of sounds in the corridor.

"You think you can just accuse him?" Walters kept his tone tamped down low, when the pressure within it must want to blast the words to the rooftops. "Lieutenant Hoyle *was* reviewing your information, and he's led the hunts for the cop-killer. You're spouting crap about him staking out the hilltop or holding you prisoner—you think you have the right?"

"I heard the lieutenant, acting on the same orders that Nurse Setter was—"

"You *heard?*"

"Taking his instructions by phone." Zara's steady, unhurried answer brushed Walters and his intimidation aside. "I had to pose as unconscious to hear it. I'm sure the doctors will confirm that there was something slipped into my water glass, as well as Nurse Setter slowly drugging Terri—and we can only hope that didn't do lasting damage to my daughter."

*Wait, the doctors* did *take Terri away? And Walters was still keeping Zara here?* Cold fear spiked through Colin's rage.

"I tried to help you and your family," Hoyle said, with what must be a smirk bending the edges of his voice. "I set you all up here where you'd be safe. I even indulged your son's concern about Terri's kidnapper. I tried to keep an eye on him, in fact I bent over backward... unprofessional, but I sympathized. Even after he and Eric Rowe were the only ones at several killings—"

"Colin is not your killer. But *he knew* about Eric first, and Josh Gardner too." Zara's voice rose as she said it, louder, loud enough that outside—

"Gardner? What about Gardner?" A surge of sound came from the people outside. Clarence and two others pushed forward.

The two cops blocked them, muttering "Please step back" and the third cop moved past Colin to join in. If their orders were to give Walters privacy, it was a losing battle, when Zara could "be overheard" any time she wanted to remind them she had friends outside.

And the cops had left the suite's second door unguarded. Colin slipped back to it.

He pulled the key card out from under his skein—and Nurse Setter stared, as it "appeared" in the air. But the others only glanced back as the door swung open, and Colin closed it behind him undisturbed.

After all, it had to be just someone inside peeking out and already back in—what else could it be, with nobody in the corridor? Colin found himself *wishing* they'd spot him, if it finally got their eyes open for when Eric made his next move.

Now he slipped from this room to the suite's other one. He eyed the three people ahead, and crouched the blur of his body down behind a well-padded chair.

*"We will* investigate Nurse Setter."

That broad-shouldered shape had to be Walters, staring down at Zara and folding his doughy arms as if he could smother her curiosity and his own anger with the same compressed motion. Lieutenant Hoyle stood at his side, lean and silent, standing as close as if his schemes were already forgiven.

Walters went on "And I'll look into what Hoyle's done and the rest. You should go and see your daughter. And, I'm sure your son is innocent, but we can clear all of this up better if you stopped involving yourselves."

*Until the next time Eric comes after us? Does Walters think he can cover this up?* But the commissioner simply waved her toward the door.

Zara didn't move. She only smiled back, and the necklace around her throat—the one Nurse Setter's imitated, he realized—gleamed as she faced him. "Of course you can. Making implications is easy, and you'll find that the hard facts are that Eric Rowe is fixated on this family among other things, and that he keeps evading you. Somehow," she added, rather than talking about the skein.

The last person they'd trusted with that secret had been Hoyle.

"The facts are that it was Colin, and Detective Bea Simms," she went on, "who found Terri, and rescued Jessie Chapman and more. And tonight it was Lieutenant Hoyle who tried to cover up what Josh Gardner and Eric were doing at the mine. I'm certain talking to his men will prove that, and talking to Nurse Setter will tell you more."

"That is *enough,"* Walters growled. He leaned over Zara, and Colin felt his own fists tighten.

Zara's smile didn't waver. "If you want. But I do hope you have some kindness for the nurse. She was terrified by one of Eric's attacks, and now someone else has bullied her. I'm certain she'll be glad to come clean if you give her a glimmer of hope."

Walters blinked. "You... you're worried about... Well, we'll look into it," and he cleared his throat. "But I mean it, this department does not appreciate being bullied by mobs. We can't give you special treatment, Ms. da Costa."

"It's Zara. And I'm not asking for any—"

"Aren't you, *Zara?* Hoyle's been guarding your daughter like it's the only way to catch the killer. I say if we stopped pampering you we could have run Eric Rowe down days ago!"

It could have been the steady stream of denials and contempt that Walters poured out.

Or just the idea that Eric was no threat.

But the next moment, Colin found himself by the window and smashing his invisible fist through it, savoring the harsh sound of breaking glass.

Walters and Hoyle spun around in shock, grabbing out guns as Colin dropped to the floor. Of *course* they left Hoyle his gun, even now. Zara ducked backward, then a frown crossed her face.

"That's... no gunshot," Walters breathed. "Some bastard threw a rock in here—but there should be more glass—Hoyle?"

The lieutenant was backing away, gun shaking in his hand. Fierce satisfaction pounded in Colin's head; at least Hoyle *did* remember how any sound could be an invisible Eric closing in.

*I wanted... I guess I wanted them on alert again...*

*Or I could stand up and reappear, and tell Walters what he's really up against.* And go back to trusting a cop with the skein's secret, and praying he didn't sell them out?

One motion, one word, one release of his skein, would start that again.

*I can't.*

"It... it's not safe here..." Hoyle said.

"I know." Walters holstered his gun. "Ms. da Costa, you go see your daughter, and think before you start any more trouble."

Just like that, he mentioned Terri—if Eric were listening he could follow them right to her. Colin gritted his teeth.

Walters added "The lieutenant and I have someone else to see."

# CHAPTER TWO

# RUNAWAYS

The cop they sent off beside Zara shot nervous glances at her supporters outside, but she only led him along with a few reassuring motions. Colin couldn't even slip in and whisper to his mother, only scramble after them and then move down the night street watching the police car pull away. Only a few other cars moved on the night streets now.

He'd jogged half a block before he realized where they must be headed. Of course it was the Lovato, the same hospital they'd kept Terri in before hiding her in the hotel. Of *course* they were back to that—Terri was still hurt, and Eric could still take his invisible time choosing a way to get at her.

Colin's eyes ached with the strain of holding them open. He might be keeping watch over Terri for hours, days, trying to still be ready when Eric struck next. His last answer to that had been to trust Hoyle, and instead Hoyle went to Josh Gardner... and the lieutenant was *still* there with the cops trying to pin murders on Colin. *This time I can't even let them see me.*

He trotted on down the sidewalk, weaving around the few people out before they could walk into him. The idea floated in his mind to slow, to reconnect his phone's battery and call Zara, but Hoyle's people had detected that phone before.

Instead he made his way to the hospital.

He knew the night crowds and the wide, cream-colored corridors here, the brisk compassion of the staff and the sometimes-suppressed fear of the people who might bring someone in here after dark. Finding where they looked Terri over was even easier—Zara's friends were already here, sitting and pacing around the chairs outside a Visitors Restricted door. Zara herself would be somewhere beyond there, no matter what the visiting hours were.

"How'd Rowe get his hands on her *again?*" That was one of the del Toro brothers, slumped in a chair.

Clarence said "Not him. It was that cop, locking them all away..." The old man's voice faded and he glanced up toward where Colin watched.

Colin froze, waiting for them to ignore the odd flicker standing in the corner.

"The nurse." An older woman—what was her name?—shook her head. "Eric must have terrorized her and made her do it. If it was Eric at all. But there's no way in hell it was Colin, no matter what they say."

Her words were a small warmth after the many shocks of the day. Clarence sighed "You think the police will listen?"

Colin edged back up the corridor. Eric could be picking his way around the far side of this wing right now. *I should take a look, get to know the routes around here again... but I'm* tired.

He reached out to slump against the wall. His blurred hands cheated his grasp of distance, and he thumped against the side.

Eric had all the cards again. He could play his waiting game as Colin fought to stay awake, or he could smash right through him and kill anyone in reach again. He could have dragged Terri away long ago if she'd been strong enough to travel. Even that only made him more dangerous.

Colin looked around the corridor, watching for the outline of light his skein would show him if Eric crept up invisibly. But Eric could be anywhere, more people could be dying. He could be going after Bea—

she was the one who'd wounded him before. A chill ran down Colin's spine, then another.

He needed help, he needed allies who could track Eric down first... and Hoyle's lies had torn all that away. Bea still had evidence about that, if they'd even listen...

*I should go search the back corridors, I can't slow down now...*

A sharp footstep drew his gaze over to a uniformed cop, walking in beside Nurse Setter.

The woman's rounded form curled in around itself, and he saw her avoid the eyes of an intern they passed. A nurse who'd betrayed a patient.

"Please," she asked the cop. "Do I have to see her?"

" 'Fraid I've got my orders," the cop said.

Colin watched them approach, starting to understand who *her* meant. Sure enough, they walked past Zara's friends and on to the door where Setter's victim would be. Colin drew back again from trying to slip past all those eyes—*I should work my way around to Terri's bedside, or go chase after Eric, if there's even a way left...*

Zara stepped through the door. She walked with the same regal confidence she always carried in public, and her voice swelled to tell her friends "Terri's going to be fine. They tell me today won't set her recovery back even a week."

Cheers and cries of relief bubbled up around her.

"That woman they brought in?" Clarence asked. "Was that the nurse who—"

"Let's not talk about that now. I'd rather just be grateful to the hospital for their quick response..."

Colin stepped back, blinking his eyes clear. Just that motion probably drew another uncertain glance from the crowd, but he made his way to a small nook behind a flowerpot-laden counter, and crouched behind it out of sight.

First was releasing the twist of light that hid him, like prying some mental fingers loose from a suitcase he'd been holding up for hours.

Then the press of willpower that made the skein stir and slide up until the whole sheath of green had tucked itself out of sight under his cuffs and collar. *I should reek to high heaven, after marching around in anything that tight—I must be reshaping it to make it 'breathe' better.*

*It, the* dragonskin *I've been wearing…*

He stood up and walked out from the counter.

Here and there some staffers' eyes glanced toward him, whether it was his face's scars or his stumbling walk that drew their notice. The dark police uniforms were still rare enough to walk right past, if he made it quick. Zara and her people waited ahead.

The older woman at the back was the first to stare over. "Colin? Where have *you* been, Terri collapsed again!"

One of the del Toros added "They're saying you kill—" He cut off.

Colin winced, but he looked back to Zara, and *her* face was shining as she looked at him.

He said "Glad she's alright."

"She is," and Zara nodded—Terri's stabilizing was more than just what people needed to hear, then. Zara added "And you are too. Have you heard from Bea?"

"Not a word." He felt something catch in his voice, some small sign that things had changed between Bea and him.

*And… Zara and I just said everything we need to.*

"I should go," he added, voice hoarse.

Clarence snapped "Hold on, you just got here—"

Colin spun away. His last glimpse of his mother showed her face creased with sad understanding.

All because of Hoyle and his accusations, all to cover up the lieutenant's conspiracy with the dead Josh Gardner and Eric himself. The thought pushed Colin's feet along faster.

Sure enough, one doctor he passed swung her gaze away from him and reached for her phone. Of course Hoyle knew he'd be here, of course he had them watching for him. Colin kept walking on to step inside a supply room, out of sight.

He started the skein spreading over him as he heard a quick, police-sharp jog closing in outside—

his skein slowed, stalled out and left his arms half-covered with green—

it wrenched to life again and flowed out to cover him, to wrap him in protection and twist him from sight again. A breath later the cop flung the door open and looked right past him.

Colin held his place as the officer ran out and moved on. There was no point arguing the evidence with one of the uniforms, when he'd already missed a chance to talk to Commissioner Walters himself. And even then, they always wanted him sitting in cuffs while they kept asking the same questions, time Eric could use.

*And I still have to search this place.* He pushed himself out the doorway.

Walking along the corridor's side at a slow enough pace was easy. What was harder was to keep from drifting to a stop and staying there, and to keep his feet from some scuffing sound that would make people look at the "empty space" again.

But he passed several staff, and moved on toward the back of the wing and the different routes Eric could creep in here.

Any time Eric wanted.

While Colin just wore himself out standing watch.

*Maybe I have to risk my phone, if I could get Walters's own number and plead with him...*

Two cops turned into view ahead, walking toward him.

He edged back, but they weren't watching him or even moving faster than a stroll.

One was saying "No, it was a bit of fire at the Gardners."

The Gardner building? Colin strained his ears.

"Fire? Not a bomb?" the other said.

A young doctor swung his head toward them. "Bomb? Hold on, what bomb?"

"Nothing, sir," the cop said. "Just rumors, and shop talk, that's all. Old cases."

Sure, *nothing to see here.* Colin let the officers walk by and moved into step behind them, but they said nothing more.

The Gardner Development building... the last thing Josh Gardner had done was confess to Eric he'd kept all his information in the room with its old servers. Was that why Eric had already broken in there once, and why Dennis Fields died there? And now Eric finished the job?

Did that mean Eric was across town wiping out his partner's records on him, not even *trying* to reach Terri tonight? Colin clamped his throat tight to keep from moaning.

The two cops halted outside a doorway. "Trouble, sir?" one of them called inside.

Looking past them, Colin could just glimpse Walters and Hoyle— and *Bea*, her calm face a beacon in the crowd—all squeezed into the room, and a woman patient stretched out on a bed. Chairs and medical monitors stood heaped to one side there as if the rest of the room were more crowded still.

A young doctor in white stood beside them, almost vibrating in place. "No trouble, no trouble, I just mean we need to identify this substance—"

"We'll keep it safe," Walters rumbled. "I'll tell you when we're done." He nodded to the two uniforms.

They stepped forward and motioned to the doctor. He blinked, then let them lead him out. "You make it quick. I don't think I've seen anything like this..."

Colin stood flat against the wall and let the three pass by. Whatever Walters was doing, at least he'd brought Bea there as well as Hoyle— instead of locking her up based on whatever lies Hoyle was spinning.

A couple of steps closer let him peek around the doorway into the room. The patient there was one of the three, the three homeless people Eric had dragged to the mine to dissolve into more skein. All three lay there on the beds, pale and worn under their bandages, but alive. Their eyes were closed, or their heads kept turning away from the police, squirming uneasily under their attention.

Two more people were crowded in there: the frightened, silent Nurse Setter, and the cop who'd escorted her around before.

Walters stepped toward her, herding her toward the only male patient there—Wesley. And Walters asked him "So you woke up in the mine. And then?"

"I... I don't remember. Sorry. Just, pain." His voice was cracked but strong enough to be heard.

"You *have* to remember." Walters spun toward one of the women. His rough voice was softer this time, almost too low to follow. "You said you saw Detective Simms?"

"I guess... all fuzzy..." the woman croaked.

Colin shook his head. Did Walters think it would be easy, getting homeless, traumatized people to talk to the police—in front of this crowd of them too? And he had *Hoyle* lurking at the back of the group as if it hadn't been his own orders that had kept the police away from this outrage.

"We found you wrapped up in this stuff." Walters reached to a counter and scooped up a small plastic tub labeled *Hazard*. Two more cases stood on the counter. "Was this what burned you, or was it some kind of treatment for it? What is it?"

And he shot a pointed look at Bea, the one who'd known its secrets the longest and hidden them. She stood unmoved; of course she'd worked out her own reasons why holding out on the town's head cop was the least dangerous choice.

The patient mumbled "I... don't know..."

Walters grunted and twisted away. He yanked open the cabinet along the wall and shoved the case inside, then the other two. For a long moment he stood there staring at the shelves, and then he locked them with a tiny key.

And he pressed in on Nurse Setter with all his bulk to all but trap her against the wall. "These people were found beside Josh Gardner's body. We already know you were willing to drug your own patient. But can you tell me you can defend this kind of torture?"

She said nothing. Her head twisted, trying to look away from his glare, from the victims.

"Go on. You have something to say to them, *nurse?*" The last word burst out like a slap across her face.

She gasped, something that had to be "No…"

"What's that?"

Back behind them, Hoyle edged a step away, pale.

"Not… this. Not this," she said.

And the nurse twisted away to stare straight into the wall.

"He said someone was dying! He had medical figures, different pieces of the case, I don't know what condition he had but… And he said the patient I did have should be dead, she and her family were hiding the secret that saved her. *And,* he said that maniac would come back and kill me too! He said he would!"

"Who said?" Bea prompted. She knew, they'd heard all about those manipulations from the late Josh Gardner himself.

"Just, he!" the nurse said. "Or maybe she—all I got were emails. But they knew me. They said I had to push my patient, or this person would die, everyone would die. I… I told myself it was the only way," she added softly. "I didn't know it was *this*…"

She stopped. Shook herself.

"I, I think I want that lawyer now," she said.

*"Good,"* Walters snapped. "Someone else can tell you how much trouble you're in. You've seen how none of this is going away—now you can have some time in a cell to think what you've still got to trade. Go."

He waved, and the uniform who'd led the nurse around moved to take her arm. They started for the doorway.

Walters turned back to the three patients. "You three were wrapped in the same stuff we've seen on both our suspects—"

*"What?"* The cop beside the nurse stared, his pale face looking right at Colin leaning in the doorway, two feet away.

He lunged at him. Colin jumped back, somehow landing with just a soft clatter and holding the invisibility in place. The cop barreled out of the room, and Colin backed away up the corridor.

"What are you—" Walters roared, but the officer was already staring around and moving closer, and Colin turned and ran.

*He wasn't sure, he just saw something moving, he still didn't get a good look...* Colin made for the next corner, heard the cop pounding after him. Part of him thought, running must be some kind of reflex, when just stopping and showing Walters might still be the best chance to fix this. But he charged on up the corridor and slid around its corner.

Then he froze flat against the pale wall. One way or another, he'd know how much that cop had seen.

The officer burst around the corner, and kept going. He ran right past the "glint of light" against the wall and on up the corridor out of sight. Colin fought down a breath of relief.

Slowly he started back. He tried not to guess how long he could keep out of sight here—they weren't giving him a choice.

Walters, Hoyle, and Bea were out in the corridor, striding away from the patients' room. Colin closed in behind them, quick as he could keep his steps quiet. Where was Nurse Setter?

"...was *torturing* them," Bea was saying, a sharp not-quite whisper to Walters. "You know what the media would say... and I *thought* Hoyle was leading the effort to stop him. You can't let Hoyle do this—he was the one giving orders to cover this up, right as it happened!" She glanced around the corridor, then back to Hoyle.

"Not true—" Hoyle stopped to let a pair of nurses go by. "Mr. Gardner only said he wanted something in the mine, and that sounded unsafe…" He looked around again, and Colin froze behind them until he turned back.

Walters drew out a police radio. "Any news?" he said to it.

"Nothing," came the tinny response.

"Better a paper-thin excuse than none, Lieutenant?" Bea said. "You ordered your hand-picked officers out there to support the man who *bought* you. They were security to let him meet Rowe and not interfere—even when they heard screams. And you would have sent them in if Rowe turned against Gardner, except that didn't work out so well. The minute the commissioner asks your men some real questions, we'll see you're in this. Deep."

"Not. True," Hoyle said again. "I've been tracking Rowe for days. Don't you bitch at me because I think your boy da Costa may be as unstable as Rowe—"

Walters cut in "We're talking about *you,* Hoyle."

His foot stamped down hard as he halted his walk, and they all slammed to a stop there. He leaned his bulk toward Hoyle, trapping him against the wall the same way he'd cornered Nurse Setter.

"I've seen the video Simms found—I know Gardner killed that man in the basement, not this da Costa. It's the rest I don't get. You needed money? How much did it take? Where does this green goop figure in, to make you sell out and made him conspire with a murderer?"

Walters stopped, pulled out a key—the key he'd locked the skein up with. He eyed it a moment, then spun to look straight at Bea.

"Well?"

"I wish I knew," she said.

A perfect, straight-faced lie. That was Bea, as afraid of more people someday turning victims into skein as she was of Eric right now. And Hoyle could expose her denials in an instant.

"Oh, you *wish?"* Walters scowled. "You think you can cover your ass now, Simms? Maybe that da Costa woman will tell me more if I—
"

He broke off. *That* had to be a hollow threat, when he'd just seen how fast Zara's friends came to her rescue.

Instead, Walters held up the key again, turning it over in his fingers. "Somebody has to talk."

*"Somebody* has to bring Eric Rowe down," Bea said. "He's killed Josh Gardner and four cops, for starters. He held Terri da Costa prisoner for two years, and Gardner still tried to control him by targeting her again. You *know* the lieutenant went over to their side, and we still have a murderer out there. All I want to know is, are you going to let me run Eric down or not?"

"That depends." Walters turned back to Hoyle. "Are *you* a cop, or a traitor?"

"Sir!" Bea said. "You can't let him—"

"I *told* you—" Hoyle began.

"I'm telling *you,* " Walters said. "I'm getting to the bottom of this, and I bet you're looking at your last days with a badge. Right this minute, do you really want to say one thing besides 'how fast can I fix this'?"

"I... no." Hoyle hung his head. "I never thought it would turn out like this."

"Finally." Walters twisted back to Bea. "Now: Rowe was working with Gardner? You're sure?"

"The two of them held us at gunpoint. I heard plenty," she said, and Hoyle winced. "That means we might find where he's hiding if we search Josh Gardner's properties, or better yet any activities that could be keeping a place ready off the books. Before Rowe blows up any more of the traces."

"All worked out? You've been planning for this moment, Simms?"

"Always, sir."

Footsteps sounded in the corridor behind them—the cop who'd chased after Colin, stumbling his way back. Colin crouched and stepped aside into the corridor, and the officer's pale face looked right past him. Now that he wasn't walking *right into him* in a doorway.

"Someone… was spying on you," the cop panted. "I know there was. And I lost him."

"Of course you did," Bea said.

"Not surprised at all, Simms?" Walters eyed her with a thoughtful frown. Then he raised his radio again. "All of you, report."

"Negative." "Nothing." "No sign of the nurse."

The pale cop stared. "That Setter woman—I let her go!"

From when he chased after Colin. That was why Bea's group was walking, they were looking for her, or trying to as they argued.

Bea said "So can I join the search or not?" *Finally,* was the word hanging unsaid there.

Walters said "There's something lurking around here. Go find our witness, all three of you. I'll be watching," and he gave Hoyle a hard warning look.

Then they scattered. Colin watched them separate, trying to think how to join the search. Walters thought Eric was creeping around the hospital, but he must have been off destroying records at the Gardner building… no, they couldn't assume that.

The uniform headed off down the corridor, Bea moving up the other way. Hoyle made for a turn ahead and walked right past Colin without a glance; his eyes were sweeping the way ahead, and stealing looks back at the others—

*Oh.* Hoyle had sold them out, and now because Walters didn't arrest him on the spot he just might try silencing the nurse who'd joined him in Gardner's scheme. Colin followed him.

Hoyle walked quickly, head twitching to look around the different corridors and doorways he passed. Colin kept his distance and kept his own eyes searching too. Where would Setter try to run… would Hoyle spot her, or spot Colin behind him…

The people around shifted, from scattered figures here or there to several milling around the front counter and another knot of them at—

At the hospital entrance.

Hoyle sprinted for that door.

Colin dashed after him. He twisted around one woman, had to shove past a startled man and ignore that *"Huh?"* and hope pure speed would make them miss the blur darting past them. Hoyle was already out of view beyond the doors.

*Did he spot the nurse out there?* But Colin knew that wasn't it, not for this sudden dash. The bastard was escaping.

Colin burst out onto the night sidewalk. He blinked at the sudden dimness, couldn't make out Hoyle in the shadows.

Some kind of vehicle entrance was near his right, and he flung himself toward it. Was this how that cop had felt, losing Colin inside? He charged past two people on the way, letting the thin light hide his quick-moving outline.

One look in that loading bay showed that Hoyle hadn't simply ducked inside there. He stared around the night. Hoyle hadn't been glancing the other way, so maybe…

Across the pavement a number of cars stood in the open parking lot, and one figure, then another, moved among those. Colin charged across toward them. His breath came shorter now. *If I were Eric I'd still have the strength to make my skein carry me.*

That figure with the darting, nervous head must be Hoyle. Jogging between the parked cars, pulling out his phone.

Colin closed in behind him. He slowed as he did, thinking of listening in—but Hoyle's head yanked around and looked right at him, tracking his footfalls on the concrete. Panic burst across his face like a blow.

Colin lunged forward. He smashed shoulder-first into the traitor, seized him, swept him forward and slammed him to the pavement… muscles burning to hit him harder.

The cop stared as Colin pressed him down, knocked his phone—a blank screen—away over the asphalt. Hoyle's gaze swept around the lot, at the distant figures around it.

Colin growled "They can't see me, remember?"

Hoyle's terrified eyes went wider. "Da Costa?"

*He thought I was Eric, until I spoke.* Colin's throat squeezed tighter and he forced out a low snarl: "Right. Not the murderer, the guy you tried to frame for it. The one with the sister and mother you held hostage. What did Gardner say, 'hold off killing them for a few more minutes'? *Remember?"* He raised a fist.

Hoyle flailed out with a punch. A clumsy, obvious thing to block—Hoyle couldn't even see where to aim it. Colin caught and twisted his wrist, with just a fraction of the pressure that hold could put on an enemy's hand.

"Now, you want to talk to me? Or wait for—"

"You alright?" Footsteps, a man in nurse's blues trotting toward them.

Colin climbed off of his prisoner, just enough to lean down and whisper "—or wait for the guy who *did* kill Gardner for threatening Terri."

Hoyle staggered to his feet. He waved the nurse off with "Just… tripped. My head's fine, everything's okay." He stumbled away, steps getting steadier as he rushed away from the nurse. Colin moved beside him.

When the nurse fell back, Colin leaned close to tell Hoyle "That's better. Now, you want me to run through all the ways Eric or me can follow you *everywhere?* How we've bounced *bullets—"*

He felt his throat tightening again, ready to force out more and more threats. He cut those off with the one he needed:

"How Eric can put his claws right through anything that tries to protect you? Anything except me."

"You…" Hoyle stopped, breathed, and in a steadier voice he said "What is it you want?"

"I *want* you to go back there and do what's left of your job. Tell Walters you sold us out to Gardner, tell them everything you know about Gardner and Eric. How he told you to kill Zara and Terri if he lost control of Eric. Until Zara blew the whistle on you." No way Walters would leave Hoyle on the loose after that confession.

"And about you?" Hoyle's eyes narrowed. "I mean, tell him all about the skein? They need to know Rowe was spying around here just minutes ago. That's right, he was, you've got more to worry about than me—"

*Just like that he's got a distraction ready? He thinks.*

"That was *me,* genius." Colin paused, tried to think who could know how much. He shook his head. "Look, you let Bea decide that. She's worked out all the ways this secret is toxic, and she knows how you cops think. And she never trusted you," he added.

He saw Hoyle scowl at that, but then the lieutenant's face hardened. "You think you can make this just go away? Gardner was willing to make a deal with a murderer. Think, that means there'll always be someone else who wants the power. And you can't beat Rowe alone."

"I'm not alone," Colin snapped. "We'll get him."

"You haven't beaten him yet. You know, you keep talking about who he might kill next..." Hoyle's voice turned lower, sharper. "If you want to save at least one life here, you better let me go. If you don't, and Rowe kills me, that'll be on you."

Hoyle even used *that?* "You lying... you threatened my sister and my mother."

*If he gets you, I can live with it...* But Colin choked down the fury and added instead:

"I want you to live with that."

# CHAPTER THREE

# ALARMS

Colin followed Hoyle back toward the lights of the hospital entrance, close at his heels. The flush of anger still kept the worst of his exhaustion at bay—Hoyle was still *defending* what he did, even coming up with reasons they *needed* him? But maybe Eric being out there could keep him in line.

Hoyle passed through the door, and Colin edged in behind him, back to the same hobbled pace of creeping along the side of the wall. Hiding and keeping watch again, with no end in sight...

Hoyle was waving up the corridor. Bea strode down to join him.

"You'll want to hear this," Hoyle told her. "I, I need to—"

Bea looked past him, right to where Colin stood.

Hoyle added "Yeah, that's da Costa back there. You guys got me. Now come on." He turned and headed on toward where they'd left Walters.

Bea lingered a moment, and Colin stepped toward her. "Sorry," he said.

She simply said "Use this and stay back," and she held up a phone.

He fumbled it under the skein at his waist to get it out of sight, glancing around and hoping none of the few faces nearby had noticed it disappear. She gave him one quick smile and moved after Hoyle.

Colin followed, until the two came in sight of the commissioner, and he felt the phone buzzing against him. Whatever model Bea had given him, the thing barely made a sound.

He ducked down behind a gurney—the tangy hospital smell was stronger down there, and a dazed thought wondered if the cleaners had just been through—and drew the phone out where the gurney would shield it from passing eyes. Bea knew Hoyle had tapped his other phone, but when had she had time to get this one?

"Alright, what is it now?" came a muffled form of Walters's harsh mutter. From the sound, it came through Bea's own phone that must be hidden in her pocket.

Hoyle said "Simms is right."

"Right? Go on."

Hoyle said nothing. *Nobody* spoke, for one moment, two... Colin thought he could hear footsteps passing near that hushed stillness. He was holding his breath as well.

"Right about all of it," Hoyle said. "I did sell out to Josh Gardner. I spied, sabotaged—"

"God! Hoyle, how could you dump this on me now? Damn, damn, damn you!" Walters growled.

"Sir..."

"How am I supposed to fix this now?" A shrill edge rose in his growl. "First a killer you can't catch, now this? Why would you even *tell* me this?"

Colin crouched lower, and his fingers tightened on the phone. Walters talked like Hoyle had sold out just to spite him.

Hoyle sighed. "I... I think that killer's going to be coming for me next. Grabbing up that nurse would be straight out of Rowe's playbook, he knows Gardner had her attack his girl. And he thinks I was part of that. I need protection or I'm dead."

Colin peeked over the gurney, at the three cops huddled together up the corridor. At that distance he could believe Hoyle was meeting his boss's gaze without flinching. He did make his reason plausible.

*Wait, he said Eric "thinks" he was part of holding Terri?* Weasel.

Walters said "You actually... what got into you? I relied on you!"

"Just, money, is all. Gardner offered me too much. And, I thought—"

Hoyle broke off. Colin watched a nurse scurrying past their little knot of whispers. When Hoyle started again, his voice was softer yet.

"I thought if I kept an eye on Gardner and whatever his tie to Rowe was, it might keep more cops from getting killed. Who knows, Gardner could have been setting him up himself. So I kept him in the loop, and hoped I'd get something that would let us catch Rowe."

"Oh, is *that* what you call it?" Walters grumbled.

"I tried to help him, and keep back anything Rowe could use. And Gardner did tell me to put security around the mine. I never thought he wanted it for Rowe to torture people."

*Liar! We showed you what he started to do to Jessie, and we told you the homeless he was grabbing had to be next.* Hoyle had fought against them even investigating that at all.

But Bea still hadn't said a word, even after she'd accused him half an hour ago.

Walters said "Oh, it never crossed your mind? When you *ordered* those men to *ignore the screams?"*

"I... I was in too deep, by then." Hoyle's voice dwindled and faded away as he spoke.

Colin heard his own breathing grow harsher under the skein. Did Hoyle expect anyone to believe that? Or that he'd worm his way into some kind of sympathy?

The lieutenant went on "Yes, I kept watch over Zara and Terri da Costa. And then I get orders to kill them on command. So I tried to stall—"

"Oh, you tried to?" Walters stopped, seemed to collect himself. "Alright then. If you got pulled that far in, tell me *why was Gardner involved with a maniac like Eric Rowe?"*

"I wish I knew," Hoyle said.

"Funny thing—that's just what *you* said, Simms. So you tell me, what was Gardner after?"

Colin peeped up to see Walters turn full-on toward Bea, like Hoyle wasn't even there.

"Sir?" she said.

"What kind of killer could vanish on us *again?* Kill four cops and counting? What the hell can I tell them that gets the whole state down here to run him down?"

Colin shook his head. With the fears Bea had about the skein's secret getting out, Walters had found the worst possible words for his demand.

"We know Eric Rowe's smart, sneaky, and he knows the town," Bea said slowly. "It makes more sense if he was getting information from Gardner, and now Hoyle. He's also crazy strong—literally, I expect. And he's got some kind of armor, since he's gotten up from being shot enough that we've tried using SWAT rifles, but we still haven't gotten a clean hit."

"Rifles with infrared scopes," Walters muttered. "I get those loaned to you, I'd like to see some results."

"They seemed like the right choice, for a night operation."

"And you still lost him! Last night and tonight! We need to *get* this animal."

"We need to get Eric Rowe, yes. So, Lieutenant, who really killed Dennis Fields?"

Hoyle hesitated, for one long moment.

Then: "Gardner said… I should blame you and da Costa if it was possible." He looked at the floor. "When you found his body, I put the possibility out there, yes. But that recording you found looks good. It does put Gardner himself right there when he was shot, and now we've got the gun we found on Gardner's body."

"In other words," Bea said, "Gardner killed him. Not Colin da Costa."

"That's how it looks."

"We still need the rest of the pieces," Walters said. "Da Costa's been in the middle of this too, and he's been wearing the same armor Rowe does. It looks like the only way we'll clear this up is to give him a few hours in a cell, until we know he's telling the truth. Odds are all we'll find is a man protecting his sister."

He made it sound so reasonable... *but those* few hours *of me help-less are all the time Eric would need to get at Terri, at me, at anyone he wants.*

Walters added "You know it's the only way to get da Costa out from under this, right, Simms? And you're going to help him, right?"

"If he gives me the chance." That doubtful but unflinching voice was pure Bea—and just this secret phone link was her already choosing Colin over him.

"Alright then," Walters said. "Now, you keep looking for Nurse Setter. She knows this place, she could still be in any corner of it. But my money's on her being spotted across the state in a few days—they always screw up.

"But not like you did, 'Lieutenant,' " he added.

"I think I know that," Hoyle muttered. Still playing the victim.

"Simms, this conversation *never happened*. Hoyle, I need you to help me clean this up, and *maybe* you'll walk away. If Simms or any-one finds one sign that you're burying any of what you did, I bury you—or I back away and let Rowe do it, his way, since you're so sure he will. But *if* you can stop digging yourself in deeper, your chances depend on if you can make yourself useful."

"I know. I'm sure I can be," Hoyle said.

So that was it, the traitor was getting a pass? Colin's fingers clenched against the phone... but, wasn't this what they wanted, Hoyle forced to work on their side again?

Bea and Hoyle walked away, together.

Colin watched them go, waited for anything more from the phone line, but neither of them spoke now.

He hung up and slid the phone back under the concealing skein. He could still go keep an eye on Hoyle... but there was still Nurse Setter, she could still be somewhere here...

His vision blurred a moment as he forced himself upright.

His feet were heavy, dragging at the slow, soft pace he needed. But one footfall here could be noticed, with so few people to cover it in the long, hushed corridors at night.

So endless, so quiet... *keep walking, watching...*

"You don't get it, do you?" a low voice snapped, from a door he passed. "You are not turning this facility upside down *again."*

Zara's voice answered "I'm sorry for the—"

"Sorry?" A short man as dark as his doctor's coat was pale glared back at Zara. "Sorry? A few days ago you brought a killer here to terrorize our patients. Now your daughter's back in our care, and next thing we've got *cops* running around saying one of our nurses was..."

He stopped short, like he'd just frightened himself. Colin struggled to wrap his sluggish thoughts around that.

"Well," the doctor started again, softer, "after all that, what are we supposed to think?"

His reason for hesitating clicked. *He's thinking we'll sue them all, after their nurse drugged Terri.* The silence stretched.

"It's frightening," Zara said. "Somehow Nurse Setter lost her way and turned against her calling. I hope they can bring her around again. But at the moment, my main concern has to be my daughter."

"Hmm." The doctor closed his eyes, and seemed to tremble a moment as a decision worked through him. "Of course. And we'll do our duty with Terri, there's no question of that. But we'll also be weighing her treatment against the safety of the other patients."

"And we're grateful for that. Can I see her now?"

"At this hour? You need to trust that we'll look after her. But... go tell the nurse you can see that she's comfortable, for tonight."

"Thank you."

When Zara turned and walked out, she walked slower than Colin had seen her move in years. He let her pass, looked around the quiet corridor—nobody was close enough to see.

He stepped ahead of her. "It's me," and he waved a shimmering hand.

Zara gasped, jerked back, but only for a moment before she caught herself and smiled. *She's already been through so much. We all have.*

He let her lead the way through the hospital. He walked a few steps behind, fighting a feeling that he'd stumble into her if she stopped suddenly. The heavy, tangling weight of the long day wrapped tighter with each step, and he tried thinking of Eric lurking around the next of the endless, never-quite-empty corridors, just to keep his eyes and his wits moving.

Invisibility clung around his mind like an armful of cold, wet clothes. His feet shuffled on, on, as he tried to make each step rise cleanly and set down softly. Once he felt his shoe scrape on the floor, and saw a uniformed cop glance over. But they pushed on.

That cop was the only officer in sight when Zara stopped at a doorway. That couldn't be right, Terri had to be better guarded than that...

"Sorry, ma'am, your daughter needs to be alone now." A nurse, a man fidgeting with a clipboard and a tablet in his hands, closed in on Zara.

Zara smiled. "Dr. Morton said to tell you I could see that she's comfortable."

"I don't care *what* he said, ma'am. You shouldn't even be back here." The nurse folded his arms and moved to block the doorway.

Zara drew herself up straighter, just half an inch. That motion was all she needed.

She looked straight into the nurse's face. "It's good to see Terri has someone like you looking after her. But the doctor did send me to see her, and you might want to think why." And she stepped right past him.

In the moment the nurse turned away to his tablet, Colin slipped by too. The room was spacious even for its two beds, but the second bed was empty—the staff must be trying to keep Terri away from other patients now.

His sister lay in bed, watching. The withered face around those bright eyes made him think the same question: would her shattered, mis-healed body ever be able to get out of that bed again?

"Showed him." At least Terri had the strength for those few words to Zara. *You showed that nurse who he was dealing with*, she meant.

"I should have let him have his way." Zara stepped closer and leaned over the bed to whisper "But look who's with me."

Colin willed the skein to split back from his face, and he peeled its mask away. Terri looked up at the head that seemed to appear in mid-air, and she only smiled back.

He moved around to crouch behind the far side of her bed, eyes on the doorway and sliding the skein back into place. "Are you alright?" he whispered.

"Sedatives. Nurse Setter just wanted me weak, they say. She's missing?"

Zara sat beside him, eyes widening. "Missing?"

"Overheard that," Terri said.

Colin said "I think she just ran. Or it could be Eric, but it sounds like Eric's off trashing parts of the Gardner building, so I'm trying to think she's alright. If he's busy covering up anything Gardner had on him."

"He might."

Terri's words made Colin frown, and eye the lines on her face again. Why was he guessing, when he had the person here who had spent two years as Eric's prisoner, watching him unravel? "You think so? Where would he really go, you think?"

"Not sure. He wants me, if I can be moved." She motioned around the bed, more just a glance with a weak shrug to echo the motion of her eyes. "Wants to show the town is dying—" She stopped again and took a careful breath. "And hide his secrets, sure."

"Like those prisoners of his." A wave of dizzy horror swept through him. "The doctors took the skein off them. He'll want to silence them, collect that…"

He lurched to his feet. But his legs wobbled, he slipped and had to twist his weight to only crash down off the edge of Terri's bed.

The *thump* echoed, faded, in the corridors. No other sound woke in response outside. *Some guards they are!*

Zara whispered "Sit down. Where are you going?"

"To get that skein. And…"

"The way you are now, do you think you'll do more harm or good? And you just said Eric wasn't around here."

"But—"

"Stop and think. Are Eric's new victims in more danger than Terri? The police must think so, and they'll keep them under guard even if they forget her."

"I guess. But…" If Eric wanted them he could go right through the cops.

Zara shook her head. "You can't keep chasing around and waiting to see when you collapse. Did you ever think that Eric might be stopping to rest?"

"Him? Funny." And Colin felt the beginnings of a laugh gathering in his chest, fighting to get out. *That's not good—*

"Think," Terri said. "Where are you needed most?"

"Here, defending you. And defending those three, and finding Nurse Setter, and…" He cut off in embarrassment, looked away from his family.

Zara sighed. "And you expect to stay on watch forever? Then all Eric needs to beat you is to stop and sleep before you do. You wouldn't have a chance."

"I *know*. But… how does that change anything?"

He glared at the two faces, his mother whispering beside him, and his sister still and watchful on the pillow. The words came pouring out.

"I mean, everywhere Eric's touched seems like it's a target now, or anything that stands for this town he hates. Today we lost a friend, Fields, *and* an enemy who thought he could control Eric—by leaning on you. Where's the part where this gets easier, even for a minute? When we trusted Hoyle?" He twisted over to look at Terri. "Are you *sure* you're alright? Because everything else we do looks like just trying to push Eric back, with no sign of it ever ending."

Zara laughed, softly. "Of course she is. We've had friends from all over the Hillside come to cheer us on. Just think how fast they rushed to us tonight when Lieutenant Hoyle got out of line. And there are dozens more waiting for news. They need us to be alright."

"Sure, but it doesn't make getting there any easier," he muttered. "And, I was asking Terri."

"After all this?" Zara said. "You think we'll let Eric or Nurse Setter beat us?"

"Beat us?" Colin thought of mentioning how Eric tore the Vargas House down, the center of everything Zara had built—just to cover his escape when he was first collecting skein. How were they supposed to recover from that?

*"You really do have to go now."*

The nurse's voice came from out in the hall, closing in on heavy feet.

Colin clenched his fists and his invisibility, staring at the others, mind gone blank.

"Understood," Zara said. "But please, look after Terri." She got to her feet, looking straight at the nurse in the doorway. But Colin knew she was speaking to him.

Then, Bea's voice:

"We'll keep her safe." She walked right up past the nurse, with a confidence in that "we" that left no room for anyone interfering.

Terri said "And I'll be fine. I *know* it." She made that one word ring with certainty.

"Then, sleep well." Zara gripped her daughter's hand once and walked out to follow Bea and the nurse.

Colin pushed himself to his feet and crept out after them. The nurse was already walking away, eying his tablet and his clipboard, but still glancing over his shoulder to be sure they left.

Bea looked at Zara, and her eyes moved in a slow, deliberate look over to where Colin stood. "I'll keep watch out here until the sun's up. If I see one flicker of something that isn't a friend..." She held up her phone. And glanced at Colin again.

Zara said "Thank you. Just... thank you."

She turned and headed away down the long, wide corridor.

Bea stayed where she was, opposite Terri's room. Colin edged toward her, enough to whisper "We should get that skein they took from the prisoners. Before Eric does, or Hoyle, or Walters—"

Bea raised her phone to cut him off. She held the screen by her face, close enough to hide her lips from the nurse in the hall as she whispered back.

"I know. But I talked to the doctor who removed it. He wants to test it, and now he knows that's evidence in my case and Hoyle isn't allowed near it."

"And that's *enough?* When Eric comes to get it he'll..."

Colin swallowed and tried to force down images of the carnage that could lead to.

"Look, let's get it now," he said. "And then, if Walters is so hungry to know what it is, we can show him. Get guards all around with IR scopes and everything."

"Tell him about invisibility? We've seen where that idea leads, with Hoyle finding something to sell out. Or Gardner: he wanted a means to heal himself, so Eric made him more skein. From their prisoners' flesh."

"I guess." He let the breath, the idea, slip away from him, and sagged on his feet. "I'm just not up to dealing with it now."

*"Now* is the operative word. But we're going to take Eric down," she said. "You're going to take him."

The last words were warmer, a flash of something more personal from Bea.

*That* kiss, *back in the mine. I'd been wondering if she felt the same, ever since we met...* Now he found himself all but alone in a silent corridor with her...

Her features looked *at peace,* alert eyes searching but no tension in that gold-crowned face, like nothing had ever shaken her. His hand twitched, wanting to rise and touch some of that strength...

He held his hand down. Touching her would just be weird when she could barely see him. *And I can't start this when I'm falling-down tired.*

Instead he said "I appreciate that. And—everything."

Saying that was easier with his face hidden, but he still heard his voice crack on the word.

She didn't glance over. The detective pretended she hadn't heard.

He slipped back into Terri's room.

Its light had gone off sometime while he was out; Terri must have a switch within her reach. That left the not-quite-dim light from the corridor, and that guided Colin to her bedside.

"She'll be on watch," he said. "And I'll be ready if she wakes me."

"I know you are."

First Bea, putting a whole encouraging message into a few words, and now Terri? But Terri had been making her statements count ever since they found her. Her shallow breath and careful words must be affecting them all.

Colin stretched out on the floor behind her bed, where it would screen him from anyone passing by outside. He set the phone by his head—Bea would warn him if there was trouble, a nurse, or anything.

When he let the skein's twist of the light finally relax, the back of his mind cramped, like fingers that had carried a weight for too long. He smoothed himself against the hard floor and tried to let the tension ease away.

Was it even safe to sleep encased in skein? In *dragonskin?*

All this time, they'd been wearing pieces of a dead myth against their skin. When Eric ran Leo through or Bea cut a hole in a window, those were dragon claws... and still Colin couldn't even risk sleeping without keeping the stuff around him.

But Terri had done it for years, and skein had kept her alive. Colin slowed his breathing, tried to pick out his sister's soft, soft breath in the stillness...

"Goodnight." Her voice stirred in the hush. "I wanted to say that."

*Maybe she would, after so long.* After so long hidden away by the man she would have married, watching Eric trying to help her but slowly coming unhinged? Or was he revealing he was always that broken, now that he had the power to act on it—

*No.* Colin pushed those thoughts away. This had to be a space, a time, where the enemy *wasn't here*, as long as Bea stayed quiet outside. *Just me and my big sister, and I can be here for her again.*

"I wanted to hear it," he said at last. "Goodnight."

Did Terri's breathing shift, or her weight on the bed, as something in her relaxed? Colin wanted to believe he could hear that.

He tried to settle his own aching muscles and worn-out nerves on the hard, smooth floor. The skein could probably pool into some kind of cushion under his head...

*Breathe. Breathe, let that invisibility fade away, let the bruises and the worries wash through me and vanish.* There were only the sounds of the hospital at night. Low voices, a few scattered footsteps, when any of them could be Eric moving closer—

No. Bea would spot him. They were always safe with her.

That peace let him simply listen to the sounds, and think of all the people around who simply went on their ways untouched by this battle. And drift away.

\* \* \*

Something buzzed in his ear.

A... phone. He stirred, on the hard, cold floor...

*Where he was* blasted him awake, lurching up and lunging toward the doorway, fists curling.

Bea stood outside, quiet and calm.

The sight brought him up short, twisting at the skein's power to stare... stare... But no secretly-glowing shape sprang out of the corridor, not even the faint, easily-overlooked outline that he might spot without skein. No attack.

Instead, one nurse here, another wheeling a patient along there—Colin ducked back behind the door and tightened his own stealth around him before he looked out again. None of the nurses had come near, and there was only the hospital, stirring to life after the night.

Bea gave him a slow nod, and walked away.

Because her "shift" was done. He'd slept to morning.

Colin stretched and tried to pull his thoughts together. The same heavy, thick muzziness pressed on him, but now it felt closer but less complete—like layers of fatigue piled onto his head instead of his whole body. *I should be hungry, starving, after working the skein all day.*

He settled back by Terri's bedside to wait for the next move.

They had to be ready if Eric struck... unless he risked slipping down to the cafeteria to build up more strength. But he held his place, waiting for Zara to join them.

Bea's phone was the main thing he had to fill the time. He studied its settings, and searched the news for signs that Eric had been out cutting some bloody path while he slept. Nothing.

Twice nurses came for quick checks on Terri, and he ducked out of sight. Terri said little, and he let her save her strength. He let Bea and Zara rest too, instead of calling them first. Instead all he had was what he could search through the phone, and the barbed, restless thoughts of where Eric could be attacking now.

Hours later the phone buzzed in his hands.

He almost dropped it, before he brought it up to his ear.

A stranger's voice was saying "—clearly it was a bomb."

*What did I miss?* His fingers scrabbled for a solid grip on the cell, as his heartbeat roared in his ear.

Then Bea said "How much of the basement room did it damage?"

Oh.

Basement room, bomb—the Gardner building basement, this was Bea investigating the damage to that server room, what the cops had talked about last night... The fragments of Colin's nerves tried to settle. Terri was watching him, wide-eyed at whatever she'd read from him.

"The *room's* salvageable, the Fields crime scene not so much. Nobody's getting blood spatter now, and they'll be earning their pay just getting his time of death. Why'd you have us locked out, we would have found the bomb and saved everything!"

"Better question," growled a familiar male voice, "is how'd anyone get the bomb in there. Since she had you locked out."

Ed Jordan—of course Bea's sergeant was defending her decisions. And he knew all about the skein. Did they have him back on the case, even after Eric put him in his wheelchair?

"Yeah, I know. We'll find out."

Colin could just make out the sound of heavy feet, and a door thumping shut, hard.

"You hear all that?" Bea said.

So Bea and Jordan were alone now. "Sure," Colin whispered back.

Was this how it was going to be, her sneaking him information on how they were still a step behind?

"Sounds like nobody got hurt, right?" he added. Terri's eyes were on him, more starved for answers than he was, and he tried to fill her in by thinking aloud. "A bomb in the Gardners' basement. I'm guessing it was mostly enough to get the old computer Josh Gardner was using? I think the bomb was already there—I saw something weird attached to the computer when I... found Dennis Fields's body." He shook his head, tried to think past the sheer waste of that death. "I mean, we heard Eric ask Gardner if he'd kept his secrets anywhere besides that machine."

"He knew," Bea said. "And he'd already planted the device."

"Fields told us he'd found traces of Eric down there. But then *he* got caught there by Gardner. And shot."

"So Eric's bomb ended up taking out two layers of evidence, Gardner's records and Fields's death too. But," she added, "there'll still be signs to prove that you didn't kill Fields. Starting with matching the bullet to Gardner's gun."

Jordan said "Is this what Rowe's up to now? Covering his tracks?"

"Cover-ups, instead of chasing new targets?" Colin bit his lip. "I asked Terri the same thing. It could be right."

He glanced at Terri. She only watched him, adding nothing.

And if they were wrong... Something twisted in his gut as he said "Tell me that's all. Tell me nobody else got killed tonight while we were sitting here."

"As far as we know, no," Bea said. "But we need—hold on."

A dull, soft roar filled the phone as she tuned the sound up.

A door rattled, just as a thought crashed through Colin. *If Eric's burying evidence, those three homeless witnesses from the mine have to be next. Zara thinks the police can watch them, but if Eric wants them dead...*

"Any news from Josh Gardner's house?" Bea said.

"Nada," said a woman—another cop. "Not a peep. The next shift is on it now. You think Rowe will be there, or are you just wishing?"

Colin squeezed his eyes shut. Was there a chance they'd catch Eric there, or would he come after the homeless witnesses? And Colin couldn't even tell Bea while her meeting went on.

"I think I want to know if he does show up," Bea said.

"But Gardner's dead. That news has to break soon. We need to tear the place apart before the town tramples all over—oh hell. Walters is trying to play this quiet, right?"

Feet pounded in the corridor, rushing up to Terri's room. Colin ducked back and held the "floating phone" down behind her bed.

Zara rushed into the room, gaze darting around to settle on her son's outline. Her voice shook.

"Something's happening with those homeless."

# CHAPTER FOUR

# THEN HE SAID

Colin twisted to stare up at Zara. Her gaze searched a moment and settled on him, as she knelt down by Terri's bed.

"You're alright?" she asked her daughter.

"Yes. Nothing here."

Sounds clashed and milled out in the corridor, murmurs and footsteps moving, growing louder. A nurse leaned in to shoot an anxious look inside the room before he rushed on.

That sight jolted Colin from shock, and he jumped to his feet. "What happened?"

Zara's face was tight as she whispered "I went to the rooms where they're looking after Eric's prisoners. But there's a crowd outside, and the guard is keeping them all away."

*We're too late!* Colin took a step for the doorway—and jolted to a stop to look back at Terri. *Eric's right in the building, I can't leave her now.*

"Go." How could Terri sound so calm? "Eric can't even move me."

"But…" His words died away. But, protecting Terri had been the one thing they'd clung to.

Zara turned and strode to the corridor. "Nurse? What's going on, is my girl even *safe* here?" Her voice wavered at what would seem like the edge of total panic, to someone who didn't know her.

And a nurse's voice tried to calm her, another drew closer to answer the stream of questions Zara poured out, and another joined in. She was gathering a crowd—Colin had to run to slip out before they blocked the doorway.

A crowd wouldn't stop Eric if he went after Terri now, but it could make him hesitate, it might even give Zara the chance to touch him and use the spell. Colin clung to that faint hope as he dashed for the prisoners' room.

It would be too late for them, he knew, but he had to see. The room was just a couple of turns ahead. He saw a head glancing toward him in confusion, another, drawn to the passing blur or the footsteps where no feet could be seen, but he rushed on.

Just like Zara had said: a half-dozen figures, mostly doctors in white rather than nurses in blue, standing back casting curious looks past the black-uniformed cop at the doorway.

Colin crouched down below eye level and edged in along the wall. The voices around were an odd murmuring of *what is* and *behind schedule* that he couldn't follow, too low and casual for them to realize there had been murders.

He pressed lower as he neared the doorway. This was the same spot where one cop had chased him away before—he halted just short of the entrance and strained to hear through the buzzing voices outside.

"…tell me how it happened, doctor…" Commissioner Walters, trying to keep his voice low and mostly failing.

"…outraged, *hrrm*…" came a rustle of another voice..

*The* how *is that we still won't tell you to watch for blurred shapes like me! And I was sleeping in the other room while these three were killed.* His heartbeat thundered in his ears.

Then the second voice, the doctor, broke through again. "But he… he was right in the room, *hrrm*. And he missed it?"

Meaning some guard Eric had dodged around? But the doctor seemed far calm for that…

"Say it again," Walters growled.

"I was… asleep…" Even soft and hesitant, Colin knew that voice. *Wesley,* anxious, homeless Wesley, one of Eric's three victims in the mine. Alive—warm relief flooded through Colin and left him sagging against the wall.

"I took *the strangest* substance off of you," the doctor said. "I spent all night thinking of tests…"

His voice faded in the babble around the corridor. Colin saw the cop waving the onlookers back, and held his breath to make out more.

"…cops insisted on splitting your fellow patients up, so that makes you the only one here when it's gone, and you sleep through it?"

Gone? He had to mean the skein, he meant Eric had taken back the skein they'd removed from the prisoners. And left the witness alive.

Wesley began "I told you—"

"You're lying," Commissioner Walters rumbled. "We know you're lying. You want us to get the medical readouts that show you were wide awake?"

That sounded like a bluff. But Wesley moaned "No… said he'd kill me…"

*"Who?"*

"The masked man, with the gun… he broke into the shelves and took the stuff, he said to keep quiet."

A gun? But Eric had used those too, to hide his secrets.

A cramp twitched in Colin's crouching knees. *Eric's prisoners are safe, I should be heading back.* But he held his place.

"Describe him. Now!"

"Just… a mask. Dark clothes, tall, big, big gun… he just took it! That stuff almost killed me, and now… it's all too weird."

"What mask? Like in the mine?"

"That was a *mine!*" Wesley's voice rose in pleading. "That was total black, just a couple lights. He chained us up, he *smeared acid* over us. You want me to remember that again?"

"But you *did* see. You heard them talk, all of them."

"I told you, I saw the detective that brought the cops back. I told you, she didn't do it, it was her and Colin da Costa that saved us."

"Saved you, from the thief with the gun?"

"I don't know! Colin and the other masked man didn't have guns."

"But *Colin* had a mask?" the cop pressed.

"Uh…" Wesley went silent. Then, stronger, he said "Yeah, he did. But it was his voice, and he and the lady tried to warn us before that freak grabbed us. They *saved* us. Colin even stopped the acid gunk from melting me."

"Stopped it?" the doctor said. "How?"

Silence. Not a sound, against the murmurs of the onlookers that the guard was still warning back. And they had to be catching more and more of the conversation inside.

"How?" the doctor said again. "Don't you realize this substance *makes no sense?* You say it's corrosive, but I hear people are wearing it for armor—and this da Costa just neutralized it?"

"I told you, they saved us. From the other masked man, and the old man, I *told you* those were the ones that—"

A voice at Colin's side burst over the sounds within. "Sorry, I can't. I've got my orders," said the cop on guard.

Hoyle stood in front of the doorway, pinning the cop with his gaze. "You do *not* want to do this, kid—"

"No, let him through," Commissioner Walters called out.

The cop stepped aside, and Hoyle marched in. If he spotted the blur that was Colin by the door frame, he made no sign.

"So what happened?" Hoyle said.

"What happened?" the doctor laughed. "Your boss just has to lock up the strangest thing I've seen on a patient in years, and now we had someone stealing it all! With a gun, *here!*"

"You think enough of them heard you?" Walters muttered. "Come on."

Colin flattened back against the wall as the three swept outside and turned away up the corridor. He twisted and scrambled around the onlookers, and saw one doctor's head sweep toward him before he darted past. No time to worry about that now.

He closed in behind the three as Walters said "I remember the man on watch. He swears he was only away for a minute. But how'd Rowe even know we had it here?"

"Read the reports," Hoyle said. "With all the places he's gotten into, this is nothing."

"Hold on here!" That voice was the doctor's—a fat man with folds of loose skin even on the back of his head. "None of this changes how you promised I'd get a look at that substance when you confiscated it. So, what are you going to do about that?"

*"What is going on here?"*

That bellow came from up the corridor, where another doctor—the same small black man that had been arguing with Zara last night—came charging down at them.

"Tell me we didn't just get *robbed.* Tell me the da Costa case didn't put our patients in danger *again,* in *one night!"*

Walters snapped "And I told you we're trying to get to the bottom of it. Not as easy with the best evidence gone, though."

"Evidence?" the first, plumper doctor said. "Try 'puzzle' or 'medical enigma.' And his people let it slip through their fingers!"

Hoyle edged nearer his boss. "It honestly could be the center of all of this," he said. "You might need to talk to Detective Simms again, or get some other line on it."

Then both doctors were talking at once, as they walked on together. Colin eyed Hoyle; was he trying to put Bea on the spot, when he knew she'd never talk about the skein's secrets? *We would have stolen it ourselves*—but this couldn't have been Bea, and Wesley had mentioned a "tall man." And Hoyle *did* know almost all the skein's tricks, but now he was playing dumb?

Walters brought the group to a stop, with his back to a doorway.

"Enough, all of you. It looks like I have to talk to them myself again. And, I know, I'm not going to kill your patients, I swear."

Patients? The patients here had to be... the other two from the mine, so Eric had missed those witnesses too? And Walters was checking their stories again...

Colin jerked back. If the people were okay, and the skein was gone, he knew all he needed to. And every minute out here was another away from Terri and Zara, knowing Eric could still be around here.

If it had been Eric at all. He glanced at Hoyle again, standing behind the two doctors, and turned back for Terri's room.

This time he walked slower, moving along by the wall and away from the sight of the people scurrying on their way. No need to raise invisible footfalls all down the corridor—Terri was right, her own frailty made her one person Eric couldn't simply carry off. But Colin had still been away too long.

Zara was still holding traffic to a stop in front of Terri's room. "So how do I know if she's sleeping too long? Please, *how do I know?"* with a blend of worry and earnestness that had two nurses and several visitors clustered around her, even with a doctor in white trying to break them up.

Rumor had it that Zara could hold court in a restroom, and had—keeping this crowd here to ward Eric off was nothing. By the time Colin slipped around to Terri's doorway, she had already spotted him and shifted to "I'm sorry, I've taken enough of your time..."

*She knew this outline was me again, just from my shape. We better hope Eric never tries rearranging his skein to imitate my height.*

A nurse was taking a bit of blood from Terri's finger—a birdlike woman with a brisk way nothing like Nurse Setter. Colin moved to the back of the room unnoticed.

Height, disguises... the thoughts set an idea gnawing at him again: *Hoyle* was a fairly tall man, like Wesley had described. He could have dressed up and seized the skein instead of Eric. It wouldn't be the worst thing he'd tried.

The nurse muttered *"Look* at that woman." She flicked a hand toward Zara, still out chatting with two of the visitors. "How do you ever talk to her?" she asked Terri.

Terri smiled. "Easier to let her talk."

*Especially now*—so Terri was making *jokes* about her condition. Colin's throat went tight.

"You may have to make her listen," the nurse said. "You know that, don't you?"

Terri didn't answer.

Colin froze. Shame at listening in mingled with a chill about what she might think Terri would need to make so clear. The chill hung on longer, as the nurse gathered up her tools to go.

Zara swept in and went straight to the nurse. "And, thank you for your help—"

"Please, don't," and the nurse brushed her aside and left the room, but Colin saw a smile trying to form on her face. Standing up to Zara was never easy.

Zara settled in the chair by Terri. Colin watched the two women, wondering if he could ask what the nurse had meant.

"They talked about something being stolen," Zara said softly. "The skein from Eric's victims?"

"That's right." Of course she overheard that.

"Everyone here is nervous." She bowed her head sadly. "We do make it difficult. First all our police protection before, and Eric still getting in, now Nurse Setter's missing, and then this."

"This might not be Eric. But if it is, he has the skein now, and he let his prisoners live. That could mean there's nothing left to bring him here except—"

*Except us. Terri.*

To smooth what he'd almost said, Colin turned to his sister. Her face didn't react—had his blurred head hidden his flinch?

"Terri? You, well, you said Eric wouldn't risk grabbing you in your condition. He thinks that enough skein would make you better...

you think that's what he was waiting for? Or could he have given up on you?"

Terri's eyes closed.

Then she opened them. "Can I have some water?"

He reached over to the side table, where a cup of water stood ready. He tipped it up to Terri's lips—*she could have done this herself before Eric took her skein!*—and waited as she sipped, swallowed, small repeated motions until the cup was drained.

Colin sank back to the ground as she spoke, her voice soft against the tangle of sounds pressing in from beyond their room.

"When I first woke up like this? He said he'd tell you I was alive."

"Eric said that?" Zara scowled.

"Soon, he said. And then... he said, he would when he was sure I'd survive."

"Oh *God.*" Zara caught her breath. "How could he, how could *anyone* just say that to, to anyone?"

Colin's fingers shifted on the paper cup, still in his hand. "Was it to... to make you fight to get better? That sounds like his kind of trick. Probably one of the ways he thinks he saved your life." *Maybe it did.*

"So I lived." Terri's words were fainter now. "And he said he'd tell you when... he could trust you."

Zara snapped "When *he* could trust *us?* That's simply insane."

Terri added "Trust you, to let him heal me."

"As if he was the only one in the world who could." Zara turned her head to look around the room, the whole hospital surrounding them. "Obviously wrong."

"Then, he said he was deciding how to break the news to you."

Zara's eyes narrowed and glittered cold—he'd never seen that kind of anger in her. "Break it to us? He said, he *dared* to say, that we couldn't stand the shock of knowing my little girl was *alive?*"

"Then..." Terri added, "he said he told you, and you didn't believe him."

"I *bet* he said that." Colin twisted on the hard floor. "And said it was our fault you ran into the building at all, right? And how the whole town's part of that too, and he's going to—"

He cut off. The paper cup felt frail in his tight-knotted fingers.

"Look, I'm sorry," he tried. "I know you cared for him, but... we know what Eric is now. I guess anyone trying to comfort someone who's always hated his life here, it can only go so far."

*"I* was leaving too, remember?" Terri's gaze locked on him, and her voice scratched as she went on. *"I said it wasn't worth changing how they saw him."*

*How we saw him.* As an undersized kid, as a failed shopkeeper's son... *We tried to protect him.*

Terri said "We wanted to leave together. Then I got caught in the quake and I couldn't move at all."

"It's not your fault—"

"He said, I could leave if I healed more. Or if he found more skein for me. He didn't find it... then he said he needed it to get more... always, needed more..."

Her voice faded in a croak and she gasped for breath.

*Always under his control.* Every step, Eric tried to fool her more. Or fool himself that only he could help her or see what was wrong with the world.

For two years.

*Crunch.* The paper cup crumbled in his grip.

"And he never listened," Zara said.

"I... never... talked," Terri forced out. "Once I could, I... knew not to."

Then Zara was leaning over the bed, draping herself over her daughter in the softest, most delicate embrace. Colin stretched over to hug them both—warm, shaking, all three of them.

Zara gasped "I, I knew it must have been a nightmare, but..." Her muffled, sobbing words faded away.

When they had to pull apart again, their hands lingered, holding onto Terri's.

And she looked from one face to the other, and her voice was ice. "So... do *you* think Eric will give up on me?"

The room went still. A pocket of silence, a cold bubble where her words had pushed back all the noise of the building around them. Where Terri was trapped now, where any of those sounds could be some blind stranger or worse, come to shatter that stillness...

A footstep fell in the room.

Bea walked in.

"Morning. It looks like you're all okay..."

Her voice faltered, as she glanced between them and the mood lying between them.

"We are," Zara said, and her voice was clear. "Eric only went after the 'evidence.' If that was Eric?" she whispered as Bea came closer.

"It wasn't me. You have any other theories?"

"Never mind." Suddenly Zara was on her feet, sliding the chair back and turning for the door. "Right now I'm feeling a need to have a few words with the three people here that were under Eric's thumb yesterday. And who can't be as brave as some of us." She turned and leaned down to kiss Terri's forehead.

She headed away, then paused in the doorway. Her head turned to pick out where Colin stood.

"I'll stop for a snack too. Probably more than I'll need," and she nodded to him.

*Food.* Colin could feel the empty space in his stomach—he *should* be ravenous after so long working the skein. But where he'd felt hungry once, these days he seemed to be forgetting that more and more.

"Alright," Bea said. "But keep your eyes open and stay near other people."

"I think I know that by now." Zara gave them one more smile, and whirled away.

Colin shook his head. At least she could show her face out there, at least she could go *do* something, even if it was only cheering up Eric's prisoners.

Bea broke the silence again, with her usual crisp tone. "I've had a look around that room. Also, we're still searching for traces of Eric around town. We'll find something—"

She yawned.

Then she frowned, turned her face away, like she was embarrassed to have simple frailties like sleep at all.

What would Zara say here? He tried "Listen, I need to thank you again for standing guard last night. I'm still not sure how you stayed awake at all."

Bea looked back. "Yesterday you ran up to the mine and back, on top of taking on Eric and Gardner. I *drove* up. And then... when Hoyle's men drove me back, and I couldn't guess if I'd end up arrested or not?"

"Yes?"

"I slept the whole way back."

He stared at her. "You're kidding. That's a joke—isn't it?"

"It might be."

And there it was, one of her little smiles. *It seems like a lifetime since I've seen those.* A lifetime and a kiss ago.

He looked away. Terri lay right there, watching them both. He swallowed, no idea what to say to either of them...

The phone vibrated softly.

He slid it out to see Zara's name on the screen. "Hi," he said.

Instead of her answer, he heard a jumble of muffled voices, background sounds around a corridor.

A throat cleared—

"What?" Terri asked, and he held up his hand for silence.

"Sorry, ma'am. Zara," the man's voice added. "But, you can't just go in. I mean, we've just had some trouble in there."

"I understand that," Zara said. "But I hear you've already looked the robbery site over, and you've talked to the witness. Is there really any harm in my seeing him now?"

"I... well, *your son* is still one of the suspects. Not officially now, but they do want to know if he was part of it."

"And is that what you believe?" Zara's words prickled like the softest challenge.

"No—" the cop muttered. Then, stronger: "No he's not. More like we owe him. Anyway, I'll be watching you."

Moments later, Colin heard her say:

"Hello, Wesley."

"Zara? You're here? Guess you would be," the weak voice added.

Colin could hear Eric's former prisoner rousing, warming to find a friendly face again.

*I hope he's alright. But is it really my place to listen in when she's cheering him up?* Except, Zara must have called him because she wanted him to hear.

"They say you're starting to recover," she said. "You had a few people worried there."

"I got kidnapped, chained up, a bit of my chest got *melted*—I just want it over. Recovering sounds good, yeah."

"We missed you at the last two Vargas House food drives. We were wondering what your story was."

"I could have come more, sure. It's just, Vinnie got nervous there."

"Your friend... oh yes, your pet. The sweetest little rat I've ever seen."

"He's gone now. When that freak grabbed me, I *lost* him. I don't even know if the little guy's alright." Wesley's voice choked up, more shaken now than he'd been about his own health.

Colin shut his eyes. This was the kind of person that got abducted, and all Eric thought was that nobody would miss him.

"Rats are survivors," Zara said. "People are too."

"I guess. But I have to get out of here and find him. You know, Colin said Vinnie would warn me if I was in trouble. I just had to notice him getting spooked, and I missed it."

" 'Would have' are painful words to start saying—"

"I need to get out of here! I know your son and that cop saved us... listen," he added.

Was that what Zara wanted, for Colin to hear some gratitude from the people he did manage to help?

But Wesley went on, his voice almost too low to pick up: "Listen, I'll tell the cops anything you want. We owe your son that."

"There's no need for any of that," Zara said. "Just tell them what happened."

"But... my head was spinning all the time he had me there. That stuff he put on me, it *hurt*. And none of what they said there made sense."

He whispered lower still, and faster.

"I mean, they called the old man Gardner, *the* boss of the whole Gardner company. And they said something about healing, like all this was some kind of test. Something about some old killings, or..." His whisper faded in the hiss of the sound, but Colin knew that sound must be "*a cop.*" Hoyle.

Zara said "It's alri—*uh.*"

She broke off, just for a moment.

"Please," Wesley breathed. "Please. I'll tell them anything you want, I just need to get out of here and find Vinnie."

"You already talked to the police," Zara said. "There's nothing to worry about there; they have everything you saw."

Something brushed against her mic, a *thump* like muted thunder. Then a second one.

"Well, some of it," Wesley said. "But it's so crazy—old history and—"

"Relax." Zara's voice was a fraction louder now. That thump echoed again, faster... anxious... "I'm sure the Commissioner picked your brain to get every last thing you could give, even the pieces you don't remember noticing. All you have to do now is rest."

That sound, some kind of tapping signal. And she kept talking about Wesley's testimony—

He turned to Bea. "Something's wrong."

The words came out louder than he meant. Bea *sharpened*, drawing herself one critical fraction more upright, her balance shifting on the chair. One finger tapped the gun at her side.

Then his hands were stuffing the phone under his skein and out of sight, and he left Bea behind to charge away.

People milled and moved in the width of the corridor—he twisted around one group before they stepped blindly into him, raced on past more, trusting in speed to hide his blurred shape one more time. *I don't know it's anything. Except...* Except Zara kept insisting Wesley had shared everything he knew, when Wesley himself said there was more.

Like she wasn't speaking for him to hear.

Colin flung himself faster, wrenching strength from his lungs to his pounding feet.

"—a ghost, I told you—"

He swept on past that gasping voice. Wesley's room was just ahead, easy to spot with the uniformed cop at the doorway. That guard was looking half into the room, but his head had just begun swinging away as Colin raced up.

Beyond that doorway—

A hulking shape, a soft spectral outline that would be a mere shimmer to someone without skein to see through. Eric stood right back there watching Zara at Wesley's bedside, his deadly hands ready.

Colin dove down through the room at just the right angle that would shove Eric away from her.

*This one more time, let me make the skein* drive *my feet and give me the strength to* push!

Eric looked up just as he slammed into him.

Arms snaked out and locked in the beginnings of a hold. Weight shifted, straining for that one point to unbalance his enemy.

Something spun off-center, Eric's momentum was already stepping out of his path and away from Zara—

An arm lashed off to the side, gave him an opening to bear down harder. Sound moved behind him, Zara closing in ready to touch Eric with the spell or get herself hit.

Colin twisted and flailed for a better hold. Eric's fists pounded at him—cushioned hits, but so *strong* each rattled his grip, while his own skein lay still and only soaked up the worst of the blows. He strained, anything to keep Eric from getting leverage.

"What the bleeding hell—" The guard.

A shove rocked Colin back. He dove back in, into a fist that flung him spinning away.

He crashed down against a bed. Against a shape soaked with blood. *I forced Eric away from Zara, not from Wesley—*

That grim sight was gone as he spun back toward Eric. Toward Zara, as the guard herded her back into the corner. Eric's huge figure faced them both.

Colin leaped at him. Eric twisted, flung out a stiff-arm that sent him crashing back.

*"Stop right there!"*

Lieutenant Hoyle stood in the doorway, leveling a pistol that looked bigger than both of his hands around it. His face twisted in fury, studying them both—they must both have slipped into visibility by now.

Two shapes covered with the same green.

Eric looked at Hoyle, and pointed a finger at Colin.

*No, he can't fall for it—*

Zara yelled "Not that one—"

The gun swung over to Colin. Eric blurred toward Hoyle.

The room exploded, with a single ear-shattering boom that spun Eric around where he stood.

Colin stared, caught by a lightning of wild hope—*lightning after thunder,* came a sudden thought. But Eric stayed on his feet, he turned.

Hoyle stood gaping. Colin's feet began to move—

Eric's claws thudded into Hoyle's chest, and the cop hurtled away to crash against the wall.

Colin stumbled, glaring at the murderer. *Nothing* they did stopped him.

And Eric turned back, he spun and backhanded the poor dazed guard, to fling him away and send him crashing into Zara.

Then he turned to where Colin stood frozen.

"Two witnesses left."

And he shimmered, and his invisible form darted from the room.

*Going after his other prisoners.*

Colin wrenched to pull his invisibility around him again. He stole one instant to glance over and see Zara dragging himself out from under the cop, safe, and started out past Hoyle's body.

The lieutenant was sitting up. Green skein glittered under his shirt.

# CHAPTER FIVE

# ABANDON

*Hoyle was alive.*

And Eric wanted the "Two witnesses left."

Colin dashed into the corridor—*how could all these people still only be* gathering *out here?* He skidded around them and headed up, toward where he'd seen Walters go to interview another of the victims.

Eric was nowhere in sight. Too many people moved in Colin's way, blocking his view and making him swerve around them. Wesley was dead. Zara was safe. Hoyle had the missing skein.

Shouts and footsteps surged around him, but the target's room was just ahead.

Two figures stood in the doorway, one in black and one in white.

The cop shouted "Isn't noticing this your job? They were your patients, both of them!"

The doctor snapped "The monitors were off. It was just twenty minutes."

*They* were *his patients... I'm twenty minutes late... but Eric said...* *Eric said. He let me hear it.*

Colin lurched to a stop and whirled back the other way, back for Terri. Eric had killed again, he must have gotten the others first. And he used that. *How could I* ever *believe he wasn't after Terri?* And Bea was there trying to defend her, alone.

Shouts were rising around the corridor, shrill fingers of fear from the patients that squirmed up against the staff's voices trying to tamp them down. Colin could only rush back through them.

He swept past a glimpse of Hoyle and the crowd, Zara standing beside him, still okay.

A tangle of frightened visitors and harried nurses blocked the way—he twisted over and ricocheted off the wall to slip past them, but he felt heads turn as he did. And nothing, nothing, he did now would give his skein the same speed and power as Eric's steps...

Through the crowd, he saw Bea standing in Terri's doorway.

He clung to that sight as he wove through the distance. Bea was safe, Terri had to be safe.

Bea eyed him warily, gun still at her side, as he slowed to a stop.

"Yes it's me," he said. "So Eric didn't come—" A chilling thought made him glance back, but no, Eric wasn't simply following him now. He slid around her into Bea's room, out of sight.

"Take a look," she said softly.

His gaze darted to the bed—but Terri looked back at him, unhurt.

Then her lined, ashen face tilted to glance down along her sheets. Something lay there, a bit of tangled metal that should be glittering. If it weren't darkened in dried blood.

A necklace. A frail little shape he'd seen before, a thin imitation of some of Zara's.

Bea whispered "Nurse Setter wore that. Eric tossed it in here and ran."

"So he took her after all. This means she's probably—"

Colin cut off, seeing Terri's eyes on him. But he remembered what had set Eric off against Gardner, what order the old man had given to Hoyle and the nurse that had made Eric explode.

"Dead," Terri finished. "Because she drugged me. Where's Hoyle?"

"Oh, he squirmed out of it," Colin said at once. "Eric tried for him, but he's got the missing skein to protect him. But... the prisoners from the mine, I think they're already..."

His voice broke. He saw the understanding jump from his face to Terri's like some awful spark. Of *guilt*—Eric had only seized those three to grow more skein for Terri.

"But, Zara's fine," he added quickly.

"I'll have to confirm those." Bea's face creased into a frown. "For what it's worth, we've learned something here. Eric retaliated against Hoyle and the nurse for harming Terri, but he also didn't risk touching her. We're still at the same stalemate, at least about Terri herself. It's people around her that are targets."

She had to say the last part out loud? Colin winced.

But Terri's eyes were spread wide with that truth. "So more people die, and more? And *nothing* changes that?"

Her voice was a broken moan. Nothing in her shattered body had drawn a cry like that from her, ever.

"Listen," he rushed out. "Let's just get through the first thing. Like... we haven't looked for him around here. We don't know he doesn't have more tricks lined up on top of these."

"That's true," Bea said. "You can see him better, so I'll stay with Terri—"

*"No!"*

Terri snarled it through her teeth. Her eyes bored into Bea.

"You said Colin needs you to use the spell and beat him. I *don't hold you back. Ever.*"

Colin leaned over his sister and flung back "Now you listen to me—"

"Quiet."

Bea's single urgent word cut through their voices. Outside the sud-denly-still room, footsteps were closing in. Walters's voice rumbled out orders like an advancing storm.

Colin twisted away. Squeezing tighter on the invisibility, he dived down behind the empty second bed—jarring it a moment and making the pulled-back curtain rustle.

Walters swept in, with Hoyle and Zara in his wake. He marched straight up to Bea.

"I do not *believe* this. Three witnesses killed—and you're still standing guard over yesterday's news here?" He leaned in, all his bulk looming toward her.

"I made a judgment call, sir." Bea's unhurried voice could have been speaking to anyone. "And Rowe did come by here—"

Zara dodged around Walters to reach Terri's side.

"—just to drop off a message. From the missing Nurse Setter." Bea held up the stained necklace.

"That does it," Walters snapped. "We *find* this animal, and I find someone who can lead this case. And *you* stay right there," and his hand darted out to grab Hoyle's arm.

For a moment, Colin saw Hoyle's crossed arms squeeze closer around himself, holding his torn shirt closed over a glint of skein.

"Please," Zara said. "Can we at least be grateful, for the ones who did survive—"

*"No.* Hoyle, show Ms. da Costa that weapon you used."

Hoyle drew it out from his shoulder holster.

Colin stared. The mass of steel looked bigger than ever—was that an actual Desert Eagle? No, the lines were off from the pictures he'd seen, but it looked like the same kind of hand cannon. How could Hoyle even control that thing when it went off?

Walters said "Hoyle says he put a round smack into Rowe, and the other officer collaborates that. So, Ms. da Costa, how does anyone get up after being shot with *that?"*

Zara's eyebrows rose. "Are you asking if I'm some sort of gun expert?"

"I am *demanding* you tell me." Walters's eyes blazed, his whole face shook as he leaned in. "If there's armor that can stop that round, I want my whole team in it. If there's a weapon that beats it... and if you want any hope, any hope *at all* of keeping any of our protection here..."

He spun around and looked straight down at Terri.

"You tell me what you know!"

Terri glared right back at him.

Colin's fists clenched against the second bed's frame. Terri had watched skein begin to devour people, she'd seen the cost of letting its secrets spread, but she also knew the threat Eric was right now. There was *still* no clear answer who to trust.

But Walters pinned her under his gaze.

Her breathing whispered in the room, soft, hesitating.

It broke into a *wheeze* and she struggled for air. Zara leaned past Walters and took Terri's hand, and in a moment she steadied again. Colin's suddenly-racing heart slowed as well—of course, Terri must have faked that attack, but it delayed Walters anyway.

Hoyle's voice broke the silence. "Really, one answer is in the weapon."

"What?" Walters spun back toward him.

"Inside it. My pistol's heavy caliber, but I loaded it with safety rounds, and I suppose they shattered on Rowe's armor the same way they're meant to do if they hit a wall." Hoyle's mouth actually crooked in a small grin. "I had to use them to prevent accidents. We're in a hospital."

"You... you..."

Walters scowled at the lieutenant as if the whole explanation was somehow his fault. When it was one thing Hoyle's scheming hadn't caused.

He turned back to Zara again. "Whatever Hoyle says, I've never heard of armor shrugging that off. And you want to think hard, about if I let Detective Simms or anyone hang around your family after this. She was your only protection today, and all Rowe did with the chance was toss you a trophy. I call that ignoring you, and it's about time I did the same thing."

"Is that a threat, Commissioner?" Zara said.

"We need to *catch Rowe*. Without tying resources down here, around a target he passed up, who still refuses to cooperate."

He turned away, and the last rumble of his words faded to let stillness settle over the room.

Then Hoyle's smoother voice slipped in. "You might let me talk to the ladies. I think I can convince them to—"

"You get out of here!" Walters moved to block him from the bed. "You already compromised yourself, 'lieutenant,' and yet you're still hanging around the case... You go join the uniforms and look for traces of our killer. While I figure out if I want Rowe to catch you or not!"

Colin bit his lip. He'd seen how Commissioner Walters bullied Hoyle—when Hoyle was enough of a backstabber without provoking him.

Hoyle slunk out of the room. Walters headed out himself, not sparing another word for the others, and moved the opposite way.

Colin slipped out behind Hoyle.

The weasel had to be up to something more now. Colin watched him march down the corridor, trying to think how long to stay with him. Doctors, nurses, and patients buzzed around them, too many. Too many chances someone would spot him, or else he'd have to slow down and lose Hoyle.

Instead he edged up just behind the man.

*"Careless,"* he whispered.

Hoyle jumped, whirled, and the shock across his face brought a twinge of shameful satisfaction in Colin's gut.

Hoyle blinked, stared. "Da Costa?" he whispered.

"So *you* stole the skein."

"Of course." The fear faded to leave a hint of a smile on Hoyle's face. He turned and resumed walking again, and Colin fell into place just a breath behind him. Hoyle whispered "You were right, Rowe did come after me. This stuff kept me alive."

"And you're sure you deserve any of that? Eric wants you because you sold Terri out, same as Nurse Setter."

"And I survived to hunt him again. If you really wanted to bring him down, you'd show me how to use the skein, not just survive."

"Like you care about stopping him. You covered up Eric growing skein in the mine, because Gardner paid you. And now..."

Hoyle's explanation for Eric's armor flashed through his mind again. The conniving...

*"You* want to be the one to bring our secrets to Walters, is that it? Or you think you can bring Eric down yourself and save your job?"

Hoyle's step faltered.

A pair of nurses walked by, close enough to halt his whispering.

When they passed, Colin went on "Is that it, you're fighting for your job? But you were too late to save Wesley and his friends."

"I know."

"Did you even want to save them? They're the victims you helped to hide up there. Did you just let Eric cover them up for you—"

"Do *not* say that!"

Was that real pain in Hoyle's voice? Guilt, in *him?*

Hoyle's voice settled lower, more controlled. "I'm a police officer. You think I spent my life on the job just so I'd have more to trade to a man like Gardner? You think I want to see cops killed? Because every time we blink, that's what Eric Rowe does."

"So you don't watch it happen, you run? Don't think I forgot, I had to drag you back here last time. Maybe I should have let you go—at least you'd be out of our way."

And now Hoyle had the skein Eric had grown. *If I let him keep it.* Colin's muscles quivered, anger simmering through him.

"I'm trying to take him down." Hoyle spoke quietly now, steady as his footsteps. "And you saw Rowe do it again: he can walk into any-where, anywhere he wants, if someone doesn't get him. Walters won't listen to me, and he's tired of defending your sister too. That means it's up to us.

"I know where the infrared scopes are," he went on, softer now. "I slowed Rowe down with this weapon, and I can load better rounds into it. That and the rifles I had the men using before. From where I sit, if you wanted Rowe beaten, you'd be jumping at my help. Instead you're letting me figure this skein out all on my own."

The man was too smooth. Colin halted his steps and watched Hoyle pull away, feeling the fury spread and set his fingers quivering.

Hoyle really thought he'd trust him again? The traitor could take anything he knew about the skein and just run—or stay and wind up a worse threat than Eric. *I could rip that stolen skein right off him... he won't be walking near people forever...*

Up ahead, Hoyle stole a second look back, an uncertain look as if he was just realizing Colin had fallen back.

Colin shook his head. Sure, just take his skein and leave the man helpless? He watched Hoyle continue on his way and wondered if the lieutenant might still do some good. *I guess one of Eric's targets having just enough skein to protect himself is a good thing.*

Even if it was Hoyle.

A corridor branched off to the side, and Colin saw only two nurses walking up there. He twisted away up that quieter space, away from Hoyle.

The anger was still dug into his flesh, even with the crooked cop left behind. His head pounded. He pushed on, looking around and glancing into rooms for where Eric might still be holed up.

This branch did seem less crowded, only a scattered nurse here and there who might stumble into Eric. Colin walked faster, wondering how long it would take to peep through all the back corners here. Eric was probably long gone. *And what if I do find him, when I'm alone and this distracted?*

Around a corner came Bea's voice: "No, you both join up and take a thorough look out front. Rowe always hides somewhere we miss— see if you can flush him out. I'll take the storage…"

Her voice faded. He looked around the corner to see Bea walking away, her phone at her ear.

One point at a time, in control, that was how she spoke. Just that brush with her words' rhythm left his heartbeat steadying again. He watched her walking along, phone ready but her head always turning slightly as she took in the rooms she passed. Ready for any glimpse of Eric.

His feet turned on the floor, eager to join her.

Or, they could sweep the place faster separately. That was the goal, to get through this and know Eric wasn't still lurking nearby, not watching Bea at work. He twisted away.

He walked faster now, watching the nurses and doctors he saw. Which way would be the emptier, more dangerous sections?

His phone buzzed at his hip.

Just one of its near-silent pulses, and then it stopped. Like a mistake or a signal… oh. Of course Bea had noticed him.

The next room was locked, but the next was open and empty enough to let him duck inside and pull the phone out. There her name was on the Callers screen.

One click called her back. "Hey. Yeah, you spotted me."

"It's only staying alert. Why did you pull away?"

"Thought I'd rush through the side where you weren't looking." Without checking which places those would be. He leaned back against a cabinet—his moment's urge to keep separate felt only foolish now. "What's the plan?"

"I'm looking through the emptier places where Rowe's more likely to stay unnoticed. I sent the uniforms to the more crowded spots; seeing them might flush him out. Then if he's not in the building, we go back to our wider search."

"Like the Gardner building, or Gardner's home? Eric has to rest somewhere." He had to be tired—Colin could still feel the morning and yesterday weighing on himself.

"Right. He seems to be wiping up signs and witnesses of where he's been. We should have seen that."

"And kept those three people safe after the mine," he sighed. "If we ever could. We haven't been *saving* much, or tracking him down either, have we? Terri said we could be doing this forever."

The last words slipped out as a tired moan. *Did I really let her hear that?*

Bea said "It's an investigation. It can change at any moment, and sometimes for the better."

"Oh, you're trying to cheer me up?" And just like that, a joke came sliding off his tongue: "You'll have to do better than that. I've been cheered up by experts."

"So I've seen." A fairly bland answer, but he thought he heard another smile in her tone.

It was time to stop and finish the search… but… "Sounds like you need more training there," he returned.

"If that's a skill I need," was all she said.

*Ugh. I tease, I flirt, and she just misses it?* He opened his mouth, fumbling at the idea of trying again.

Bea said "Hold on. It's Zara," and her voice snapped to full alert again. One blip sounded on the phone, and new sounds flooded in.

Zara was saying "Now please, will you listen to her?"

"To your police friends, Ms. da Costa?" That voice was the doctor, the short, prickly one who'd challenged Zara last night. "None of that changes this. Your daughter needs to leave this facility."

"Please remember, Terri was being *poisoned*. Do you want to ignore what that could do in her condition? Also, Bea, will you explain?"

"I already said—" Bea started, before Colin stuffed the phone back under his skein and rushed back.

This hospital had already turned Terri loose once, and he'd had to watch her grow weaker and sleepier every day. That was with "help" from this place's own Nurse Setter, but now they were kicking her out again?

His dash through the corridors slowed as more people streamed into view again—busy staff in their uniforms, visitors in brighter colors, all people who just might spot him and begin whispering about "ghosts," an hour after Eric's rampage. He moved on for Terri's room, not sure what he could even *do*.

He was closing in on her doorway when he caught sight of Bea, closing at a run. She looked straight at him, and waved him to move aside.

Head pounding again, he edged back up the corridor, back around a quiet-looking corner where he could crouch down and risk pulling out the phone again. Lurking at a distance seemed to be the only place left for him now—and what stung most was, Zara had called Bea, instead of family.

Their lines were still open, and he heard Zara saying "Dr. Morton, each time I ask, I've been told the effects on Terri are still uncertain."

"And now they're certain enough," he answered—Morton, she'd called him. "We've done what we can for your daughter. And I told you, we have to consider the needs of all our patients. You've brought a *murderer* here again, and what looks like more police disruptions every hour. That's not something that can continue."

"And putting anyone in danger is the last thing we want," Zara said. "Even though Eric might have come to silence those witnesses no matter where Terri was. But Terri is your patient too. The last time you discharged her, you worked with us to see that she'd have help."

"I think you'll find your daughter meets all our guidelines for discharge."

"I'm. Right. Here," Terri breathed. Her faint voice only just came through the speaker.

*"What is this?"*

Walters's voice crashed into the line, into the room.

He added "Someone's talking about discharging the girl?"

"Guidelines, they call them." Zara didn't lose a beat, even with both of Terri's doubters in the room. "I think we should both look at these rules that let them throw out someone in Terri's circumstances."

" 'Circumstances,' " Walters growled. "Doctor, Terri da Costa is an important witness in the worst murder spree this town has ever had."

Colin let out a breath. Of course, Walters knew he needed Terri safe, in spite of all his bluster and bluffing.

Walters went on "I understand Lieutenant Hoyle has insisted you support her before?"

"Hoyle?" Morton snapped. "You really want to mention the man who fired a *gun* in a patient's room? If that thing wasn't a bazooka— we're getting requests for hearing tests now."

"The lieutenant was trying to subdue your patients' killer. But I assure you, you won't have to worry about him again. As for this girl supporting our case... it looks like the witnesses have been less than useful. And today just proved she's the only one *not* in danger."

Colin's fingers clamped hard on the phone.

Zara said "With all due respect, your files should give you a different picture of what Eric Rowe—"

*"Due respect* would be leaving the police decisions to the police!" Walters's voice boomed down the corridor. "This manhunt has nothing to do with you or your family anymore. Or with *anything* the doctors decide for your daughter. And I've got a killer to catch."

And he marched away. Some of those hard footsteps came through the phone, over the pounding that grew in Colin's head.

*Witnesses less than useful...* was Walters still trying to pressure Zara to talk, or just turning on her out of spite? He could actually just leave Terri defenseless...

"It seems like this hospital may not be safe for your patient." That was Bea, still there. "We've worked this out before: you can help hide her somewhere, along with the care she needs."

Dr. Morton sighed. "I'm afraid we still have to think of our other patients, and where we can make the most difference—"

The roaring in Colin's ears swallowed the rest, that and the sound of Walters storming by outside.

Zara's voice swelled in his ear, that small rising that caught people's attention. "Is it pampering to give a patient what she needs? You've seen the number of messages Terri got when she returned. We should all be pulling together here."

"Together? I'll say it again, we have *standards* for this, as the best way to help everyone. Not keep struggling over one patient or put everyone else at risk. I wish—"

Colin shoved the phone in his pocket before he could slam it into the wall. Sounds, doctors, drummed and rattled all across the rooms around him, and Walters was still stomping down the corridor—

Colin rushed after him.

Startled gasps sprang up as he passed. The cool presence on his skin, the invisibility, *flickered.* He clenched his thoughts tighter around it and closed in. Walters stepped into a side corridor, and slowed.

Colin let the stealth drop before Walters turned around.

The big man stared, and his hand edged toward his coat pocket. He growled "Rowe?"

"No," and Colin yanked the skein mask back. "But he will be here sometime, because Terri's here."

"Colin da Costa." Walters frowned. "I heard you'd be around here—"

"You should have 'heard' that Eric will keep coming after Terri. He kept her locked up for two years, do you seriously think he'll just get over that?"

"And *you* may have heard, we have limits to our resources." He held up a hand with its fingers spread, and leaned toward Colin. "Hoyle tried camping out around your sister and still managing a search, and that only..." He spread those fingers wider, and loomed closer.

*Like he's talking to a child!* Colin stood his ground, his mass against Walters's bulk. "Eric *will* come after her again. He only left her this time because she's not safe to travel. But Eric will always be back..."

He was repeating himself, he knew, and his voice died away. The murmur of voices in the hallway filled that silence.

Walters said "So you're saying she works as bait?"

"No!" Colin gritted his teeth. "I'm saying you try protecting the victim here. The only way to stop Eric is if we're all on guard—"

*"We?* My men could have had the whole town searched and run down every trace of Rowe by now. The big reason he's still out there is those cops watching your sister. That and *you,* and that body armor."

Walters's eyes narrowed. His upraised hand stretched a finger, slowly, toward the skein.

"Is that stuff like Rowe's? Where'd you get it? What caliber does it stop?"

"It stops anything *you're* carrying. You'll find that out, if you abandon my sister." Colin leaned in to stare straight into the commissioner's eyes. "If you let Terri get one more scratch, I'll show you what—"

A punch slammed into his stomach.

His breath *whoofed* out, and pain flared, real pain. Even through the skein, he felt it.

But Walters crumbled backward, yowling as he clutched at his hand.

Colin glared down and dragged in a breath to finish his warning, but those moans were already draining his rage away. *And I came after* him…

"What's that—"

The shocked voice sent Colin spinning away, running. He grabbed the mask behind his head and yanked it up to make it settle in place again.

*"Get him!"* Walters, screaming through the pain. Shouts echoed behind him.

The next doorway was waiting. Colin ducked inside, out of view for that one moment. He wrenched his skein at the light around him, and slipped out to move on.

Someone gasped.

The skein flickered. For one instant, the invisibility gave way.

He clamped control down and bolted.

Feet pounding, path twisting, turns weaving and leading him deeper into the building, he flung himself away. His control slipped again and again, and he ran trailing louder and louder shouts behind him, for what had to be flashes of him appearing.

At last he got the power steady enough to duck around several turns unnoticed, and finally settled in an empty room to slump down and breathe.

*I lost it. I lost it with the skein, and so much worse picking that stupid fight with Walters.* Heat flooded through him, dark and helpless shame, burning at him as he tried to stand.

Bea. Zara. One call to them would get him some kind of help… but he couldn't bear to touch his phone yet. Hospital staff trundled by outside—someone would glance into here at some point.

He willed the skein to invisibility again, and he could feel his control flicker. First he couldn't tap into its strength, now he was losing its stealth and its protection too…

Safer not to wear it outside at all, then. That one chance to do *something* pushed back the confusion for a moment. He willed the skein to slide in under his clothes, and at least that well-practiced move still worked. His stomach looked, felt, undamaged too, but a simple punch should never have hurt him at all.

Then he was walking out and strolling away. Walters couldn't have many men looking for him—he'd been trying to pull them *away* from the hospital.

And it felt good to walk around in real clothes again. One nurse saw him and simply waved him toward the front corridor, another stream of visitors in their varied clothes let him drift in among them... Besides, he could call Bea any time.

He only realized his destination when he saw the cafeteria ahead. Of course he'd come here, when the best guess they had about keeping the skein working was to stay fed.

The brunch crowd moved around him, as he filed past the first of the plastic plants along the wall. *I'm Colin da Costa, I'm a friend, supporter, defender around this town.* He thought he saw eyes glance toward him, but those had to be because of the scars on his face, from fighting Eric. Not just throwing his temper away against Walters.

He heaped plates with pasta, sausage, fruit... what would have the best nutrients for fueling dragonskin? The thought started him chuckling, even when people began glancing at him again.

The empty table he took wasn't in the middle of the room, but it felt like it. Even the smells of the huge meal in front of him didn't spark hunger—instead he mechanically shoveled each bite in. The skein used to make him and Bea ravenous, but now it seemed to deaden his awareness of food. Eric might have gone through this too, not that he could ask him about it.

At the corner of his eye he saw more faces turning toward him. Some must be for the scars and some for the portions he was putting away, but someone could be getting word back to Walters. Colin dug into the carbs and meat, food he couldn't pocket, and tried to work faster and still keep it all down.

When the uniformed cop finally appeared in the doorway, Colin only had to scoop up his last apple and work his way into the crowd. He made for the back door at a quick walk, no faster and no slower—even his speed was different with him moving in plain sight.

The cop closed in behind him. A turn off the main corridor twisted him out of view, and he broke into a run.

"Hey, hold on there—" a nurse called. He dashed on, fighting down the queasiness in his stomach.

*Just get* away. *Get time to get the skein working again, get back to the real enemy...* At least he knew the hospital better than the cops. He twisted around another turn and slowed to a walk again. The food lurched inside him.

"You can't be back here. Do I have to call Security—"

He scrambled on. Which way, which way would get him out of the building and away, or just in deeper and away from prying eyes? The sounds behind him moved faster.

His feet ached. His stomach churned, as he spun around another corner...

They ran past him.

When he moved on, it was with slow, fragile steps, afraid of disturbing that one pocket of peace. For one moment he was *not* digging himself in deeper, and he could believe in staying clear long enough to get his strength back or fix the bridges he'd burned.

Something pulsed against his side.

He started, his footsteps clattering louder than the phone had been. Of course, of course it was simply his phone.

He drew it out, closed his eyes for a moment: *Please, is it Bea?*

And her voice filled his ear. "Where are you? They think they spotted Eric across town."

# CHAPTER SIX

# WAIT AND SEE

With reports of Eric across town, Bea had no trouble sending the police out from the hospital to reinforce their trap.

Too easy, maybe. Colin tried to trust that they had found their enemy, that Eric wouldn't simply circle back while Terri was unprotected.

The hospital exit was only two short minutes away, by the quick walk Colin took. His worries about being spotted settled back into perspective: if Walters did have people here, the truth was still that the commissioner had punched *him.* But to stop and argue that now, with Eric out there…

Then he stepped into the parking lot, climbed into Bea's trim black car, and she sped them away.

"Trying to get me out before Walters sees me?" He meant it as a joke, but the question came out all too straight.

"Let's say all of this will be easier if the troops don't," she said. "Just, easier."

More softly, he came to the real question. *"Did* they find Eric?"

"The facts seem to fit. We kept Josh Gardner's home under surveillance after we searched it. It should be empty, but now there's someone inside that they never saw enter, and he's avoiding the windows."

"You thought he'd come looking for any more information that Gardner had on him? That does fit—Eric wouldn't blow up one computer and think that was all there was."

"This has to go step by step, now." Bea's thoughts sounded miles ahead of the car, and deep in her own element. "To build up a perimeter that Rowe can't slip through."

"We tried that before, with Hoyle in charge. Now it's Walters?"

"Now it's me. Odds are the commissioner doesn't want his name on this if it goes bad. And he mostly trusts me, with the 'actual case.'"

Meaning chasing Eric without Terri in the picture. "If he's picked you, then he's got one thing right. But... I won't be much help."

He reached under his shirt to wrap his fingers in skein. Then he held them up, and wrapped *light* around them to shimmer them from sight. They stayed a blur for two seconds, four, five...

They flickered back to sight, just for one moment. Still useless.

"Sorry," he groaned. "But I did grab a meal, a big one, so maybe I need time for that to settle in. Or I have to get my focus back—or it just won't work for me again, I don't know." He looked down at the dashboard, hearing the forced cheer in his voice begin to sag.

"Focus on what you can do," Bea said. "We need to spot him when he's hiding, and not just as a blur. Can you do that?"

Colin peeled the skein off one finger. At least it still flowed to match his needs, and he spread it out into a gossamer fold over his eyes. For a moment he thought of the sunglasses he'd used to camouflage this trick before, and wished he'd taken better care of them.

He shimmered his other finger away again, but looking through the skein he saw the clear halo of its power. It held, held... the image vanished, an instant before the finger itself fell back into full view. Then stealth and sight both locked in place again, flickered...

"Not too bad," he said. "At least a sense that blinks off now and then is safer than an invisibility that gives itself away."

He shook his head, looked around. They were just driving past a group of children waving a *Car Wash* sign, and two cars being soaped down. Laughing in the summer sun.

Colin shut his eyes. Zara had helped people set up a few of those over the years, so of course they'd spread through the town, even this far from the Hillside itself.

One more part of the town that Eric hated, blamed, for Terri and everything else. *Please, please, don't let me fail now.*

When Bea slowed the car, he realized he hadn't used any moment of the ride to tease her, or just say how glad he was to face what lay ahead with her. No hint of that kiss, not now.

"The third house up," she said.

She motioned up the block, up along a wide stretch of lawns, bright green even in the summer. *Thanks to Gardner's gardener?* Colin pushed down the random thought. But if Rayo Hill could have anything like a rich neighborhood, this was it.

He could barely see where Josh Gardner's house itself would be, with two other homes and their different trees and walls screening the car's position from it. What he saw was the broad two-story size of the other houses here, and the amount of open space between them, even with the lines of landscaping breaking it up. Too much visibility, to crowd police into a net to catch someone that always saw them and slipped away.

Bea held up her phone to show him a neighborhood map, and a picture of the deep brown house itself. Then she brought the phone to her ear.

"No changes? Rogers, Garcia, Jonas, Woo?"

She listened, for one long moment.

"Then wait for Jonas," she said. "Do *not* spook the suspect. Stay off the radios, in case they're tapped. Keep binoculars on that house at all times. We're bringing in the infrared scopes again—remember my orders, once you have one, keep looking through that scope, never mind that it's daylight."

When she looked back at Colin, he said "Scopes? You're using those, but not saying *because there's a near-invisible man in there?*"

"It's the most they'll believe. I sent an officer out with Hoyle to pick up the scopes and the SWAT rifles."

"Wait, *Hoyle—*"

"Not my choice," she said. "But he's the one who had them stored last night. And he wants to win this too, he's got no reason to hold back. But until we have them…" She held out a hand, palm up.

"Right."

He peeled off a piece of skein and passed it over, and she set it across her eyes. She was the one who'd shown *him* he could see through it, and she'd used skein in small amounts for weeks before she met him—Eric would never slip past her.

He said "That map looked clear enough. I guess if you're up here, I cover the back?" He reached for the door.

Then he stopped, fingertips just touching the handle. The skein wasn't working for him, not any use strong enough to match Eric… so *why was he wearing so much* when all it did was keep him from using the spell? If he went out with just the bit for his eyes, he could use the best weapon they had—if he could survive getting in reach of their enemy.

*Bea let me carry all our skein, but am I better without it now? If I can't get control back…*

"Colin? Anything?"

"I'm on it." He swung the door open.

His steps came quick and sharp against the sidewalk. His head felt clearer now; leaving his skein would have been accepting that the bulk of its power really was lost to him.

The street curved slowly around away from the Gardner house. Colin marched along, watching for any glimpses of the house's brown—not the family's signature pale green, for once—through the patterns of trees.

How long before Eric spotted them?

It might all come down to that. More time for the police to close in, for Colin's meal to work into his system, for Hoyle to bring the tools to trap Eric. If Hoyle didn't find a way to cheat them again.

The streets seemed so *quiet*—more space and trees than people here, if that was how someone like Josh Gardner lived. The air was clear, more smells of the plants than the town around them.

He caught one more glimpse of the Gardner house, just another sliver of it between the screens of trees and buildings. He drew out his phone and called Bea. "I'm rounding the block now—"

A dust-covered little car stood parked on the street ahead, and two figures stirred inside it, looking right in the direction of the Gardner house. Some of Bea's cops in plainclothes... he paused on the sidewalk. To come closer would be testing whether Walters and his grudge were still at work out here. But the only other way to help would be to creep in right past these houses and up behind Eric.

A woman, graying hair, strode down from one house toward the surveillance car. Of course strangers here would stick out.

As the police moved to talk to her, one of them turned to look straight at Colin. He swallowed, but none of them closed in on him. His phone to Bea was silent.

This had to work. Bea would keep the police off him, keep the neighbors clear of the crossfire, close their grip around Eric... it had to work.

He glanced through the trees again: still just a glimpse of brown walls through the gnarled branches at the back end of the block. No chance to see Eric, no chance of being spotted himself.

The phone beeped, someone being patched in.

A new voice said "—opened, repeat, the front door is wide open. No movement so far."

*It's starting.*

The rustles and motions along the street froze, as the world locked into a moment of sharp clarity. Eric was moving, he'd seen them, they were out of time. Colin clutched the phone, stared back up the street.

"Hold position, every one of you." Bea's calm was the eye of a rising storm. "Report any movement, even a blur. I'll move up and cover the front."

The front? Was there *anyone* in sight of that door now who could see if Eric just strolled out? His legs burned to rush back, to stand with Bea... but she'd said *everyone* should stay in place...

A car slowed to park some a distance from the cops, and Hoyle stepped out.

The disgraced lieutenant walked straight in among the trees. In one hand he held one of his IR scopes to his eye; the other carried a briefcase.

"That's *Hoyle,* " came one of the cops' voices on the line. "What's that case for?"

Another cop said "What about our SWAT rifles? Hell, we can go right in now."

"Still looks quiet," Bea said. "Report any movement."

Those cops still didn't know, what Eric could do...

Colin plunged into the line of trees, angling toward the house and Hoyle. He steadied the phone as he ran and said "Hoyle's going in himself!"

Through the tree row ahead, he saw a high-up glimmer of glass, and an aura-marked figure moving behind it. The next moment, that reflection shattered with a gunshot.

"Sniper, top window!"

"Take cover!"

Police voices crackled on the line, as Colin dropped for the dirt. Something moved between the trees near him—Hoyle, crouching low, fumbling open his case for what had to be a rifle of his own.

Because that broken second-floor window made a perfect sniper perch, to cover the whole open space between the house and the trees at its back border. *But since when is Eric a marksman?*

Colin pressed himself low and crawled nearer, scrambling from behind one gnarled tree to the next. The window waited out across the yard, one open gap in the brown-painted wall that glared back at him.

Or this could all be a distraction, while Eric walked out that open front door. But Eric knew someone would be watching that door too, like Bea was rushing there now.

A haloed shape hurtled from the window.

Eric had leaped headfirst into space—his side cracked against the frame as he passed—for one frozen moment Colin watched their invisible enemy dropping toward the ground, knowing none of those collisions would touch him through his mass of skein.

He still had to cross the open backyard. Colin leaped to his feet and racing toward Hoyle. *Move, move, push my legs and give me* speed! But his skein still churned sluggishly under his clothes, weak.

Hoyle watched Eric land through his scope. He fumbled to open the "rifle case," then stopped and instead yanked out his massive pistol.

Eric charged.

One skein-powered leap flung him whole yards to the side before another zigzagged him into a lunge toward Hoyle that sent dirt flying. Colin raced toward them, twisting around a tree trunk and still too far away.

Hoyle turned, trying to swing the scope in one hand to catch a clear glimpse of what must still be a dodging blur to him. His other hand strained to hold up the huge handgun. Eric twisted zigzagged again, closer, too fast.

Hoyle ran. His face broke into a ruin of fear, as he whirled and bolted for the street.

Eric slammed to a stop. He turned to line up straight at his prey's back.

Colin was still too many seconds away—but he flung all his breath into a bellow of *"Got you!"*

Eric glanced over.

Colin charged in. *My skein's got no strength, I'm still carrying too much of it to risk the spell's touch, I'm* helpless.

Eric stopped. His masked head darted around.

Colin stretched his hand out as he rushed in, knowing he'd never close the gap.

Eric flickered, for one moment his image changed from a magic-marked outline to a fully visible shape of green. Then he snapped back into invisibility and leaped away. Just bluffing about the spell had made him hesitate.

"What the hell—"

Two men, cops in plainclothes with guns ready, rushed toward them. Eric swung to the side and off among the brush, just a blur to them—and neither of them even glanced at him.

Colin's phone was still in his grip. He jammed it to his ear to bring Bea into earshot, looked at the officers, and pointed after Eric. "There he goes! Come *on!"*

For what that was worth—their simple handguns wouldn't scratch Eric. Colin glanced over at Hoyle and his giant pistol. The lieutenant was only trudging past the cops now, eyes downcast.

Colin rushed after him as he headed for his car. From the corner of his eye, he tracked Eric leaping over the wrought-iron fence around the next property, distance already making his shimmer harder to notice and harder still to chase.

From the phone came Bea's voice, calm and firm. "Pursue him, but keep your distance."

"Pursue *what?"* a cop snapped.

"Watch for the sniper!" The second cop crouched, stared up at the broken window. *No, no, that was all just to give him an open window to jump out!*

"Watch for the smallest movement," Bea said.

"I saw *something..."* the first officer said.

Was that it, Bea was asking them to walk right up to Eric's shimmer and spot it themselves? Instead of telling them there was a barely-visible man there?

Hoyle reached his car. He was just pulling the door open when Colin reached him, slammed it shut again.

"Tell them! Tell them he's over here!" he yelled at Hoyle. Eric was still crouching behind the fence's bars, *right there.*

Hoyle groaned. "It's no good. I… I tried, I should have got him. If I got one minute, one more minute to put my rifle together… I missed my chance. Of *course* I did." The last words twisted his face, from hollowed-out despair to pain.

Or guilt. If Hoyle could feel that much…

Colin pushed that away, and roared in the lieutenant's face "So it's all about you, *you* nailing the killer?" Did Hoyle even bring the scopes and rifles for the other cops?

He looked out at Eric again. Their enemy was gone from the fence.

The other cops stared around, one looking right at Colin.

"No time!" Bea's voice cracked in his ear. "Garcia, your team's with me. The rest of you hold position around that house, but watch all sides and be ready to follow us. Move!"

And they moved. The two cops took places to watch the back of the Gardner house, but they did sweep their gazes around them as well. Bea's clarity and her pretending the house still mattered had broken through their confusion.

Eric slipped across the yard, drawing further back. Colin left Hoyle and dashed along the sidewalk.

And a car, that blessed little black car with Bea at the wheel, swept up and pulled up beside him.

"There!" Colin waved at their target.

Bea nodded. The band of skein around her own eyes glinted as she moved. Then the car surged forward to lunge down the street, and he charged after her.

The property's fence flew past him. Its far end, a driveway, rushed up but an ornate iron gate sealed that off. Eric was heading inward now, alongside the big house.

Bea reached around behind her seat.

Then she swung up a big long shape, a gleaming black rifle, and she twisted to lean back against the inside of her door as she aimed it across the two seats at Eric. The passenger window slid down to give the muzzle room.

Eric lunged away around the back of the house. Too fast.

Bea snapped "He's fleeing onto Acacia. Hoyle, head him off!"

*What? She still expected anything from Hoyle?*

Bea's horn honked. Colin saw her waving to him, and he yanked the car door open to dive inside.

The door's slam launched them into motion: in the next heartbeat Bea's rifle landed across Colin's arms, and the car screeched forward and made him flail to stop the weapon from bouncing in the too-tight space. His feet and shoulders braced and did their best to stop *him* from bouncing.

The end of the block swept up already, and Bea swung them around the corner. A tree-lined sidewalk raced past them.

One thought stirred under the frantic jostling: Bea was *leaving* Eric there in the middle of the block, so certain they'd catch him on its other side, when he could just pull in and take cover in the fences and trees?

A boy stared at them from a window, a woman looked up from trimming her garden. If Eric stayed on the inside of that block, how many new victims would he run across?

They swerved around the corner. Other cars, fast-moving ones that had to be more police, moved at the edges of his sight.

There Eric was—his aura dashing away up the street. Just openly running along it, as if putting distance from them invisibly would let him slip away.

Bea raced the car after him, all their engine's power to close the gap. Colin wedged in place and grappled for his seat belt. They roared past a lawn truck full of branches, one house and then another of different fences and trees around them. Eric's running shape came closer, closer.

The street beyond Eric churned with people.

The even lines of the street and sidewalk ahead broke up into varied cars, figures, people and families and *children* milling around— the *car wash* event they'd passed on the way in. Colin braced himself tighter, stomach queasy.

Eric dashed straight ahead, on course to run right by them.

A car closing in ahead of Eric, that would have moved blindly past him, slowed. It slowed, it U-turned around toward the car wash crowd on the other side, and its course cut Eric off.

Its lumbering motion should have been no obstacle; Eric could easily veer to the left around it. Instead he jerked right.

Right, and in beside the crowd. One invisible arm lashed out—not forward, not at anyone in his path. An old man went crashing back against the side of a car.

And Eric raced on, away.

Colin gaped, at the enemy, at the crumpled, still-moving shape that filled his vision as they slowed.

Bea brought the car up beside the fallen man. Colin wrenched the door open and slid out from under the rifle to leap in among the milling, muttering crowd.

The old man struggled for his feet. One hand gripped the other arm, where it hung at a lopsided, *wrong* angle. His gray beard twisted with the pain on his face.

"Stay still, don't move," Colin said. "There'll be doctors on the way, I'm sure."

"What… what hit me?" the man groaned.

A young woman moved to ease him back to the pavement. "Something must have. You didn't *fall* on that arm."

Colin looked at them, words tangling helplessly in his head. "Keep still," he said again, and he swung back to their car.

Bea was already settling at the wheel again. The seething rage on her face had to be a match for Colin's own.

"Hold this up," she snapped, and held out her phone.

Colin grabbed it, and the next instant the car peeled away. Her siren wailed to life.

"Suspect turning onto Seventh Street," she barked into the phone. Colin looked up, saw Eric twisting away onto that other street ahead.

That "suspect" had the full brick-shattering power of his skein, and he'd turned it loose on an old man... because... of just a moment of frustration that a car happened to wander into his path. Colin flexed his arm, tried to feel the strength, *strength,* of his own skein under his sleeve. He *had* to reach it.

"Get up to Seventh and Oslow," Bea was telling her cops. "While you can!"

She swung the car around an oncoming minivan. Colin clutched at the rifle, trying to keep the barrel over his shoulder and his hands clear of the trigger.

*"Oslow?"* a cop's voice came through the phone's speaker. "How'd he get up there?"

"Do it!"

Bea hauled them around Eric's turn in a squeal of rubber.

There he was—still *running,* right down the street in the open, trusting to speed and invisibility. Already half a block ahead.

Colin held the phone up for Bea, clamped the rifle with his knees, braced his feet until he fumbled the seat belt into place. The engine's roar swelled beneath them. Eric charged straight on down the street, as trees began to thin and houses took their first steps toward sitting closer together. Every block meant more people.

Colin called the skein out from under his sleeves. His fingers flexed inside the gloves, clenched against the seat cushion, as he dug at his memories of the skein's power. How easily Eric had lashed out and struck that old man down.

"Closing in," some cop reported.

*Eric moves like* nothing *can stop him. He crippled Bea's partner Ed Jordan... killed Andy Anderson, Leo Tozier, two police and then another two...* The gloves squeezed tighter. *Joe Martin, Phil Balan, Dennis Fields, Josh Gardner, his three prisoners, he could have killed that old man...*

And he'd held Terri prisoner for two years, and this was their one chance to catch him away from her.

A police car lurched into the street, more than a block ahead.

The phone squawked "What're you doing, where is he?"

They couldn't *see* him. Eric would just breeze past them all.

But the ghostly figure slowed. Circled. Turned and headed back up the street at their own car.

Bea slammed the brakes. The seat belt caught at Colin, the tires squealed around them—a car behind them swerved around and past with its horn blaring. She grabbed the rifle from his grip and stepped onto the street as Eric charged in.

One chance, one chance... the weapon came up to her shoulder...

Eric leaped aside, away, on up a side street. Bea swung the rifle around, tracking...

A groan tore from inside her, and she dove back into the car. People stood around the street, two of them on the sidewalk Eric had darted past. Some were already staring and pointing at Bea's car, its flashing light, the glimpse of her rifle.

"What was that?" a voice through the phone demanded.

Bea passed the weapon to Colin and raced the car for the turn.

"Should have given you the wheel." She swerved them around a slow-moving pickup.

*Or I could take the weapon—no, she's had real practice, and they'd never forgive a civilian opening fire out here.*

The open space of the street broke up into smaller and smaller patches, as more cars came in view for them to dodge.

Eric swerved off the street.

He ducked in under a tiny red sign, in onto the pavement of a small gas station, in among two cars. Right among where their drivers stood.

Bea slowed as they pulled up. "Close in around the Verdugo gas station," she told the phone. "What happened to Hoyle and that gear?"

"Uh, haven't seen him…"

But Eric was simply standing there, leaning against the low brick wall at the space's back. Watching the two customers by the pumps.

Bea tapped her phone once, and turned to Colin. "Three civilians, one in the office. I can't shoot anyway, this near the gas fumes."

"Got it."

The words were right there for him, like the skein already running up his sleeves to shield his fists. He opened the door.

One young woman was pumping gas and staring at the car's flashing light, an older man was blindly wiping windows on the pickup that sat behind her—at a pump with an "out of order" wrapper around it, he saw. And there was the clerk moving inside the tiny office, alone.

While Eric only stood against the wall, like there'd be *amusement* under that mask. And this was only one spot along the street. More hostages would always be just a dash away.

Colin swung wide around the woman with the pump, to put himself in Eric's path before he moved toward her. He could almost smell the tang of the gas—and Eric had once collapsed a whole house, *their* Vargas House, to cover his escape.

"You need to go," he told the woman.

"That police car—"

"Trust me. Go."

She looked at him, eyes widening. At his scars, the gauze-thin wrap across his eyes, at Bea inside speaking on her phone…

She dropped the hose and jumped in her car. As she roared away, Colin turned to the man at the pickup.

Eric paced toward them, with slow, menacing steps.

The man tossed his washcloth away and climbed in his vehicle. Colin turned to face Eric. The pickup pulled forward.

The next moment it *stopped* at the working pump.

Colin stared—couldn't he hear the siren screaming? He sidestepped toward the driver to wave him onward, eyes staying on the enemy.

The pickup's door creaked open. "What's your problem?"

Then another young voice came rushing up, the clerk from inside: "What is this, what do you cops want—"

Eric rushed at the clerk's back.

Colin was closer. He shoved past Eric's target and charged, and Eric came in slow, slow enough that Colin had an instant to pace his steps and time his punch.

His gauntlet crashed into Eric's stomach. The impact's *boom* rang off the pavement and the huge shape staggered back.

There's *my strength! But he's holding his invisibility, something's wrong.* He let Eric fall back against the wall.

"What was *that?*" the clerk yelped behind him. "That bang, was that a *gas leak—*"

"Yes!" Colin snapped, what they should have said from the start. "Get out of here, both of you!"

Footsteps scrambled away, both the clerk and the driver.

Eric drew himself inward ready to strike. His fingers spread, stretched into claws.

Bea's voice broke into the moment's stillness. "All units—"

Eric lunged—too fast, swinging wide around Colin and angling toward her.

She ducked behind her car, her empty hand coming up, ready with the spell that was her only weapon here, if she could survive to make that touch—

That instant broke as Colin's shoulder slammed into Eric and flung him away.

Then pain burst along Colin's side.

He toppled. Eric's punch had hammered him right through his skein, and just falling down jolted him... he dragged himself up, fighting for breath.

Eric was standing already from where he'd thrown him. His head looked around, still hidden from ordinary sight.

Bea rushed at him. *No, don't—*

Eric twisted away. He spun and darted behind the tiny station shop, and away up the street.

Colin shook his head. Why, why did Eric keep running?

Bea reached his side. "You alright?"

"Go... get him," he forced out.

"You think I'd give up on you?" She slid under his arm and helped him to her car. He sank into the passenger seat—*no, she had wanted the shotgun spot. The rifle spot. Too late now.*

His breathing eased as they roared forward again. He managed to hold up the phone for her, and she ordered "Get up on Angel, repeat, Angel!"

"We're trying," a cop answered. "There's *something* out there."

Eric came in view, still racing up the street again. Colin tried to push through the pain and think. Eric could have dodged their cars by staying back inside Gardner's block... instead he kept running down the middle of streets. Why, just because he had a taste for more victims? Was this *fun* for him?

The engine growled and the gap between them began to dwindle. Motion multiplied along the streets, with a parade of signs and shops tangling their colors together as they raced by. More and more businesses, and too many would have people right in Eric's view.

"Angel! Can anyone get to Angel!" Bea called again. Only unclear mumbles answered her.

Eric raced on, weaving around what traffic came at him. The bastard could dash all through the town and just keep killing...

"What the hell are you doing, Simms?"

The pain in his ribs went numb with shock: that voice was Commissioner Walters.

Eric's shape already looked smaller, pulling away again.

A shape slid into the street ahead of him. A huge black and white police van, figures in black stepping out to face them, a rifle in one officer's hands.

Even at that distance... that long shape only pointed at the sky, not down the street. *They still can't see him!*

"I said explain!" came Walters's roar, pitched like he was trying to shatter the phone in Colin's hand.

Eric swept up toward the police. He'd killed four of them so far.

Colin grabbed for the car door, as he felt Bea tapping the brakes. Too far, Eric was too fast.

The car screeched to a stop. Bea caught at the rifle, grabbed at the door. But she halted, and the weapon slumped as she sank back in her seat.

Eric was too far to shoot, with too many cops in the line of fire, all ready to fire back at her instead of seeing their real target...

Eric reached the police, and leaped, he sprang upward and sailed clear over their heads, over the van, before he dropped down beyond it.

And a cop voice asked "Where's the suspect? Where?"

*"Simms?"* Walters bellowed.

Bea took the phone from his fingers, and switched it off.

Colin watched the shimmering, mocking figure shrink away up the street. "Eric played us. He suckered us into chasing him around like maniacs. We have to tell them what was..."

His voice died away, before the sternness on Bea's face. She had to be thinking of Hoyle again, how he'd sold their secrets.

She said "My badge, for one chance to stop him. A fair trade."

His jaw fell open. "You *knew?*"

"You should go," she added. "It just gets worse for me, the more Walters sees you."

" 'Sees…' "

Colin eyed the police up ahead, as he summoned his skein to flow out and surround him again. There was always one way to make people believe in invisible men.

"Don't," Bea cut in. "We can never guess what they could do with the skein's secret. Or who they'd tell. And if Walters decides you're the key to all this, who keeps watch over Terri?"

Colin's breath hissed out of him.

When he sucked in a new breath, he muttered "Cheap shot."

But she was right.

He twisted at light to wrap himself in stealth… at least that seemed to work again, just as his strength did.

He slipped out of the car.

# CHAPTER SEVEN

# WHAT WE WISH FOR

People, half a dozen at one street corner, another few across the street, gathered and whispered and pointed at the police van. Colin stood in front of it, looking through the windshield that couldn't hold in how Walters shouted at Bea.

"…rampaging down the street, pointing rifles at thin air…"

Whatever Bea answered him, her face looked unafraid.

"Chasing *what?*" Walters snapped. "It's one killer, or were they everywhere?"

Her reply was still too low to hear.

But her hand twitched, a faint *away* motion toward Colin out front. *Go away, you can't help me, Eric could be going after Terri this minute.*

A cop in uniform said "…think I did see something…" and motioned along the street. So Bea wasn't completely alone.

Another chimed in "…killer was at the house. We found what was left of the nurse's body…"

A few words, that should have been too soft to hear—and Nurse Setter was dead. *Eric terrorized her, Gardner preyed on that, and now she's just* gone. *I don't even know her first name.*

"How'd he even get her there?" Walters boomed through the glass. "How'd any of this… I thought you had the place under surveillance… I thought I could trust *some* of you to cover *any* of this…"

Colin turned away from the van, before the fact of the woman's loss tore his last tolerance of Walters to shreds. And Bea's answer to that bully was to just sacrifice herself?

He looked over the crowd as he turned. One fierce, frustrated tangle inside him *hoped* he'd spot Eric behind those onlookers, still gloating over his work. At least that would keep the bastard away from Terri, away from all the other havoc he could be causing somewhere.

Colin started toward the hospital. Bea was risking everything she had, all over again—first for shooting Eric when the police didn't know what a threat he was, now for chasing him when they couldn't see that threat.

He pushed on faster. He could make the skein's strength, dragon strength, carry his weight again, but Eric still had enough power to kick him all over the street. *There's enough skein in the mine to change that, but when do I get to go back for it?* Eric had every edge there was here—he could just pick targets off any time he wanted, but Colin was leaving Terri unguarded every time they took another shot at Eric.

Like they'd even get those chances, if Bea lost her badge and her eyes on the street and…

*Move faster.* Faces along the street were already glancing toward him, and he could only push the skein harder trying to outrun their notice.

\* \* \*

The Lovato Hospital again—the same smells of cleansers and hidden pockets of sweat among them, same pace of sliding along the side of the corridors, never sure if his outline caught their eyes or not. And now Walters might still want Colin on charges for getting in the way of his fist, if he wasn't satisfied with yelling at Bea.

He closed in on Terri's room. At least they couldn't finish throwing her out in an hour, could they?

The room had no guards, no doctors, no Zara in it. Instead, Hoyle thumbed through the clipboard chart from the foot of Terri's bed.

*They left* him *alone with her?* Colin's fists clenched. The man had been part of drugging Terri and worse, but Walters let him walk right up to his victim?

At least Terri looked awake and unharmed in her bed. Silent as he could, Colin crept toward Hoyle and the chart he held.

Right in Hoyle's ear he said "Where's Zara?" and flashed into sight.

Hoyle jumped, staggered backward. Colin faded from sight again—the shocked look on Hoyle's face felt *so* much better than it should.

"Not... here." Hoyle's voice steadied as he spoke. "She was gone when I got here."

Terri added "Some idea of hers, to help me." Her frail voice sounded calm enough her.

Colin moved to keep between Hoyle and her. "You abandoned Bea and the whole chase. We might have *got* Eric, if you'd passed out the scopes like she told you to."

Hoyle straightened his coat, slipped his hands in his pockets like he always did. "Those IR scopes were my idea."

"So?" He took a step toward the traitor. "What, the police can't use them if you're not in charge?"

"When I was in charge, we didn't make reckless runs around the street and set off panics."

"So you bailed out of the chase." Colin pressed closer—no, Hoyle was doing it again, using anything he could find to distract him. "What are doing *here?* Another try to catch Eric yourself, or did failing at that mean you're ready to sell Terri to him?"

Hoyle flinched. He set the chart on the chair and snapped "I don't need to explain myself to you."

And he walked past Colin to the doorway, eyes avoiding him.

Colin's hand reached after Hoyle, but he pulled it back. Maybe he'd touched an actual nerve in the traitor—and anyway, he could feel the flames of his own rage spreading the more he pushed Hoyle around.

Instead he sank down beside Terri's bed. "He didn't hurt you? It'd be nice to find one time he didn't screw us. Did he even say what he was after?"

"He didn't. Either of those."

She said nothing more, and Colin shifted around to his old spot, sitting at the back of her bed. The start of more *days* waiting for Eric to make his move, or worse. *While there's a whole mass of skein waiting up in the mine, if I could just go after it again.* But Eric could be anywhere, going after anyone, and Bea wouldn't even get word…

A voice pushed out of the sounds in the corridor: Zara, with all her warmth engaged: "…wish I had time to ask you more about that."

She and a nurse, a withered-looking older woman, stepped into the room. The nurse answered "It's good to see you so determined to lift her spirits."

"It's what I always try," Zara said. As if her smile could fix anything.

The nurse stopped, looked at the waiting chair, and picked up the chart Hoyle had left there. She tucked it under an arm and walked away with a last nod to Zara.

Silence fell, the small, hollowed-out quiet in the room that left the corridor's many sounds lapping outside.

Then Terri said "He's baa-aack."

*Ghost jokes now?* But Colin let himself appear for a moment, to let Zara see him.

"You're alright?" she said. "What you went after, it didn't go well, did it?"

She could read that just from what, the way he sat by the bed?

He let the words sigh out of him: "Nurse Setter really is dead. They found her body."

Or what was left of her body, they'd said. Zara didn't need to know that.

"Oh, Rosa…" Zara whispered—of course she remembered the rest of her name. "I'm sorry. I still had hopes that she'd turn herself around."

"Hopes." He thumped a hand on the floor. "Eric got away. He might really have ruined Bea this time, the way he suckered us. And he ran down the streets striking people down or letting us see him come at them, and nobody else can see one glint of it!" He glared at the hospital wall, knowing Eric was out there beyond it, somewhere. "It's like he's having *fun,* not going after Terri at all."

"I wish I could help you with that. But I think I have one idea. Something that could make this part of it easier," and she took Terri's hand.

He groaned. "You think you can make Walters put her under guard again? Not him, not the way he hates us now. There's *nothing left,* just me waiting around until Eric thinks she's strong enough to take again. Or, you think you can sneak Terri out of here yourself?"

"I think we should stop Eric from looking." Her hand tightened on her daughter's. "Terri, listen to me, Eric knows pulling the skein off of you was a mistake. His fear of making that worse has been holding him back, so far. That's something we can build on."

Terri's hollow eyes narrowed. "What are you thinking?"

She leaned closer. "That it wouldn't be so hard to let him believe you'd passed away."

Terri's eyes flew wide. "You… you're serious?"

"She's not!" Colin shook his head, felt his neck hurt. "We'd, what, get the doctors to fake Terri's death, and hide her somewhere? You know Eric—what's he going to do to those doctors? What does he do *to the whole town* if he loses her?"

"We don't know." Zara lowered her eyes, then looked right at his still-blurred face. "It's the only way I can think of that will stop him coming after her, and keep you from wasting away on guard. How does you standing guard forever help this family, this town, or anyone?"

"It doesn't. I know I can't." He sighed.

"Then isn't it time," and she smiled a small, reluctant smile, "that you stop splitting your attention? That you took the fight to him?"

"I'd... need time, before you made your move..." *Before Eric heard and went berserk, but maybe I could stop that if I got the skein in the mine first...* anything else was waiting for him to strike anyway...

"So you sneak me out?" Terri breathed. "Hide my doctor too?"

"Of course. If we can work out how to manage all the parts." Zara's smile pushed a fraction wider.

*She's forcing her smile,* Colin thought. If they did this, it could mean Zara and Terri hiding, even leaving the town she'd given everything for, all for the hope that he could free it from Eric.

"...I've seen what your *security's* worth..."

The word in the hall caught at his attention.

"Is visiting open or not? We want to see Terri." Voices, several of them closing in outside.

Then Zara was stepping out to meet them. Colin peeked out: Dr. Morton was standing in the way of Clarence and a group of children. Clarence didn't wrangle his grandkids around often.

Zara told them "I... thank you all for coming out here, but it's not a good time..." Her voice was shaky, with so little of the life it should have—working up to the bereaved tone she might need soon, he realized.

The visitors sensed it too. Zara spoke a few more, softer words to them, and they turned away.

Then she and Morton drew back into the room. Colin scrambled to duck behind Terri's bed again.

"What was all that?" Morton said. "The worn-out act, and that crowd of friends showing up? Kids? I knew you'd pull something to fight Terri's discharge, but this?"

"If we wanted to make noise… but, that was none of my doing," Zara said. "But, there is one way you can look after all your patients, and Terri too."

"No! This hospital can't keep her here. How many times do I have to say it—we can't keep endangering the other patients."

Colin hunched tighter where he sat. It was that simple, for Morton to throw Terri out again without even seeing what Eric was doing in the world outside his little kingdom?

Zara took a step toward the doctor. "So let's remove the danger from all of them. Send Terri out of the hospital, and also free our friends up from guarding her so they can stop more victims from coming in. The only one to sacrifice would be you."

*"What?"* Morton stared at her.

"You, and Terri." She stepped aside from Morton, leaving him looking straight at her daughter. "The only way to buy time for her, and everyone, is for you to announce that she died."

The doctor's eyes went wider, but they stayed on Terri. "You're serious…"

"You've been keeping Terri's medical facts close to yourself—please don't deny it." Her voice sharpened, a cat showing a glint of its claws. "Part of making her seem safe to send away?"

That sounded like one of Morton's manipulations. Colin glared at the little man.

"No need to be so suspicious—"

"I saw it all," Terri said, a single low, certain whisper.

"Here's your chance to do just that," Zara went on. "You simply use that chance to announce something different, that your problem patient has passed away. Just think: if you push Terri out your door, that only makes her more vulnerable to her stalker. I *see* that you're trying to choose between her and everyone else. But…"

She stepped closer to his side. Morton's eyes were still on Terri.

"You can say you missed the signs, *because* you were hiding her records as part of your plan to push her out. We have this one chance, just one, where you can say your staff never knew. And after every-thing Eric's done to whoever crosses him, people would *expect* you to go into hiding within the hour—no, faster. You stay far out of sight until Eric is caught. And everyone else, everyone, would be safe."

Dr. Morton only stood there, still gazing at Terri in the bed.

Colin slid the few feet down that put him beneath that bed, out of Morton's view for a moment. The mask and gloves folded back. His invisibility fell away.

He rose up behind Terri, and he said in the gentlest, surest voice he could find, "And we *will* catch Eric."

Morton's eyes swelled, he staggered back. "What... you weren't here, I know you weren't... this is more of your tricks?"

Slow as he could move, Colin spread his hands. "Those tricks are how we can catch Eric. And how he can reach Terri any time, as long as she's here."

"Unless you be the bad guy," Zara added. "I swear to you, we'll be sure everyone knows the risks you took to hide Terri, when it's all settled. And everyone will be alive to hear it."

Morton turned away, staring at the wall. "You're all crazy. I... I don't even know if we could sneak a 'dead' patient out of here."

"Not just sneak her out." Colin kept his words soft, somber. "You'd have to find help around here that nobody would connect with this. Imagine Eric's next untraceable visit here, sniffing around for what happened to Terri's body, and who knew. It would have to be foolproof."

"It... I'd need time, to think if this is even possible." Morton still looked away. "One doctor could never arrange it all. And my other patients, I'd be abandoning all of them too and dumping them on my staff... but, remote consultations... let me *think.*"

He spun away and stumbled from the room.

Terri turned toward her mother. "Martyr himself? That was your pitch?"

Zara shook her head. "Not a martyr. But Dr. Morton has wanted to look after everyone here fairly, and I think if he can do that he'll pay any price to himself. I know the signs," she added, with a smile at Colin.

He looked away from that not-quite-joking gaze. "I need to call Bea."

If Walters wasn't still screaming at her. He dug the phone out, wondering if he could say anything in a message.

Instead, he heard Bea's quick "What happened?"

"Nothing yet. Can we talk?"

"If it's quick," she said.

*That* was never good. "What's Eric done? You need me anywhere?" From the corner of his eye he saw Zara start, and Terri's head turning toward him. Now he was scaring them too.

"He hasn't been seen. Or anything. So far," and he felt his breathing ease. "From what they tell me," she added.

Oh.

But they told her *something,* at least, Walters and his rage hadn't wiped out her whole career. "What did they—"

A shape moved into the doorway.

Colin froze, too late to duck down, and his face was showing—

Then he relaxed. The man in the wheelchair already knew their secrets.

Zara said "Sergeant? What brings you out here?"

"They've asked me to coordinate a few things." Ed Jordan looked the same as ever, so focused that he seemed ready to step out of that chair the moment he needed. "And, I already know it's not the whole force that's written Bea Simms off. Or all of you."

"Good to hear." Colin kept the phone up, for Bea to hear it too. "I know Bea appreciates her partner's support—and I know she'd never tell you. And we could all use some of that help. Maybe soon."

Zara added "We're looking into a way to get Terri out of here in secret. One thing we'd need is a place to hide her, that Eric would never connect with any of us."

"But not yet," Colin said. "If we do this, there's still too much to set up with it, and me…"

His jaw stretched into a yawn.

He snapped it shut, tried to meet the other three's eyes after that moment of weakness.

Zara said "I think you need to work on something right now: rest. Why don't you let me fill them in? You had a long night and a crazy morning—unless you think it's going to get easier," she added with a rueful smile.

"But—"

He could be one shout away, if Eric really came after Terri right this hour. *And, I wanted to sneak back to the mine for more skein before this happens.* He had a sudden image of himself making the trek back to get that overpowering weapon, and then standing there just as helpless to control it he'd been last night, when more food or more sleep could have put it all in his grasp.

Bea was still waiting on the phone. He told her "It looks like I'm trying to grab a nap. While I can."

"Understood," was all she said.

"Don't do anything crazy while I'm out," he added.

"No promises," said Terri.

The playful lilt in his sister's voice lingered in his head as he moved to the room's back. Zara and Jordan shifted over to talk in the doorway, to guard it and delay anyone who might come across him.

Instead of curling up on the floor hidden behind the second bed, he found himself stretching out openly on the bed itself.

*Eric's been by here just this morning—that makes right now as close to safe as it gets. And he's busy discrediting Bea…*

*No.* He dragged his thoughts back from the streets, the people, the opportunities Eric could be preying on. They couldn't watch *everywhere.*

And what if Zara's plan happened? A way to shield Terri and give him the time and power to run Eric down. If it worked, if Eric stayed quiet long enough to get it moving—

And there was that rabbit-hole again, pulling at his attention.

*Just, be still.*

He felt his breathing seep in and out, let the voices in the doorway wash over him. No reason to think this would work anyway. He'd caught hours of sleep just last night, and spent most of today just sitting and worrying.

He wasn't even tired...

\* \* \*

"Colin?"

Zara was leaning over him.

"Nurse at the door," she whispered.

A thought made the mask and gloves slide back over him, another snatched him from sight—Zara's sharp breath told him that worked. He rolled down from the bed, letting the skein soak up the fall.

An aging woman in nurse's blue strode in at the doorway, the same one he'd seen here before. Zara moved to Jordan's side and said "Why don't we go for a late lunch? I want to stock up while I can."

*Stock up.* The words pushed the last of his sleepy thoughts into motion. She might be speaking to him, promising him she'd bring back another round of snacks for him too.

Zara and Jordan made their way out, leaving him to watch the nurse work with Terri. They started a round of familiar tests. Colin thought of Nurse Setter again, trapped and bullied into abusing that same trust, and now killed for it.

Colin stretched, felt his muscles had lost some of their heaviness from before. Stealing naps here was awkward, but anything was worth it if it left him more ready for going after more skein, and then Eric.

The bustling beyond the room almost swallowed the nurse's words: "I had to insist to get in here. And I showed your chart to Dr. Morton, and he wouldn't let it out of his hands."

"Sorry," Terri said.

Colin smiled. Zara wasn't the only one with friends here, and that was one reassurance about leaving Terri here while he went after the skein.

The nurse's wrinkled face stretched in a sad O. *"I'm* sorry. I wish I'd never seen it."

Terri only looked back at her, silent.

The nurse leaned closer. Her voice choked as she whispered "But… it's all in there. I don't know how we missed it…"

Terri nodded. Gently she said "Someday it won't matter."

*The hints of her coming "death."* The nurse must be already finding clues about that, and Terri had found a way to comfort her. Her words might even do that twice—if the nurse remembered them again when the whole truth came out, and why the reports "didn't matter" after all.

The nurse pushed on through her tests, checking Terri's eyes, then the movement of her fingers.

"But last night—" The nurse's whisper came out of nowhere. "We should have seen it when they brought you back in. Your organs aren't responding right. Too many reasons to think you might not have another month—"

*Last… night…*

He couldn't breathe.

And she mentioned Terri's chart, but she had taken it *before* Zara had even talked to Morton…

Terri said "I know."

Something thumped against his back. The bed, he'd stumbled backward—

"What?"

The nurse whirled, she *stared.* Then the skein twisted him out of visibility again, an instant late. *What did she just say, what did* Terri *say?*

The nurse blinked and turned back to Terri. "I, I thought I saw something there... My mother said if you're the first to give bad news, you never know what might hear you." She hung her head. "Then I must really be tempting fate..."

Her head darted up again, staring out the doorway. A sound, a distant voice sharper than the other murmurs down the corridor, and a second voice beside it.

"Please try to remember," she told Terri, "I only wanted someone to know there was more than what Dr. Morton was telling. No good deed goes unpunished, I guess."

And she rushed out of the room. Those voices hung in the distance, still out of reach.

But those were a world away, a lifetime. Colin shuffled, stumbled, across to where his sister lay.

"You. You're dying, already." *Already*—wasn't that always the word? The walls felt like they were spinning. "A month, she said?"

"Seems like it. Zara won't hear it," she added.

*"How?"* The word gushed out of him. "How could you, after all the ways I fought for you, you turn around and—"

The petty, useless sound of his words brought him crashing to a halt. He sucked in another breath, stared at his sister. Still no hurt, no anger in Terri's face, only a strained silence growing between them...

Footsteps closed in outside.

He stumbled backward, hidden again.

Two men walked in. Doctors, in white surgical masks, wheeling a gurney between them. Colin edged back, watching them.

One of the upraised voices outside broke through the sounds: "Just let us see her—"

The taller man leaned down over Terri. His voice was gentle. "Miss da Costa..."

"Do what you have to," Terri said.

They turned to setting up the gurney.

As they did, Dr. Morton stepped into the room, his own face bare. He nodded to the others, and set the chart clipboard in his hand—the one the nurse had taken before—back at the foot of Terri's bed. The voices clamored on in the distance.

The masked men lifted Terri onto the gurney, with such sure, careful movements. *Not careful enough, not anymore.*

The thought sank in: this was their plan starting off, because the nurse had leaked Terri's condition, that was what had brought the people up in the corridor. The doctors' masks were so no word could leak back to Eric about just who else had been with Terri. In these "last" moments.

Terri gave them a smile, before they laid a sheet over her face.

Colin had to squeeze his mouth closed over a moan. Morton knew, he knew about Terri, and he could still have them *fake* what was all too real?

He stood watching as the two left Morton behind and rolled her out... suddenly she was out of view beyond the doorway and he had to scramble to catch up behind them.

Dreamlike, he moved in their wake—some part of him wondered if his footsteps were still silent, but a dull roar filled his ears. As long as he stayed close behind them...

Stares. Somewhere around them were people watching, trying to take in the covered shape. Not like the voice calling *Terri, Terri*—but no, that sound wasn't simply in his head, it was the people somewhere up the wing, still out of sight. The ones that pushed Terri and the plan into motion too soon.

The gurney stopped in a small room at the back of the hospital. Ed Jordan was already there.

"Could be the timing's for the best." Jordan's no-nonsense words were a steadying force. He slid the sheet back from Terri's face. "We just had an 'accident' at the church you were first hurt in. No deaths, but it has Eric Rowe's earmarks."

"So speed this up," Terri said. "And get him."

Jordan turned to the two doctors. "You ready to wheel her out? The minute I get word that the van is waiting?"

"Um. Yes, ready." The bigger doctor had to shake himself to answer that, faced with Jordan's firm gaze and this hurried scheme. He and his friend stepped over to the door—a moment to breathe in the middle of the strangeness.

And all of it could be wasted, Colin realized. He forced his thoughts away from Terri's secret and leaned down to whisper to Jordan. "Shh—"

Jordan only raised an eyebrow at the phantom voice.

"Terri's nurse was in the room. She'd just seen her alive, she knows..." She knew Terri didn't die minutes later, *it wasn't* that *soon...*

"Don't worry, Zara got to her," Jordan whispered. "Maybe this time she'll keep her mouth shut." Then he looked over at Terri, and added aloud "Looks like it's time."

He held up his phone.

A muffled, low-tuned sound breathed from the speaker. Zara's voice, from her own phone, pushing back against a murmur of voices around it:

"I'm... sorry. You've given us a great outpouring of support, and I've never been more grateful. But..."

She paused, and the sound around her went still.

"But Terri was pronounced dead a few minutes ago."

The stillness rippled. Voices washed back against hers:

"No—"

"She was safe, she had to be—"

"I'm so sorry, Zara—"

"Even when she came back once, it's like it wasn't—"

"Sorry—"

"Sorry—"

The sounds faded, as Jordan thumbed the speaker down. "Weird thing to hear, I know," he told Terri. "I can shut it off if you want—"

*"No."*

Terri's voice cracked, from somewhere deeper in her than her shallow breaths. Colin's throat went tight. For her to listen to this, knowing…

Dr. Morton's voice was the next to speak, a somber professional tone. "I've just come from Ms. da Costa's room. We did everything possible, but we had to respect her wishes about resuscitation—"

*"You killed her!"*

Zara's shout was fiercer than any real sound she'd ever make.

"You see, 'doctor'? You see what happens when you're so afraid for everyone *except* Terri? You wanted her out of here, you covered up her condition so you could toss her out—I saw it!"

Morton said "I understand you're grieving—"

*"I* understand you covered it up. Now admit it!"

Her voice trembled, even through the phone, and those tremors reached in and shook through Colin. Those had to be real fears tearing at his mother.

*And she still thinks she's playing.*

"Enough, yes!" Morton flung back. "Yes, I was afraid the other doctors might see something. So I took steps to make me the only one with the complete data. Yes, I did it to protect the rest of our patients, and yes, our staff are blameless. The responsibility is mine."

"A lot of good that does Terri," Zara said.

"I can only apologize for that. But if it helps, I may be paying for it any time now. Excuse me."

A burst of angry voices flared up—that would be Morton making his escape. Betting his life that he could vanish before word got to Eric.

Tears filled Terri's eyes.

Another voice on the line, Clarence, tried speaking now: "Zara... you mean, she's really..."

"Please, enough," Zara sighed.

Then the only sound in the room was the tone that said that call had been cut.

# CHAPTER EIGHT

# WHAT WE FEAR

A simple dark van waited at the back of the building. Somehow the two doctors worked their way through the corridors with Terri's covered gurney, and brought it all the way to the van with barely a glance from the people around them. Colin crept along behind them.

Then the two loaded her into the van. They spoke only in the briefest, lowest whispers as they moved her, as if any noise or hesitation might jinx them and bring attention crashing down on them.

When they finished and stood back, Colin eyed the closed door, wishing he could slip in and whisper something to Terri. Wishing there were anything to say.

That ended when Jordan rolled up. The doctors passed him the keys and retreated back into the hospital.

Before Colin even reached his side, Zara swept into view around the corner of the building. "Just get us out of here," she said.

Colin hefted Jordan's chair inside, and the sergeant strapped it in against a seat. Zara took her place beside Terri, and Colin took the wheel.

He'd driven bigger things when one of their projects needed him to, so pulling the van's bulk out into the noonday street was familiar enough. Behind him he saw Zara next to Terri, rifling through a bag of medications they'd left with her.

*How much will those really help her now?*

Smoothly, steadily, he tried to move the van through the streets without jostling his sister, following Jordan's directions. But he nudged the gas down every chance he could, every time he found a clear space to push forward... racing against time. Jordan spent more time watching his phone than guiding Colin, probably watching for those first signs that Eric had heard about Terri's "death."

Pull past one car. Settle into the traffic's flow, no point in battling it with the block half over...

His muscles shook, ready to race the van away to safety and fling himself on after Eric. He didn't even have time to get to back to the mine and the skein, Eric could get the news any moment because they'd rushed their whole plan—

The van pulled up at a stoplight, and bitter, barbed truth caught up with him again. *No, none of this is like we planned. But that nurse could be wrong about Terri's chances. The records weren't certain.* Except, she saw a pattern even back when Dr. Morton wanted it covered up. And Terri believed her.

He looked back at where his sister lay, with their mother sitting by her—he blinked against a sudden blur in his eyes.

"There's a second *Remember Terri* site going up," Zara said, looking up from her phone. "I knew it would be hard for our friends, but... I wish we'd let more of them visit you sooner."

"Hmm," Jordan said. "Simms says there are no signs of Rowe yet. From what they'll tell her, anyway. Pull in left, the empty house," he added.

Colin eased the van around. The house was a common site in Rayo Hill: small, with patchwork signs of rough repair around some of its trim, and the last telltale scars on the way to its being abandoned. On this one, the garage's door waited yawning open for them.

When they closed themselves in and wheeled Terri inside, the boards creaked. The rooms looked empty but clean enough, recently cleared. Had this place come to Jordan's notice because of some crime, or did it belong to someone he knew?

Zara set the medications down on the narrow kitchen counter. "I'm amazed you found this so quickly, Ed. But I should really thank Dr. Morton and his two friends—if he'll ever let me know their names," she chuckled.

Jordan twisted his chair to turn away. "Thanks are fine. But how about we finish this?" He looked at Colin. "I need to be in the station, coordinating information so you and Simms can stay in the loop. We wait much longer and Walters will give up on trusting anyone with this, anyone but himself."

"We're sorry," Zara said. "We never meant to pull you out here—"

"Enough. It's been good to get some sweat on my hands for this."

Colin caught a small grin from him. "Then let's get you back there. And there's a weapon I need to get."

"Good. Let me check... oh hell." He stared at his phone.

"What?" But Colin knew, he could see they all knew who it had to be.

"Our killer's been at the hospital. The parking lot." He tapped the screen. "Tracking Morton's car, looks like."

Terri's voice was a whisper. "He would. He would."

"No time for me, then," Jordan said. "Go."

Colin dashed for the van.

*　*　*

"Pulling in now," he said into the phone.

"Remember, I'll be there in five," Bea answered.

*Like she thinks I'm reckless. Or that Eric's giving us a choice.*

He faded from sight and stepped out onto the edge of the sun-baked hospital lot.

The signs of Eric's work lay at the lot's other end. A handful of people thronged around the orange attendant booth by that entrance, with one cop there shooing them back. One of its windows lay shattered, and as Colin edged closer he saw a streak of red sprayed against the remaining glass.

*First blood. Because of what we made Eric believe.*

Then he spotted another officer on guard, standing in front of the ambulance bay entrance. A second guard for a second site, maybe a second victim… Colin steeled himself as he moved around the cop to slip inside.

A ring of cops stood beside one vehicle. The man sitting in their center wore a hospital uniform, with bandages on his arms and face—but he looked more pale and shaken than cut up. They hadn't even brought him inside the hospital itself.

"Tell the doctor, tell the doctor," he was muttering. "Tell Morton I didn't tell him about his car…"

"Yes, yes, we got that," one cop told him.

Colin looked at the victim, the officers. Was this the man from the parking booth? How long had Eric had in here, where would he go now?

"All right, all right, one side!"

A voice rolled through the garage, and Walters marched right past Colin to reach the victim.

"So this masked man cut you up? The man in green?"

"I hit him. I did!" The victim held up his hand, bandaged all down his knuckles.

"And he was after Dr. Morton. So where's the doctor?"

Something moved, under the ambulance beside them.

The secret glow of an invisible hand, lurking down in the shadows where even its shimmer would be hidden—like some animal paw poised to pounce. But none of the people here were the prey Eric was after.

The witness moaned "He's gone, gone. Tell the doctor I never told him about his car."

Colin's teeth ground. With Eric sprawled under that ambulance, he might not have spotted Colin at all. *But I can't dig him out, I can't make a move with all these people within reach of those claws.*

"Listen to me," Walters said. "That maniac thinks Dr. Morton killed his girl—"

Eric's hand shook against the asphalt.

"—so you tell me. Which car did Dr. Morton take? The Range Rover, the Lexus?"

"Lexus. Gray." The attendant's voice fell into a dazed monotone. "License started with I think DMM…"

Blood roared in Colin's ears. It drowned out what Walters said to the officers, that had to be some call to start a search. All he could do was stare at the sliver of their enemy he saw, knowing Eric and his eavesdropping had outsmarted them all *again*…

One of the officers said "Sounds like the car they found uptown. Abandoned."

*Morton left that car, he got away.* Colin felt a grin spreading, and it grew wider as Eric's hand pulled back—defeated. Colin slipped up around the vehicle, watching the cops for one sign of Eric crawling out toward them. Instead he heard a faint footstep of the enemy moving on the far side of the ambulance.

Colin froze, looked around. Eric walked past the vehicle, straight for the door, without once looking back.

"He could be anywhere," Walters was saying. "Morton thinks he can just run and he's out of reach?"

*He might be, if we could tell you what you're trying to catch.* Colin crept toward Eric's back. If he rushed him, maybe he could shove him out past the sentry and try to take him in the open.

"Huh?" A gasp from a cop behind them, an *alerted* sound—he'd glimpsed someone—

Eric leaped past the front guard and twisted out of view.

Colin rushed after him. But the parking lot looked clear, only people and cars and no glimpse of Eric. He stared at the people, the corners, every place Eric might have twisted behind. Where had he gone, what was he after now—

"Up there!"

Bea's shout caught his gaze. She was jumping from her car, pointing upward—

He spun around and stared up, to see Eric crouching up on the roof, looking straight down at him.

*Can't stand still!* Colin dove away from where he stood, but instead of leaping at him Eric only held his place on the roof. To the side, Bea was running toward Colin, ready to combine their tactics against Eric if she could reach his side in time. Colin dashed toward her.

A blur of motion at his side, and he whirled clear of a car—*someone almost ran down the man they couldn't see!* He reached the sidewalk and spun to look up again.

Eric was gone.

He twisted, stared around. Bea was closing in, the lot looked clear, despite the people staring at Bea as she ran.

Far off to the side, *Hoyle* leaned against a car, holding up his scope to search the lot.

Eric struck.

He leaped face-first from the roof, flinging himself outward through space with the skein's power and the certainty that no pavement could harm him. Not aiming at Colin, not at Bea…

Eric hurtled down at a woman walking in the lot, her arms crowded with flowers. One moment she stood there—then the unseen threat slammed down beside her, and one claw stabbed out.

If she screamed as she dropped, the weak sound never carried across the pavement. Colin charged toward them. Eric spun, loped toward him…

*Why so slow, like he's stalling, drawing me away—from Bea!* Colin halted, stole one glance over to see Bea rushing toward him.

As his gaze darted back, Eric surged toward him.

"Sniper!" One shout, one moment of déjà vu, this time spoken in Hoyle's voice that reached Colin in the instant before Eric struck.

The avalanche glanced off his hands, off his block and his whole body twisting it away—he swung Eric around and scrabbled for a wrestling hold. A kick caught his leg and sent him tottering, straining to keep his grip on that arm.

Bea darted in, hand reaching, lips moving in the spell.

A surge of strength Eric wrenched free. He dove back, crashed against a car and leaped clear of them.

Just a few steps behind Eric, a man crouched down beside a car, blind to the enemy so near him. Before Eric could focus on him, Colin rushed in.

"Stay down, all of you!" Walters was shouting somewhere. "We'll find—"

Eric leaped out of reach, too strong, too fast. His shimmering head swept left, right. Picking out more victims.

Colin screamed *"Stay down!* Stay low between the cars, I swear we'll stop him—"

That head shifted to orient on him. *I just reminded Eric how much everyone he attacks hurts me.*

Colin charged, anything to hold his attention. From the corner of his eye he saw Bea closing behind him.

Eric leaped up, one step booming down to skip him off a car's roof, another step to the next, down the row and out of their reach again. When he dropped to the pavement, he took another slow look around, at the scattered figures huddled around the lot.

The police crouched behind what cars might give them cover, stared blindly around the crashes against those car roofs, most of them still looking for where some sniper could hide. Colin eyed Eric, tried to map the ways he might spring toward one of those helpless targets and which of them he could block.

Three cars down behind Eric, he saw Hoyle move.

The lieutenant's face and the scope in his hands peeped over the hood of a car and lined up on Eric's back. He brought up his huge pistol, fumbling for a grip that could manage both.

*If I just keep his target still—* Colin bellowed "Eric!"

The halo shape paused, looked at him.

Thunder boomed out—and Eric stared *around,* untouched, at the car's window beside him and the hole in the steel beyond that, where the miss had gone. Hoyle's face twisted as he wrestled the hand cannon down. The scope had fallen from his grip.

Walters roared *"What—"* before the screams swallowed his voice.

Screams and shouting on all sides, rising in panic. Eric dove away between cars and out of sight, as Hoyle stared around for his fallen scope.

Colin rushed toward the clump of cars, but Eric was already dashing on to another next spot. Using extra cover for his near-invisible form, or searching for where people tried to hide? A man and woman were crouching right in the next row from him, unaware.

Walters shouted again "All of you, stay down—"

*"No!"*

Colin ducked behind a car, yanked back his skein mask, and let himself drop into visibility. He stepped out into the open.

"Don't hide! He'll find you all—*RUN!*"

Motions flickered around the corner of his sight, people moving, scattering. Bea moved toward his side.

Eric whirled and rushed at the couple as they broke into a run. Colin charged to head him off.

Eric spun, one scrabble of his feet to stop and turn again—angling at Colin, no, past him toward Bea—Colin was already sidestepping and turning, ready to head off his enemy's trick.

Again Eric twisted. He leaped out through space and slammed onto a van's roof and sprang on, upward, to a hospital roof a whole story above them.

*God, he's that strong—*

That still blurred shape peered down at the lot, moving, looking as the screaming people spread out below him.

A car's roar tore through the human voices. The tiny vehicle whooshed past, too close to Colin—but still steering around, of course, now that he was visible.

Eric's head twisted to track the car. He leaped.

Colin charged, knowing he was far out of reach, watching Eric slam down and smash claws into the wheel.

Metal boomed, tires squealed as the car skidded and spun helplessly around... The little thing veered too close to the streams of panicking people before it halted, and Eric was still advancing on its immobilized shape.

"Da Costa, get down!" Walters screamed. "We'll find the sniper!"

*What is this for you, Eric—rage or just play?* Colin rushed at him.

Eric spun away.

Toward the crowd, toward the backs of the people scattering onto the streets.

Colin bolted after him. He flung his power, his will, at the skein around his legs to *carry* him forward, long leaping steps still no match for Eric's. The shimmering shape darted away behind a corner.

*No, no,* anything *but losing sight of him—*

He skidded around the corner, but Eric was already out of sight.

Instead he had to hear the shouts, the dozens of frightened voices, watching the people in view run and hearing the sound spread, spread, seeping into the quiet streets of the town.

He raced down the street, on the familiar summer-hot pavement. Voices ahead spiked from a yell into a scream—he rushed closer, but he saw only a knot of people fleeing, no sign of Eric himself.

More cars raced by, but a few cars stopped and played havoc with the thin traffic as drivers gawked at the rush of people. Horns blared, and frightened shouts built, built like some ragged wind blowing through the streets. *Why did we ever think we could risk faking Terri's death?*

He must have halted in his tracks, because Bea's car swept up beside the curb and found him standing there. He dove inside.

Bea shoved the pedal down and brought them rocketing down the street. Her face was a hard stare of focus, on their surroundings and on the tangle of voices on the radio.

She scooped up her phone and passed it to him.

Zara's voice burst into his ear. "—said, what is *happening?*"

"Street panic," he said. "We can't find... oh God no."

A figure lay on the pavement, face down, that could never move again. Short hair, but hard to tell if it was a man or a woman—the body looked smaller, surrounded by all the sprays of blood.

Eric only needed an instant to do that.

"They have to get away," he moaned.

The engine's roar swelled. Colin searched the streets, the doorways, the movements of the people they passed. No more bodies, no killer. The radio chattered as Walters's voice tried to beat the scattered reports into some kind of order.

Then the car slowed, as Bea brought it to the curb. A cluster of people stood there, milling around and slumped panting for breath and shouting at each other. Still barely a block from the body.

He yanked the door open. Sounds flooded over him.

"Some kind of ghost, they've been seeing it all over—"

"Crazy with a gun—"

*"Just back there!"* Colin yelled at them. "It was just back there, Eric left a body, he could be right around here now! Get out of here, go, go!" He pointed, waved, shouted in their faces until the first of them peeled away and ran.

When he sank back into the car, he felt like Bea yanked them into motion more abruptly than ever.

The phone was still in his hand. "What was that?" Zara demanded.

He stared around the street for Eric, for any signs of people fleeing him. "I'm warning them about..."

*I could have* asked *them, if they'd seen him. Instead I'm... evacuating the town?* Eric would love that, more than any body count.

Walters's voice broke through on the radio. "What are you *doing?* Simms? Hoyle? We need riot control here!"

One block passed, then another. The sun seemed to grow brighter each moment, stinging his eyes as he looked around. How could they lose Eric?

They screeched around a turn.

Another vehicle roared in beside them—the police van, with Walters leaning out the window waving his arm at them. To pull over.

Bea eased their speed back and brought them to a not-quite-jolting stop. The van slammed to a halt just ahead of them, and another police car pulled in behind them.

Bea looked out her window. "More victims?" she said.

"We've got the sparks of a goddamn *panic* spreading!" Walters climbed from the van, waving at Bea and the other car. "You get downtown and—"

Movement. The familiar, ghostly shape of Eric stepped out between buildings. He was moving around the street, around the van... toward a clear shot at where Walters stood.

Colin rushed for the pavement. Around him he saw cops, and beyond them onlookers watching the cops gather. If Eric cut the commissioner down in front of them all...

He flung himself at Eric. Walters broke off his stream of orders to stare, but Colin rushed past him, keeping his balance light and ready for any direction Eric struck in.

Eric pulled back, back between the buildings and out of sight.

*Still playing us, making us look crazy,* a part of him thought. He could hear Walters bellowing "Da Costa, get back here—"

But he plunged on into the shade between the walls. His mask slid back up into place, and he twisted light to vanish. He still had a chance to *catch* Eric.

Bea had stayed back with the cops, he realized. But a scream came from up ahead, up out on the street beyond. He raced for it, for the chance that he could still be in time.

A toppled cart, figures scattering—and Eric was darting away around the corner. He rushed after him, grabbed the corner to swing himself around it. The bastard was gone again.

Colin ran on, strained his ears. A feeling took root in him: he was racing against the *next* scream, trying to head off something that could come from anywhere in the blocks around him.

He swung around again to the street where he'd left the police. Those cars were gone, even Bea's—at least Eric hadn't circled back to come at them again.

*But if they moved on, how long was I busy chasing those echoes?*

He sagged to a stop and grabbed out his phone. Bea didn't answer, of course she couldn't. But he stood on the sidewalk hearing it ring, feeling the ache in his muscles, even when it was the skein around his legs that pushed him along.

Then Bea's voice came on: "—seems to be thinning out as it spreads. Unsure what injury reports are from panic and which are the suspect." Another cop answered her, something about keeping the channel clear. She had to be patching the radio through to him.

One car, then another, sped past him on the street. More parts of the panic, or would a few ordinary drivers look that different from over here? *I was trying to get them to safety... but Eric must love this terror.*

Bea and the other police crackled through different reports. Scattered voices, movements, rippled around the streets beyond his sight.

"Ambulance to Lawson Corner."

"The cause?" Bea said.

"Just get to downtown in case there's looting," Walters snapped. Always, always interfering with Bea.

Colin watched another car roll by, a couple hustling along the sidewalk. Either the worst of it was settling down, or most of this block's people were already gone.

"Traffic isn't downtown," a cop said. "It's heading down Silverlode for the state road and backing up there."

"Accident?"

"No reports of that. Just a woman out there telling them not to run."

*Of course she would. And that house we left, it* was *near Silver-lode.*

Zara answered him on the first ring.

"Colin?"

"That's you out at the exit, right? What the hell are you doing?"

"Keeping part of the town together. While we still can." The fierceness in her voice sounded more certain than she'd been in days.

Of course she would.

And Eric would hear about her making her stand, and…

He ran for the street.

* * *

It was a mile to where Silverlode joined the state road, the easiest route to put Rayo Hill in the rear view mirror. Traffic was light at first, but it soon grew thick enough for Colin to ease the distance by jumping onto the rear of one station wagon—an anxiously-driven thing that had to slam to a stop at the next intersection. The skein's protection and the strength in its grip made holding on to the back comfortingly easy.

Until he remembered Eric could do the same thing.

The wagon honked and slowed as the cars ahead lost speed, until Colin could step off and take in what lay ahead.

Just beyond the empty Moon View Diner—where Eric had *killed* old Phil Balan, two nights ago—the intersection with the state road stood backed up. Cars sat parked along the side, a dozen or more people circling around at the curb. A heavy pickup truck stood, not sealing off the street, but blocking the outgoing lane and making cars squeeze by it.

Zara stood in the back of that truck, and called out as one car eased past. Her voice rang in the summer air: "Lou? Your brother's safe, right here! If you run now, are you sure you'll come back?"

*Safe?* She's *making herself the biggest target Eric could wish for.*

Colin jogged closer, angling around the crowd and staring through it, around it, for which ways Eric could move in. More people joined the crowd as he watched, as another car pulled off to the side. Music, some bright festival song, played in the air, and he saw two men setting up a small, person-tall tent that would be shelter from the sun.

That one-lane roadblock shouldn't even slow them, he realized. The ground was flat enough, anyone could pull right off the road a few yards and drive by, if they were frightened enough. And yet none of them did.

Instead a pickup bigger than Zara's paused behind her and honked, instead of trying to scrape by with its load of branches. And Zara climbed down and waved to her truck's cab, and that truck edged forward and toward the curb to make room.

And Zara meant to just *stay* out here? Leave Terri with Jordan and hope she'd come back to them alive?

As the truck moved, he spotted a familiar black car parked near it. Hoyle stood beside that, gazing around the crowd.

Colin worked his way closer, still circling on the fringes of the crowd. Still no Eric lurking between them, no invisible shape out in the slope beyond them or even gliding down from the air...

Zara's head turned and settled on Colin. She stepped away from him, back toward the overloaded truck waiting to start past them, but she angled herself to keep Colin in view.

*In case I'm Eric.* Zara wasn't completely helpless, she was *trying* to keep her guard up. And she had the spell.

The outgoing truck began rolling past her.

Zara shouted, her voice against the rumble of its engine. "Would you go if this was just another day? Would you?"

People shouted, cheered, added "Would you?" and "Wimp!" to the noise. An old man stepped out of the tiny tent, watching the movement on the road.

The truck slowed. Its engine eased back, and the shouts rang out clearer.

Colin circled outward, watching the truck, the slopes, the sky. Hoyle held his place by his car.

Then the truck's rumble swelled, and it drove on past Zara.

But the car behind it, a dirt-stained white thing, pulled over and the woman in it stepped out to join the crowd. Cheers burst into the air. The music swelled as someone cranked it up.

Something moved in the truck that had passed.

The piled-up branches in its bed shifted, as the aura of an invisible shape pushed out from underneath them. That figure looked around, searching.

Zara was climbing up onto the bed of her own truck again. Into plain sight.

Colin bolted at Eric. He angled past one couple, then a kid waving his shirt like a flag... Eric jumped down to the road, still up beyond the people... off to the side, Zara stared at Colin's motion and began to drop for the ground...

Colin burst past the fringe of the crowd. *Stop him now, don't let him get in among them, stop him* right here.

Eric turned and charged to meet him.

At the last instant Colin let his balance shift, his steps flow to ready him for—

They crashed together. Colin swayed into the block and the spin to deflect his enemy's momentum, felt his grip clamp down and his weight twist *perfectly* to force Eric down—

Pain exploded. A wave of shock blasted it all away, kicking him away, *he hit me again...*

Slumping, falling—*hold that invisibility, Zara doesn't want a panic. Zara...*

The blurred world slowed its dancing enough to make out Hoyle staring, one fixed point in the wavering figures around him. Colin braced a foot against the ground, forced himself upward.

Eric started toward Hoyle—didn't he want him dead too, wasn't there a reason...

Hoyle stared. Turned. Ran.

Again.

Eric spun away toward Zara.

Colin stood, swayed, the motion twisted inside his head and made him stagger.

But he could see Zara look straight at Eric, her back to the truck she'd stood on, hands ready to strike out, her lips moving in the spell. Eric swept in.

Eric twisted away. A surge of speed and he was gone—swerving *around,* a twist of motion that tore at Colin's balance just to watch. Zara stared, spun, struggling to track where the shimmer had gone.

A shape clamped around her face. Eric's hand sealed her mouth, blocked the spell—he stood crouched up on the truck bed behind her. With one rush he pulled her, led her, across the ground and into the little blue tent.

Colin scrambled after them. Faces stared, voices murmured and shouted.

"She fell—"

"Some kind of seizure—"

"The ghost—"

A big man started uneasily toward the tent. One surge of Colin's strength flung him aside, out of the way and safe.

Colin ducked inside, and froze.

Even steeling himself for it, to see Eric crouched over his helpless, trembling mother, with those claws poised above her...

The voice was a guttural thing from deep under Eric's masses of skein. "This worthless *town?* You love this town so much you'll come out here and tell them about hope—an hour after SHE DIED?"

Zara's face twisted. She had to be straining to speak, with his hand locked crushingly tight over her mouth.

Zara couldn't say it, but Colin did. "She's alive! Terri is—"

"*Liar!*"

The claws struck.

They dug into Zara's chest, tore in and flung her away, left her staring and clutching as the blood began to come.

A gunshot roared.

Eric toppled forward. A tiny plastic window was in the tent's back, and beyond it Hoyle aimed a massive rifle—

The tent came cascading down, pulled over by Eric's fall. Colin stumbled back and clear of the collapsing blue folds. His heel caught, his head spun as he fell backward, but his gaze stayed on the collapsing tent.

It crumbled down to a tangle of sheeting and unclear shapes inside it. Whatever ropes or pins had held them up, were useless now.

The tent's folds flew back.

Eric pushed them back, a shimmer-less figure revealed in solid green, shoving the tent away with one arm while the other hung limp and bleeding—*bleeding!*

Colin pushed himself up, swayed.

He stumbled, into the man he'd pushed aside before. His head spun, he strained to shove that man away from danger again. Shouts tore through the air.

Eric glared down at his bleeding arm. The skein around it rippled, covered and thickened over the wound.

Then he spun, moved, flung himself straight at Hoyle. One motion swatted the gun away, another slammed a kick up into the lieutenant's stomach.

Hoyle crumbled. But his eyes glared back at Eric, and his hand fumbled for his pistol. Hoyle's own skein, he still had his own armor.

Colin staggered toward them.

Eric looked down at the lieutenant. "You killed her, you and the nurse. And you think you can save them? *You??*"

Hoyle glared back up. His battered chest had the breath to wheeze "I can… try…"

The claws burst through his throat.

Colin leaped. Eric's arm lashed around, knocking him away.

Eric's claws slashed down, deeper into the shape that had been Hoyle. They brushed the skein around his chest—Colin saw that skein shimmer from sight, then slide up through the torn shirt and come loose from its old master.

Colin brought a fist back to start a slow, clumsy punch. Eric's foot kicked his leg out from under him.

Eric leaned down over him, more enormous than ever with the mass he'd just stolen.

"Now you get to wait," he whispered. "You and your mother. Next time you both pay."

# CHAPTER NINE

# WHAT WE HATE

He never saw Eric leave. One moment Colin was staggering to get to his feet, the next Eric was gone. Dashed away to some moment of cover and gone invisible again, of course—though none of the shouting around them was shrill enough to mean he'd gone *through* anyone more.

Colin wobbled toward the fallen tent, heavy steps trying to steady the swaying world around him. Faces, figures, shifted in and out of his view, more and more of them turning toward him.

"Where'd they come from—"

"He wasn't there, I know he wasn't—"

One took a half-step toward blocking his path, and he stepped around him as the man coughed *"Look* at him, he killed them—"

Friendly hands were peeling the blue plastic tent off of Zara.

Her fingers clutched her chest, clamping her blouse tight over her wounds—dark fabric turning darker by the moment.

*I should be at her side...* His legs had no strength to move closer, *he* had no strength, no right, after he'd let this happen. The nearest of her rescuers was already crowding into his path.

Zara stared out at him, eyes alert, features shifting with pain as her hands moved, trying to hold the blood in. More people gathered in the ring around her—of course they would for her. But she should be *speaking,* joking and thanking them and leading them on...

*Eric will be back for her, and me.*

Where was the rage at that, the fire he should have? All he felt was a great echoing hollowness inside.

That hollow whispered and resonated with the rolling sounds around him, the sight of their ranks thickening around her as he drew back. Back toward Anthony Hoyle's body.

He gazed down at the broken shape. A man who'd fought with them, led the hunt for Eric—right on this road, only nights ago—but sold them all out for Josh Gardner's schemes. And he'd tried to make up for that, his own way. He'd *hurt* Eric.

More than Colin had. Fingers tightened, feeling too weak to even make a real fist. *I eat, I rest, I use every move I have, and Eric's still too strong. Even grabbing him is worthless if just his blind thrashing around breaks me.* And now Eric had more skein than ever.

He looked at Hoyle, at one more person he'd watched die. The people around that body crept closer and drew back again, none of them sure what to make of him. Colin glanced around for where his rifle had fallen, but the weapon must be lost in the rows of people.

A siren howled. An ambulance, and police cars.

Now *they show up!* They heard about Zara on the radio, *Bea* heard, she knew Eric would be here and she let him come. And Walters had only roared about any chance they'd start looting the *shops—*

Heads turned in the crowd, looking from the police to him. Too many, just too many to face now. He stumbled away between them, faster, faster, until he'd slid around a car and out of sight for that one moment he could still leave them unsure how he'd vanished. Twisting into invisibility grated in his aching head an instant before he faded away.

When the medics came to help Zara, they cleared the crowd around her—enough that Colin could move up and peer between them as they watched. Her eyes stayed open, aware, and he thought her gaze latched onto the shimmer of him as some kind of lifeline. Until the drugs closed her eyes.

\* \* \*

His fingers shouldn't hold. The thought kept buzzing at him, that clinging to the back of the ambulance should wrench his poor, clumsy clawtips out of the metal and fling him into the street. But the ride was swift and smooth—they had a wounded woman on board.

Then they reached the hospital, and he had to fall back behind the police, the doctors, all the friends that began to gather for Zara.

Just *too many,* and every one of them would want an explanation, a promise, someone to blame, all of them cutting the truth of it up into more and more pieces to pass out among them… and none of it would budge the truth that they were here at Lovato Hospital *again.*

Colin swept his gaze up, down, along the same wide corridors he knew Eric could come stalking down. They were here because Eric *always* broke them, and he could be out slashing through more people all across town and nothing they did stopped him.

And Terri was broken already. No matter what they did.

He whirled away, away from those babbling voices and rushed up the corridor, testing every quiet-looking door he found until he stumbled into a room with a promise of silence. And he yanked out his phone.

"Jordan here."

The sergeant's greeting thrummed with alertness, readiness. All Colin had to answer it was a tired "Hi. Terri alright?" The name of the "dead" girl seemed to echo in the silent room.

"She is. I heard it… got crazy out on Silverlode. And, you're on speaker," he added.

Was that some kind of warning? Colin's thoughts couldn't mesh, he only said "I'm okay. Hoyle, Hoyle was killed, trying to help us."

"I'm sorry." Terri's thready voice was even fainter through Jordan's speaker. "I should never have faked this. I knew what he'd do."

"Doesn't matter," Colin snapped.

*This wasn't Terri's fault, it was all Zara's idea… can't say that, I can't tell her about Zara, that's what Jordan hasn't told her…*

He forced a smile onto his lips. "We had a shot at Eric. We'll get another. If, if you'll look after Terri a while longer." Those words to Jordan came out almost calm.

"If that's how it works," came the answer.

Colin's voice went lower, fiercer. "I swear I'll get him." There had to be something more, something else he could say...

Instead the afternoon stretched on.

People gathered.

Police came and went—with no clues to Eric.

Until, at last, a tangle of doctors and nurses wheeled Zara out, away, and Colin slipped around behind them, all the way into the room they put her in.

There was one doctor still there, a woman in white looking over records in a corner.

But there, Zara lay there, so still...

*"What?"* A scrabble of metal, the doctor grabbing in among her instruments for some kind of weapon. He'd fallen back into sight.

She edged away toward the door.

"Please! I need to see her." He turned back toward his mother.

The doctor stepped in his path, staring up at his face. "Well. You stay back, I don't know who you are or what muck you might have tromped through to get near her and I don't care—"

What he'd tromped through. Those words penetrated his haze—she meant contagions, she meant Zara needed a clean environment.

And his mother's still, still lips moved as she breathed.

Colin stepped back, looked around the doctor. He could see them now, the traces of bandages under Zara's operating gown, the IV line he'd somehow missed. He thought he saw motion under those closed eyelids, as if her eyes were still searching for their enemy, even now.

Eric said he'd come back, finish her, when they'd done enough waiting. Probably after he'd killed enough of the town that Zara had fought for...

*No! No more scrambling around, no more guarding one side and losing another.*

His fists curled, he heard the doctor gasp, but he spun away.

The plan. The whole damn scheme to hide Terri, they'd only risked it because they *had* a way to let him crush Eric—and instead they'd let that nurse's leaks rush them into action. Without first getting that wealth of skein from the mine, from the dragon itself.

He shoved the door open and marched out.

Right in front of Bea.

She looked at him, so calm, like *nothing* startled her. Quietly she said "They say she's holding on, isn't she—"

*"Where were you?"* He jabbed a finger at her. "You *knew* he'd come after Zara. But you, we, just had to run around chasing everything!" He leaned in to glare at that stubborn, familiar face.

"Colin?"

Her voice quavered.

The wrongness of that pushed him back, just a step, enough to shake his head. "No, no, I'm the one who did that. I should have gone to get what would beat Eric at his own overpowered game. That ends *now.*"

On up the corridor, people spilled aside as Walters pushed through, closing in.

"Listen to me," Bea said. "We've had new attacks at—"

*"Too late!"*

The words burst out of Colin, too easy.

"Too late, I've got no time. I'm trying to save my mother—"

Walters snapped "You're not doing a thing. We're the ones taking Rowe down, and anyone who still counts as a cop can start by getting away from here and—"

Colin's arm swung up, his body lunged to slam the arm across Walters's throat and sweep him back against the wall.

*This* man, he'd ripped away Terri's protection and now Zara's too... Colin's arm shook, skein against the man's folds of flesh, more than powerful enough to crush it. His other hand rose, slowly gathered in a fist.

With the skein fingertips growing *sharp.*

Power. One motion, one impulse, it made it so easy. But his arm couldn't pull back, he couldn't drag it away from under that pale, shaking face that never listened...

*"Eric,"* and he forced the word out at Walters, "Eric will come here after Zara. You're going to protect her, with everything you've got. And if Eric gets here before I make it back... you'd better hope you go down fighting."

The words, the momentum of the threat, pried in between his arm and the man's throat. He dragged his arm back and let Walters slide down the wall.

He turned away... and awareness crashed in, of all the people around him. Hospital staff in blue and white up the corridor, two cops in black just beginning to push through those and toward him, the doctor looking at him from the door. And Bea, Bea gaping at him. And yet she'd *let* him tear into her boss.

Time to move.

He spun away down the corridor. Shouts, footsteps, gathered behind him, wiping away the last chance that he'd dreamed those moments of madness. *I got into Walters's face* again. *I could have crushed him.*

Dazedly he flung himself past the shapes around him, scrambled around a corner a few feet ahead of their sight, and crouched down behind a janitor's cart to vanish. His heart pounded, his head whispered that they were all too close. But, the police dashed on by with barely a glance at the space behind the cart.

"Out of the way, he attacked a cop—" someone shouted.

He had. He'd really done that to Walters, with Bea right there to share the blame... He couldn't think about that, only pushed himself on for the nearest door out.

Then that door came in sight, wide and bright with real sunlight beyond it—and as he made for it a tall cop beside it glanced toward him.

Colin ducked backward, back behind the corridor's corner, but the man was already starting toward him, following up on just the movement of his outline.

Instead of running, Colin dropped to lie out on the floor. The cop charged into view, glanced around, and raced on past him. Because an odd-shaped glimmer on bare tiles was nothing... but a shape that moved like a man could catch their attention.

That should make them *a little* better at protecting Zara. If Walters had learned his lesson, under Colin's grip.

*No escape from what I did,* he knew as he charged out into the daylight. The long downtown streets opened up around him, calling him out onto the road he had ahead. Hospital staff, visitors approaching with their flowers and worries, cars on the street, all moved around him. All the people he'd have to move on past, on the way to their only hope.

He froze. He was on his way to take the dragon's skein... and Eric could follow him to that too. *Just like he did to the Vargas House.*

The fierce afternoon sunlight was suddenly ice-cold. Colin stared around at corners, cars, rooftops, every scrap of cover an enemy could be crouching behind, and every figure on the street that might be Eric just hiding his face instead.

Nothing. And Eric didn't even know he *had* found more skein.

The van he'd driven back here was still in the lot—but he needed a full sense of his surroundings now. Instead he took off at a long, skein-boosted stride up the street. One block, another. The hospital itself was the one place Eric might know to watch for him, so if he could slip away from that...

One more block, and then tiny little Laredo Alley split off between a cluster of buildings, and Colin darted into it. The walls stretched high enough to make it almost a cool, dark tunnel in the middle of

downtown, and pressed close enough that his invisible footsteps echoed off the bricks.

He slowed to hush those sounds. The long alley should let him spot
anyone behind him, even though it left him helpless if Eric did come
charging up this path with his dragon-claws out.

*Dragonskin.*

*Eric wrapped himself in dragonskin, and he's tearing around like a
monster himself. And now I'm going to take on more of it...*

Colin shook his head, snapping his thoughts into place. Any more
of that doubt and he'd be making excuses for Eric's savagery, or
flinching from what he had to do. Still, the dim path behind him and
the high walls seemed to grow longer and darker with every step.

At last he reached the next street and the sunlight again. He took
one long glance around that Eric wasn't somehow lurking ahead of
him, and bolted away through the downtown blocks.

The skein around his legs hurled him forward, letting him simply
shift his own muscles to ride its motion as he wove around the few
people on the street. One street led to the next, twisting him along. He
could feel the ground begin to slope upward, on out of downtown and
nearing the Hillside, his home streets.

Here and there he saw signs of discarded food, an overturned
sandwich sign, a black tire mark on the pavement. Not signs of a
"panic" this morning, only a momentary rush away from danger.

And Eric was still out there. "New attacks," Bea had tried to tell
him. *I'm turning away from that now, after all the times I said nobody
else should die...*

*I can't even save Terri.*

That thought was a jagged thing lodged in him, something that
could tear loose and rip him open if he touched it. *So I do what I have
to.*

Another turn brought a shape rolling into view. A food cart, a simple wood and metal push-cart, one touch of normalcy still rolling
along through these shocked streets.

Food. Just that morning, that huge brunch had given him the strength to control his skein again, and now he was out to master more of it than he'd ever carried. Colin ducked between a pair of close-parked cars—it was cover enough to let invisibility drop and slide the skein back under his clothes.

The man at the cart was young, not the graying figure Colin thought he'd seen around town before, but already weathered from the sun. Colin caught him looking away from his scars and the wisp of skein over his eyes, as he scooped up a peach, carrots, everything he could fit in his hands.

*I'm still part of the lives here, aren't I?* Colin made himself smile. "Long day."

"Sure is," the vendor answered.

Colin handed over his money—almost the last scrap he had on him.

A siren screamed. Behind him, right on the street, too close and coming closer. A piece of fruit slipped, almost fell from his fingers before he caught it.

The vendor's eyes narrowed at that. But Colin kept still, kept his face turned away from the street—one minute earlier and he'd have still been invisible—until the police car raced by behind him and the tone fell away in the distance.

It shut off... was that four, five blocks away? That sudden hush could mean Eric was *there,* people could be dying, not so far out of reach...

And if Eric crushed him and kept his promise, who'd be left to save Zara? Colin grabbed his armful of food and wrenched himself away, turned up the street to swing far around that spot. *I do what I have to.*

He pushed himself up the block, his teeth tearing off chunks of food, feeling the rush of juices in his mouth. He was betting every-thing on that mass of skein in the mine, and him having the strength to control it this time. Even if it meant terrorizing Walters and turning away from that siren.

The mass of food in his stomach churned, uneasy. And the skein, that hidden layer he'd pulled in under his clothes again... should it really feel so familiar on him?

"No, the window just broke, boom!" A young woman was walking toward him on the sidewalk ahead, arguing with her friend. "And the glass never came near me, but look!"

She held up her hand—wrapped in cloth, streaked with red.

"So? You think the ghost cut you?" her friend scoffed.

Colin's mouth opened, to warn them about "ghosts" and the dangers of being on the street at all.

But if it had been Eric up there, the way they'd come from...

He spun around to walk away from them. He caught a flash of surprise on their faces, maybe a spark of anger at the avoidance.

*Do what I have to.*

He scrambled down a block, then swung around two, three blocks to the side, panting past low, sparse Hillside houses and walls that left so much of the street in plain view. He gulped more of his food down, and turned another block.

Between the branches of the tree ahead, an invisible figure stood up atop the next house.

Colin dropped, pressed against the low brick wall beside him. *No, no, I can't have run right* into *Eric!* Cold, strangling rage twisted inside him.

But from that glimpse, the one image lingering in his sight... Eric had faced away from him. Looking away along the street, not back at anyone moving along under the trees behind him...

Colin crouched still. One sign, one thing that made Eric look back could ruin it all. And he saw one old man across the street glancing toward him, maybe ready to walk over and look at the man who was cowering from empty air.

He counted thirty too-slow seconds against a frenzy of heartbeats. At least he risked peeping up over the wall.

Nothing stood on the roof.

Colin stood, walked, ran the other way. His feet rang on the sidewalk, but he held the pace until he'd cleared that block and the next, and finally looked back. Nothing.

He sagged against a fence and gulped down the last of his meal with shaking hands. If he even needed that now, if he could dare go toward that mass of skein power with Eric nearby.

It was a long way around the Hillside.

Emptying his hands let him step into the first corner he could find to call his skein out around him again. But even that speed and stealth only cut through the distance so much, to put enough blocks around where Eric had been, always watching around himself on every side.

Still, at last the town thinned away. The rambling houses gave way to scattered things on a narrowing road.

*Me, a road, and the sun, again.* He'd climbed this way twice before, up the slope that had truly made Rayo Hill—first partway into the countryside to get Terri to safety, then chasing Gardner and blundering into the secret he needed now. Unless the dragon's remains had been *drawing* him both times… but that was crazy. This would be his last time here, it had to be.

The last traces of the town faded behind him, faster now with so much food to drive the skein around his legs. It all fell away except the hill, the scrubby growth around the dirt road, and the distant birdcalls that disturbed the open air.

Finally the road branched up into a trail up the bluff itself. Toward the "mine" where the creature lay… Josh Gardner had said the whole town had been shaped by either getting or hiding that secret. And Eric would destroy that town unless someone had enough of that power to face him.

The switchback trail led up toward the smaller mine entrance, an easy open path now that nobody up at the hillcrest was watching for intruders. His legs and the skein's strength dug away at the distance.

The tunnel entrance stood blocked.

Where there'd been a shadowy gap just yesterday, a heavy metal mesh lay wrapped around the remains of the iron bars he'd cut through.

Colin glared at the stopgap barrier. He could slash through it even easier than the bars… but that would leave proof that there was still something in the mine worth taking.

Instead he walked on up to the crest, toward the larger entrance beyond it, all too sure what he'd find. *They've been chasing Eric all over town today, but they made time to block this place off again? Seriously?*

Down on the opposite slope, he saw the other entrance, and the two police. Two men, sitting right against the side of the entrance, just playing with their phones as if they meant to sit there *forever*.

He worked his way downward and around the slope toward them. First Hoyle had sent men out here to keep Gardner's scheme safe— now even with Hoyle dead, killed trying to make up for that, they still couldn't keep out of the one place Colin had to be. Instead they had to waste manpower just to protect the scene of a crime that he and Bea had already solved for them…

He froze. Those two leaned right *against* the mine's side, he'd never slip in behind them. So he was creeping toward them to, what, knock them out? Risk whatever damage that did to their skulls, and prove the cave still had its secrets?

*But every minute I lose could be Eric killing someone.*

He stared at the glimmers where his fists were. He'd dodged all over town, left Eric on the loose, left *Zara,* and all of that was blocked by two grunts lounging beside the cave? What were they doing, chatting about some game app? The nearer one wasn't even turned toward him.

Colin stopped with his fist drawing back.

The air was still. No voices, no birdsong, only the faintest sound of the two guards working their screens, until Colin crept away.

*My responsibility, my choice, no flinching from that. The skein's not trying to make me a monster, it's not.*

Instead he crept around to the trail up between them and started forward. Slowly, silently, taking one stretched-out breath just to reach a foot out. Their gazes peeped up right at his approaching shimmer, again and again. One of them was round-faced, young, the other older with a bandage hidden on the other side of his head.

"So you Check again? Why do you even have a Bet button anyway?" the young one grumbled. Deep in a game of online poker.

He inched closer. A shimmer, an outline, would be nothing to them if their eyes didn't recognize it, didn't notice it move…

Under his foot, a pebble *cracked.*

They glanced up. He froze—so close they could have kicked at his feet.

Then they looked back to their screens.

Colin clamped down the urge to sigh. Even when he eased forward again, he moved without breathing until he'd slipped between them and on out of the sun.

Somehow his steps grew steadier as the light thinned away behind him. What small scratches his feet made on the shaft floor seemed swallowed up, ignored. The odd dry smell of the mine hung around him. He let his invisibility fall like throwing off a silent weight. *It's just me here now, no enemies, and I'm leaving that anger behind.*

Traveling in the dark was only part of that. His armored fingers traced along the wall's roughness—what branches the mine made were clear in his memory, and a flash of his phone's light could orient him if he doubted. He took the wrong way only once.

Then the tunnel opened outward, and that light showed the nearest sides of the great sloping basin. Now that he knew what lay at its bottom, he wondered how he'd ever thought this cavern could be natural.

He picked his way down using just glimpses of light. The rocky side held together better than it had before, but that risk felt oddly removed—no rockslide could harm him in his skein, so it giving way now felt almost pointless.

His feet reached the clutter of rocks at the bottom. He flicked on the light again—

From down here he could just guess at the edges of the cavern around him, all pressing down at him from beyond his sight. Now he felt his heartbeat begin to rise, the only living thing under all this.

He crept along the rocks, peering between the stones of the cairn. His steps clattered off the shifting stones.

A glimmer of silver-green shone through the cracks. His battery flickered.

He crouched down beside the spot and flicked the light off.

The dragon's resting place... all this skein had lain here for so long. And yet some of it had been out there killing, while Matt Vargas used it trying to shore parts of the town up... until he ended up killing himself for that...

*Stop that, we need this to beat Eric. I need to make this skein join my own, not fail like I did last night.*

He let out a slow, slow breath, and reached toward the gap in the rocks. This dragonskin did *not* make Eric a murderer. Or Howard Strickland a "monster," or drive his son into the Beast Killings. *Or make me attack Walters.*

*Or else it already has.*

His hand jerked back from the rocks.

And, Bea had told him on their first day how she'd been telling Jordan that she couldn't remove her skein. All a lie to make him keep her secret, and she always could separate from it.

But she'd never worn as much skein as him, or for so long, or had to fight to keep control of it. If that *was* what happened over time...

He couldn't move. He might be sitting alone in the dark with the monster itself wrapped around him, and he'd come here for more...

*Let go!* He swung his arm down, flung his strength into the command. The sheathe of dragonskin shook, trembled around him—was it shaking, or just beginning to tighten against his flesh in the darkness—

No. Fear was just fear. He breathed in again, and breathed out "Let. Go."

The skein split open and sloughed away, fell away to the ground.

He stood shivering in the blackness. His bare face tasted the dark cool air against it, as if the ghost of his movement left air stirring against his sweat, his tears.

A sob tore from his throat. *Attacking Walters, that was all me.*

And Eric was simply being Eric. Colin reached down and pulled his pool of skein back up and flowing in to encase him again. Then he thrust his hand between the rocks—finding the opening in the dark without a moment's fumbling—and gripped the remains of the dragon.

The thing felt nothing like skein, or even rock. It felt like the indomitable force that had burrowed through the mountain itself just to die... and he thought he could command it? *I already failed once.*

But Bea had done it.

He let that image fill his mind: Bea, so easily drawing up a handful of the dragon's skein, never a doubt in her mind. And yet, the same impossible woman who'd taken a moment to apologize to the remains of the beast. *And she kissed me here, a minute before that.* She made it all look easy.

Except she only took one piece of skein.

But, he needed enough to *win.*

His fingers spread against the body. His skein flowed outward—he could never feel the motion he willed it into, but this would have been his fingers stretching, clamping hard against the resistance.

Against the mountain, cold and still and silent.

*Not* the mountain. Fingers dug deeper, into the same stuff he'd controlled, that he'd seen Bea use. *Come here, you can, you* want *to join with me—*

His heart stuttered a beat. This thing *didn't* have wants, did it?

*I do what I have to.*

Those fingers dug deeper, sank into the skein or called it up, pulled... for an instant he *could* feel through it, feel the dragonskin coming away, both joining one self and coming free of his other...

It flowed up around him. A great mass of ready power surged up and flowed and joined to thicken his armor, layer over his muscles, give him strength.

# CHAPTER TEN

# WHAT WE LOVE

Step by step, Colin walked back out of the mine, with a new weight of power thrumming along his body. The nearer he came to the light outside, the more he slowed and relearned how softly those steps could move. The two guards were still outside.

He flew past them with one leap. They flickered in reaction as his shimmer blurred by, but his next footstep was two dozen feet away, too far for their eyes to catch up to and confirm, with all this open space to lose himself in.

Looking around at that open hillside... one unsettling idea stirred in him. *And it might be more frightening if this works.*

Still, every minute he lost was another minute Eric could be using. He swung around and climbed back to the hill's summit.

Spreading his arms, he sent the skein stretching out beyond them. He willed it to thin, to broaden, to spread behind him to join his sides, guiding it as best he could as he twisted his head back. It would have been easier to manage in full sight, not eying this ghostly outline—but this shape was nothing he'd dare let anyone see.

He stretched his arms, felt the membrane catch at the air. Not so much thinner than a sheet that would block bullets.

The hillside sprawled away below, shadows from brush and rocks growing stark as the sun lowered ahead, beyond the town in the distance. A faint breeze tugged at the folds of skein.

He'd already leaped partway down this slope, and the skein had protected him then. And he'd seen Eric ride the wind—*but it's easy for him, not knowing the skein really is all part of a dragon.*

He flexed the membrane one more time, wishing he could feel its strength as it moved. Then he leaped.

Like catching in some net, he hung in the air, with the skein around him dragging him to almost a stop. Except, shouldn't there be more motion...

*A hundred feet down* and more, the ground drifted by below him.

Those rocks pressed closer, he felt himself dip—his stomach lurched, helpless in the air. He craned his head back; the wings were bending, spilling air away, and he couldn't *feel* if they began to give way. He curled his fingers, locked his will into making the shape hold.

Colin hung in the sky.

He shifted his legs behind him, tested the angle of the skein searching for balance. The breeze was gone, as he floated along it, as the ground slid by below him instead. Those gnarled trees and knobby ground seemed to be growing, slowly, as he sank toward them.

A stretch brought the skein up—and his air slipped away, the world began to spin, and he slammed the wings into a downbeat that still left him tossing and spinning and begging for just one moment when he could stabilize, until he rode it out and held the wings steady again.

Better to stick to gliding. So, one step off a cliff didn't make him move like a dragon... That one fear smoothed away from shivering at the back of his neck, as he dangled and strained to hold the wing-framework together, and the ground slipped by.

He could see the land inching along even while it dipped away below him. The rumpled lines of the town drew closer, and a chorus of sounds began to fill the silent air. He tightened his grip on invisibility.

The first of the Hillside neighborhoods slid by, roofs and telephone poles reaching up toward him. He forced his gaze away from the remains of the Vargas House, and how many blocks looked so empty from above.

Instead he looked along the roofs, the corners, the streets for any telltale glimpse of Eric darting around. This might be his only chance to get the altitude for a wide search. *And I guess if Eric sees me first, all that my direction tells him is that I glided down from the heights, not that I had to go there for enough skein to do it.*

Another telephone pole scudded by below him, too close. He looked around again, tried to spot a way to the hospital ahead. Was it that larger structure there, with several more shapes filling the clear space around it?

But the street around it had too much *motion,* too many flashing lights even for a hospital. Trouble.

And right when he'd been away. Colin's stomach twisted, even before he shifted his weight toward an empty street and let the wings relax.

He thudded down on the pavement, skein easily catching the impact. The sound brought a woman on the sidewalk glancing toward him, then shaking her head in uncertainty and walking on. What could she make of a dim outline like his, a sprawling blur with great flopping shapes stretched behind him?

No time to be tied down. He wrenched the long, clumsy folds in toward him until they flowed in and melted along his body again, back into the shape he knew. Then he set that power to flinging him down the street in a run.

He saw the hospital in bare minutes—three police cars clustered right at the entrance, and the uneasy motion of the people around it sent tremors inside him. *What did Eric do, I had to leave Zara here, I had to...*

He scrambled in and slipped around past the front desk, away up the corridor. He twisted around the first turn, right in front of two cops. One turned to look straight toward him.

They were *that* on edge? Colin ducked back behind the turn.

"Hold it there—"

"What'd you see—"

He heard the two march toward the corner, and he could only press flat against the wall and wait.

A moment later they stepped into view. The lead cop glared around, past the "blur" on the wall, and turned back.

"Well, I'm not letting my guard down again," he grunted.

Again?

Colin whirled and walked, forced his legs to simply walk, back up a turn and swing around past those guards toward Zara's room. Or the last room he'd seen her in, she had to be there...

Another cop stood ahead of him, but this one's attention was fixed on arguing with a doctor.

"I told you, nobody's seen your partner," she told the cop.

"You don't help me, you'll have to tell the commissioner."

Colin stepped around them. Neither looked over, and he headed on.

"Look, if he can get through here to Zara, we should figure he can be anywhere."

Oh.

*God.*

Colin ran. One thought tugged backward at him, demanding he turn around and drag answers out of them, but he charged on toward Zara's room.

"Who's there!" rang out behind him. Feet raced after him.

Another two cops stood outside Zara's door.

Fists clenched—he blocked that urge, shoved himself into a side-step as the other cop closed him behind him. But smashing through them felt right, *too* right, even if it was just to see the site with his own eyes.

"What did he want?" Walters's bellow boomed out from beyond the door. "Rowe broke in here again, we've got a man missing—you tell me what he wanted with you!"

What Eric wanted… if that wasn't simple murder, if Walters had someone in there he was asking…

Colin slid along the wall. Faster than he should, too much motion to catch the eye with the three cops looking around, but he couldn't hear through their noise. And *everything* was behind that door.

Then he heard her voice.

"…was ranting about the town fading away, and it going faster now without me to pull it together. What Eric always wants."

Zara, alive. His mother's rich, resonant voice thrilled through him, pinned him in place with relief. A weight he'd feeling from the moment he left her slipped away.

"Just to *talk?*" Walters said. "You think I believe that? We've been running ourselves ragged trying to find Rowe all day. They're calling him a goddamn ghost now, and that's some of my men too!"

"I suppose they are." This time Zara's voice was harder to hear, lower and regretful. And he heard a twinge, what could be a flash of *pain.*

Walters plowed on "But your son, your son said Rowe was coming after you. Instead we get a missing officer, and you still here—and now you think you can lie to me?"

"You heard my answer. But have you heard from Bea? Has she had any luck finding him?"

"Oh, I've heard. And I do not believe this—you hold out on me and then think you can ask *me* for information?"

Heavy steps sounded, and Walters slammed the door open.

He waved to the two guards. "Move out. It's clear the bastard is done with everything here."

And Walters stomped away, with his officers falling into line behind him. He actually pulled his guards *off* Zara, *again.*

Colin stared at his retreating back. A few steps closer and he could try hearing what low orders Walters snapped at his men… or grab him and make him explain…

None of that mattered. He looked at the other figures in view—nobody too close or really looking this way now. He nudged Zara's door open and stepped in.

There she was. Lying in bed, slowly viewing her phone screen with weary-looking eyes, but Zara was alive. Colin stood, drinking in the truth of what had passed them by.

She was alone, he realized at last. He let his stealth drop. "Hi again."

Her eyes shot wide, she shrank back against the cushions—

Then she relaxed, as he finished splitting his skein mask back from his face. She sighed "It's you."

He stepped closer, slowly, trying to wish away that flash of fear he'd seen on her. "Sure it's me. And you always recognized..." No, no excuse was enough for scaring her.

"For that one second, I saw Eric instead of you. He's been the one carrying that much bulk around."

"Until now. Fight fire with fire, was the plan, remember? And at least this means I got enough of it." He tried to smile, but that startled image still floated in his memory. "You're okay? Really okay, when he came after you *again?"*

"Yes. Really okay." Her voice was shallow, careful of where Eric had torn into her, but she kept it firm. Her eyes held his.

For a moment it was too much. Colin turned away, then he stepped away to set a chair against the door to give them a fraction of privacy.

Then he crouched beside her again. "I'm so sorry." Her hands were cool under his grip. "I never should have left you here. Or let you get hurt at all, nothing matters if we lose you."

*Or lose Terri, and we already are*—the thought stabbed through him, made him twist away from his mother's gaze. How much did that tell her?

"Colin. Do you know what I'd say now?" A smile crooked on her lips, nudging him along.

"That it's not my fault? I don't know about that. I thought he wouldn't come after you again so soon."

That or Eric simply had him afraid to face him again. But after so many times just being outclassed, this time he *had* to be a match for him. Colin drew his hands back, looked at his skein-coated fingers. If they could be strong enough, sharp enough, to win next time...

He saw Zara following his gaze, and he asked "Eric said he'd be back to get us both. But then he let you go?"

"A puzzle, isn't it? And he hasn't forgiven me for standing up and asking people to stay. When he appeared here," she added softly, "I honestly thought I was dead. And then he —"

The door rattled, pushed against the chair Colin had set there.

He yanked his mask up and faded from sight, twisted in his crouch to face the doorway—

A nurse, a reedy, pockmarked man in blue, stepped in. "You alright, Ms. da Costa?"

"Zara. I'm fine, and it's Zara."

The nurse stepped toward her. Colin edged away from his line of sight, and he saw that gaze twitch to follow his glimmer, then back to Zara. People here were right to watch for shadows, after Eric had already slipped into the room once, but what would they believe?

The nurse cleared his throat. "Time for your meds."

"To help me sleep? I'd like to be awake a little longer."

He waggled a finger in the air. "And what about our schedule, and all our work measuring out what you need?"

"There's nothing life-threatening, you've all told me." Zara's voice steadied and settled into a gently persuasive rhythm. "It should be safe to give me a few more minutes. After everything, Harry, letting me take a scrap of control back would mean a lot to me."

'Harry' frowned, eyed her a moment. "A few minutes? Only that, and no arguing then." He turned and walked away.

Colin watched the door swing closed. All this hiding, was it still to keep the skein's secrets, or keep him near his family, or was it doing any good at all?

*And we may need all the help we can get.*

"Eric simply… appeared here," Zara whispered.

He slipped to her side, touched her hand again.

Her softer voice let a strain show in it, a haunted sound. "I have no idea what he did to get past them, besides hiding himself. I hope that one missing officer is all we lost."

"Hoping there's just one death." The words came bitterly. "That's what we've come to now."

"He came to… to lord it over me that more people were leaving town. And then, he asked if we'd been fooling him about Terri dying."

"He did? 'Asked'—what did he do to you?"

Zara's eyes were shut, her face still. "Nothing much. I suppose your trying to tell him the truth only made him wonder. I stuck with our story."

Colin nodded. "You didn't have to. I mean, you could have said we hid her somewhere, just not where. His whole rampage did happen because he thought she was dead."

And when Zara started that lie, she chose Terri's safety, even knowing whatever revenge Eric might take on Rayo Hill. *Like I did by spending time going after the skein.*

"I know," she said. "I came up with the deception, and I chose to keep silent, whatever it cost our people. But I'm not so sure it makes a difference." Her eyes opened. "Would knowing he'd been tricked make Eric any more forgiving?"

"You mean after the years he let *us* think she was gone? But I guess not," he added. "Either way, anything we do is feeding his hate."

"He's got plenty of that already. He was ranting, wild, worse than I've ever heard him." She glanced around, eyes tracking around the room where Eric had been. "He said he'd done it all for her, and now he didn't know what he had left."

Except killing. That was what Eric always fell back to, even before today's carnage. And yet he'd had Zara right in his grasp and... Colin shivered. "Then he let you live?"

"He thought it over."

Her eyes twitched, flinched away in what had to be fear.

"And then, he asked where you were."

"Right behind him ready to cut his head off, I wish. I hope you told him that a few times." He formed a fist, willed the skein fingertips to sharpen though the clawpoints only pushed uselessly against the skein over his palm. Not a promising sign.

"Colin. What I'm saying is, he asked about you." She shifted on the bed, and her eyes looked straight into his. "I think he let me go because it wouldn't be finishing me *in front of you.* You're the one who hurt him the most."

Colin forced a laugh. "Me? You're the one who blocked up that exit on Silverlode—and after he attacked you, the people you stopped lined up to come in and see you. I'm just the one that can take a punch from him."

*More than* take *punches, now.* He squeezed his fist again, trying to feel the power encasing it.

Zara's eyes tracked that motion, and they clouded. "So you say. But you and Bea are the ones who keep chasing him off when he makes a move. And, I'm afraid I haven't seen Bea since I woke up."

"She was here, right outside this room." *And I yelled at her.* "Walters must have her off chasing Eric. What are you thinking, that he'll target her next?"

"It might appeal to him. She's been in his way too, and he could think he'd hurt her to bring you to him." Zara shook her head. "Or he might not care, and just go on tearing his way through Rayo Hill."

"He could." Regret and pain gripped Colin's voice, a match for hers. "I just... I *have* to get him this time. Now I've finally got the strength. But... we keep struggling just to track him too."

"If you want bait, I'm right here. But that would mean we were trying to bring him in among these other patients."

Colin gritted his teeth—for an instant he found himself considering it, risking *her*. "He's already turned you down. But it's true, nothing's going to stop this if I can't lure him out, or track him down. And then trap him, even after all the times he's slipped away from us. If we can just do that, Bea and I might be enough to get him, if I can just hold him down this time."

And Eric always knew Bea could finish him with the spell, just by letting Colin handle the skein side of the fight. And she was still out there somewhere...

"You're thinking of getting help?" Zara said. "The commissioner and his men?"

Colin's eyes flew open. Walters *hadn't* crossed his mind, but— "We may have to."

Footsteps moved through the doorway.

"I said a few minutes," the nurse said. As Colin, still invisible, slid away from Zara's bedside again.

"We did say that." After Zara's whispers to him, her full voice sounded too loud, and too much of a strain for her. She looked at her phone as if it had been the only thing on her mind, and then she set it aside.

The nurse stepped closer, a paper cup in his hand. "Zara? I am sorry about your daughter, and that Nurse Setter was part of that. But you do need to trust us."

She gave him a long, measuring look. Then she nodded, and took the cup and the pill inside it.

Colin slipped out behind the nurse's back. As he did, he wondered if Zara had meant that nod for him as well as the nurse, or even about the last idea they'd been speaking of. *Could I trust Walters on this after all, even after I attacked him?* It might come down to whether his temper outweighed his sense as a cop.

Colin started through the corridors, wondering if Walters really had removed all his guards. The only police he passed were two talking with a nurse, about their missing officer.

But when he stepped outside the building, he saw the police van still in the lot, and another black-and-white at the far end of the pavement. So Walters hadn't pulled his people out after all, not yet or not all of them, in spite of his bluster.

Colin watched the van, and the two officers visible in the window. From a distance they seemed to be sitting quiet, but still too conspicuous to be staking the place out...

*I'm stalling.* The police were right there, if he could walk up to them and talk with the commissioner he'd attacked. Give him an apology, or the truth, or...

He turned away. At least he could check with Bea first.

He moved up past the parking lot, toward the half-empty buildings behind it. That gave him dozens of yards' distance between the cars and the backs of the buildings, and a couple of scraggly bushes at its border to hide when he pulled out the phone.

The battery *was* low, drained from guiding him around the cave. There were two calls from Ed Jordan—because they'd left him with Terri. Guilt prickling at him, Colin called back.

"There you are, da Costa." Jordan's brisk tone sounded like the closest he'd come to mentioning that Colin might not have made it back. "Someone here's been asking about you."

Then he heard Terri's voice: "You didn't answer."

"Busy, I guess." It was better than mentioning a *dragon* on the phone. He glanced around at the motion of cars, people between the buildings, still none of them close enough to overhear him. "Sorry I kept the phone silent."

"Sorry I worried," she said. "Jordan's been a good host. Heard some about your chase."

"The chase, yeah. Zara thinks—"

Zara. If Terri was this calm, did she still not know their mother had been hurt?

He went on "—well, she thinks I'm Eric's favorite target now. Or else that he'll just lash out wherever he wants, because…"

"Because he blames the whole town. And when Eric's angry, he kills. I know."

It was almost a matter-of-fact thing, the way she talked about what she'd seen festering for years. Except for one hitch in her voice.

"I hate to ask this," he said. "But, which do you think he'd really want? Me, or all of them? Or Bea?"

"Bea. Or you." The answer came right back. "Don't think he'd unravel enough to forget his enemies. Either of you."

"Thanks. I think," and he tried to chuckle. She had to be right, they couldn't keep watching Eric just storm through the whole town.

"Or maybe Zara," Terri said. "Why hasn't she come back?"

Just a few of Terri's short, blunt words, all it took to have him trapped. So they hadn't told her yet—*we don't hide things from family. But Terri's already fading away, they think she only has a* month…

"I was just talking to her. She had a near miss with Eric, but he didn't do anything near what he could have." That was reassuring enough, and almost true.

"I see."

Was that a touch of suspicion thickening her voice? He said "Any news from Jordan?"

"Not much," came Jordan's answer—they must have been on speaker. "I hear them beating the bushes for Rowe. And yes, Simms keeps putting herself in the thick of it."

While he was still looking after Terri, from his own wheelchair, when he was supposed to be back among the police. Jordan didn't even mention that.

"Thanks," was all Colin could say. "I'll try to break the stalemate soon. One more thing: you have any ideas how I could get through to Walters?"

"From what I hear now? Don't try it," was all Jordan said. And he hung up.

That left Bea herself to check in with. But she didn't answer, he heard only her voice mail—the dry, empty name of "Detective Bea Simms" that could have come from any officer in town.

*Don't try it.* But they needed *everything* right to take Eric down. Colin looked out at the police again, still doing their own best to watch for an enemy they barely knew. He could try to change that, he could offer Walters anything from a solid plan to a real look at how Eric got away from them. And more.

He looked down at his arms. Even from just the invisible halo, he could see the new thickness layered over him, all the skein ready to give him its strength. More of it than Eric carried, finally.

He stretched his fingertip-skein out into claws.

*Sharper. Needle-tipped, with mountain hardness behind them...* He pushed his need, his rage into the blades. Then he stretched the skein between his other thumb and finger out into inches of webbing, and laid that down against the sidewalk. As just a hint of what Eric's armor would be.

With all the strength his arm could gather, he slammed the points down at the membrane.

Nothing broke. He couldn't find one scratch in the concrete below.

What was it going to take? He strained to hone the claws to something even finer, harder, and brought them down again.

The crash echoed dully off the backs of the buildings like some pocket firecracker. But he still hadn't pierced one bit of his own armor.

He let out a slow breath, looked at the cops again. *Stalling.*

He drew back among the buildings, out of sight of the police. Then he let the invisibility drop, and called the skein in under his clothes.

It wouldn't fit.

The stuff squeezed in under his shirt and pants, and he felt fabric straining, stitches pulling. His clothes looked like he was hiding a mass of balloons underneath, and that still left heavy chunks of green coating his hands with nowhere left to go.

He could only draw it out again and settle it openly on the outside. It covered all of him but his head, hands, and shoes, like some gleaming jogging suit.

If someone wore about four layers of winter suits, in the summer sun. He stood up and walked out to the police van.

The first motions inside that van came when he was halfway across the lot. First they watched him approach, then one cop climbed out and eyed him as he drew near. The cop stood silent—so still that Colin thought, *Is he trying not to spook me?*

"Please." Colin pushed soft calm into his voice. "Please, I have information for the commissioner."

The cop frowned.

Then the side door slammed back, and the cop stepped aside as Walters erupted from the van.

"You! What are you doing here, da Costa?" He stomped forward, one hand fingering his collar. Or his throat where Colin had caught him last time.

Colin stood his ground, and swallowed the apology he'd thought to start with. Instead he spread his hands and said "I came to talk. What's important is, if you want to catch Eric Rowe—"

"You have the balls to—" Walters stopped.

He flicked a glance up and down Colin.

"What is that thing? That's a suit like Rowe's, you mean you've got *more?*" Greed thickened his voice.

"Something like that. Can you check with Bea? She can help me talk through the police tactics. How we can make this work."

"You want to make demands?" Walters's voice rose. "You want updates about *my* detective? Where's Jordan? I called him in to coordinate the search, and the last anyone hears he was talking with your mother! Simms, Hoyle, Jordan—how do you even keep getting to people, good cops who know their job?"

*Because they know what the enemy is. I'm* trying *to tell you.*

"Look, I told you we can catch Eric, it all comes back to that. And we can. We set it up right, your men surround him—"

"Oh, like we haven't tried? Or are you offering yourself as bait, da Costa?" His eyes sharpened at that. Was that an insult or curiosity?

"Maybe. You'd need your rifles—" he caught Walters glancing at his skein again— "and those infrared scopes Hoyle tried."

"Those? You know how many favors I had to call in to borrow those once? Just to track one man?"

*No, no...* "You said, you've tried trapping him, and that hasn't been working. And night's going to be here soon, so why wouldn't you want them?" Colin took a deeper breath, tried *not* to think of all Bea's warnings, or Jordan's. "And, there's more than that. Those scopes are the only real protection your men have—"

"They do *not* need your help. And I don't need some punk trying to take out his grudge on our suspect."

Walters's head twitched sideways. The tiniest gesture, but it was echoed by other movement at the corner of Colin's eyes. Other cops, closing in around him. Three of them.

As they did, another cop, a hard-faced veteran, stepped up behind Walters and whispered to him.

*"Gone?"*

"What happened?" Colin said.

Walters's face split in a sneer. "Those scopes you wanted? They're missing. And it was Officer Evans that stashed them for Hoyle—nobody's seen him for hours either."

The missing cop they'd had. Of *course* Eric would grab him, if he overheard he had the scopes. *Now there's nothing left that can get a good look at Eric, except our skein.*

The cops closed in.

"I've had about enough of your interference—"

With Walters in midsentence, Colin bolted away past the nearest cop.

He had one instant before they reacted, before their thoughts caught up that he could still think of escape. Then a weight shoved against his back, and he felt arms trying to lock and drag him down.

His strength shucked the cop off without breaking stride.

Every step came faster, flung him further and stretched the distance from his pursuers. He heard them shouting, steadily falling back. Only a couple of turns later he found a moment to bring the skein out over his face, vanish, and race on, no longer certain *where*.

# CHAPTER ELEVEN

# WHAT WE CAN'T LOSE

*Now that I've got the strength to fight, I throw away my best chance to find Eric.* Colin slogged down the sidewalk, wending toward Terri's hiding place and pausing at the few times he passed someone on the way.

"…crazy with a gun, he could be anywhere…"

But that group of old men only kept talking, repeating fragmented rumors that told him nothing.

A woman scurried by, herding two young children. Colin stepped wide around them, but she still glanced over in his direction and shooed her family on even faster. He wondered how hard his outline was to overlook now, bulked up with all this skein.

"…right off Cherry Street, and she never came back." A young man whispered to the woman beside him.

*Cherry Street—where Eric had taken Jessie and searched for the Beast Killings?* Colin leaned closer.

"I mean it, she—"

A buzz vibrated in Colin's pocket. The couple froze, looked back, at the faint sound of the phone coming from a mere shimmer in the air.

Colin twisted away and dashed up the street, kicking through discarded boxes as he went. Somehow after missing Terri's calls he'd left

the phone on Vibrate instead of Off, even while he ran around "invisible."

The sound shut off after three buzzes, but he kept moving until he
found a back corner to pull the machine clear of his skein.

The call had been from Bea.

He called straight back. The moment she answered he said
"There's an Eric sighting near Cherry Street. I'll meet you there."

"That was hours ago," Bea answered. "Where are you now?"

"Off Holt and Santos." He glanced around; yes, the streets were
just starting to rise into the curves of the Hillside. Except— "Hold on,
I'm okay, don't you need to stay with the cops and…"

She'd hung up. She just hung up, no explanation, no debate, nothing. He stared at the phone, until he remembered to tuck it out of sight
again. The battery was still low.

Some five minutes later, Bea's car pulled up beside him.

Instead of getting in, Colin moved around to the drivers-side window. Bea only raised an eyebrow before she slid the glass down an
inch to let him speak:

"You shouldn't be here. Walters just had his men trying to grab
me, and he was throwing words like 'interference' around. You can't
risk sneaking off to meet me now."

She didn't answer. She didn't speak at all, only looked back at him.

He tried "Think about it. Can't you get more done staying with the
manhunt and hearing everything the police pick up? So it's only when
they find Eric again that you let me know. Don't you see that?"

"Are you done?" she said.

Then she picked up her phone.

"Got a chance to talk to some people on Santos," she said to it.
"They're not on my schedule, but worth a try."

"Got it. We'll cover for you," a woman answered—on speaker,
Bea had *let* him hear that answer.

Bea hung up and smiled at him. "Don't burn bridges. You think I
haven't figured that out?"

"But... you didn't see how Walters was this time, he *hates* me. And word's going to get back to him, you can't keep hiding from—"

A giant's hand roared past him.

There and gone and battering him with the wind in its wake before the engine's sound registered. *A car, that's a car that pulled past Bea's, and it just missed where I'm crazy enough to be standing out in the street* invisible.

*"Colin!"*

"That was... close." He gave her a wave, something to push the shock back from her face. His knees shook as he swung around to the sidewalk and climbed in the seat beside her.

Bea's face was ashen, even while her eyes and mouth began smoothing themselves back to their usual control. She looked straight at the street and pulled the car out with a delicate touch.

She wouldn't talk about that near accident, not Bea. Instead he looked at the street ahead and said "You, you really want to risk your career hanging around me now? You know they're going to put it together, if you keep ducking out on their assignments." He glanced over at her.

Her face was perfect calm by now, if it weren't for the pallor clinging to her skin. "Not important what they do by then. By that time we'll have nailed Eric. Or we'll be dead."

"Don't *joke* about that." His words came out louder than he meant, reverberating inside the car.

"I'm not. Staying with you is what I need, the rest is irrelevant."

"As long as we get Eric."

*—Or were you talking about me for other reasons?* The joke was right there on his tongue, but he held it in in time. Neither of them were fit for teasing now.

The car glided on past one block, then another.

Then Bea broke the silence. "So now you're stronger than Eric?"

"That's the idea. I've finally got enough skein to stand up to him. So I either beat him myself, or I grab him and knock him around until you can slap the spell on him. I haven't worked it all out yet."

Even a familiar thought like that couldn't lift the pall hanging over them, not when he'd felt knew how hellishly painful that spell could be. In a lighter tone he added:

"But, remember that time Eric made some glider wings? I did that too, all the way down from the hilltop."

"Gliding? I don't see much use for that in a chase. Eric can look right up and see you coming."

Colin heard himself chuckling. Even the thought of flying was just another tool to Bea?

"So you have the weapon for the center of a plan," she said. "The step before that is, how do we get our hands on him?"

"That was supposed to be Walters and enough cops, surrounding him." He hung his head. "Walters just... I really screwed up there, I know it. Anyway, Eric must have grabbed the infrared scopes, so they'd have nothing but shadows to look for."

"I heard."

"That just leaves bringing Eric to us, meaning bait. Meaning me."

"Or me," she said. "But I'd be a softer target. You're more likely to survive."

"I plan to." He let out a slow breath. It did depend on that, didn't it? "Then the step before that one is, how do we find where to put that bait?"

"Exactly. So, patterns about where Eric's been."

"Like the police know." *And I went and attacked their boss...* "I should check in with Terri," he said.

Jordan's phone only rang twice before they answered, and it was Terri's voice from the start: "Any news?"

"We're making plans to track Eric's location down. And," he swallowed, "if you and Jordan hear about Walters wanting to lock me up—"

He broke off. Bea was swinging the car toward a driveway, at the same old house where they'd left Terri and Jordan.

He looked at Bea. "You were bringing us here all along?"

"Of course. We put our heads together, and give Jordan a hand with Terri. This way he might even take it," she added.

The car settled in the garage, but he didn't move, could only sit there in the sudden silence beside her. *Bea keeps finding her own ways to look after us...*

The most he could say was, "I truly am sorry I yelled at you after Zara was—"

"After Zara was stabbed?" She sighed. "I know you better than that. Nothing you'd say at a moment like that counts."

She climbed out, and they swung the garage door down to hide the car.

When he opened the connecting door, Jordan was waiting. He twisted his chair around and led them on in, through the emptied-out corridor inside.

He spoke the first words too: "Ready to get to work?"

"Ready," Bea said. "Except this guy here was trying to talk me into cutting ties with him."

"Idiot," Jordan muttered. "You think we're going to back down now?"

Colin managed a grin. "Shared strength. That's what Zara would say here." Since she couldn't be here, the only one who wasn't.

Terri lay in the same bare room he'd left her, opposite the kitchen. She was still on the gurney they'd smuggled her out on, but he saw blankets wadded up and wedged in around her for cushions. That was Jordan at work helping Terri... when he couldn't stand up himself.

A pang of guilt stabbed at Colin, and even anger for Zara running out on them too. He looked away, and fumbled the phone into an outlet to start recharging.

"So how do we find Rowe?" Bea said.

"I've been plotting his attacks."

Jordan held up his phone, and they crowded in around the screen. The thin, spidery outline of the Rayo Hill map appeared.

"A 'sniper' here, more like a stabbing." One red dot appeared, by Cherry Street. "An accident here an hour later, a possibility. Then a killing here." New dots spattered around the map. "You see the problem."

"This is in a few hours?" Colin growled. "They're *all* the problem."

"Besides that," Bea said. "Rowe's not simply rampaging up a straight line. He picks one target, then he zigzags away over enough blocks that we can't trace a pattern. To whatever catches his eye next."

"And to the people?" Terri said. "Looks like he's everywhere."

Colin groaned. "And how can they trace him, they can't even see him."

Jordan tapped his phone again, searching one screen after another.

Colin drew back a step and held up his fingers. A quick thought brought the skein stretching out, narrowing into solid claws again.

Bea glanced over, eying his work.

She'd done better than this herself, back when she was holding all their skein. *Alright, how about something more useful. When I'm grappling with Eric...*

He flicked his hands outward and willed the skein at his palms to move with it. The green rippled out, out into inch-long spines, but only for an instant before he saw them shrinking back into his gloves.

"A way to hold onto our target?" Bea said. "That would do it. Try using the movement to trigger your thought, faster."

He struck out again. The spikes stabbed out, shriveled again—not fast enough, not strong enough for that one chance he might have to lock Eric down.

He felt Terri's eyes on him. She could see the tension in his fingers, whatever rage was on his face. Eric was a murderer many times over—but these people shouldn't see how the thought of stabbing him felt so good,

Then Terri said "To hold him down for the spell." Her lips curved in a small, dark smile.

*Never forget, Eric's* already *left more of a mark on Terri than on any of us here.* Colin swallowed, tried the spikes again. More than anything, he'd wanted his sister to be free of this, but she'd never be unchanged.

"Keep working on that while we plan." Jordan tapped his phone again. "It all starts with finding where Rowe pops up next. I'm tracking the reports, plus I've got a friend or two where I need them."

Bea's eyebrows went up. "And Walters still thinks you're off the grid? Impressive. So we keep watching until we have a definite sighting, then we head out and set the trap." She nodded to Colin.

" 'Definite sighting'?" Colin frowned. "That sounds like you're waiting for him to *kill* someone else. If we know where he's been, we get out there now and use that."

"When the trail's already cold." Bea shook her head. "Eric would be gone by then. Or you'd be walking around the next dozen blocks just hoping he's somewhere and ready to bite."

"Too suspicious," Terri added. "You'd scare him off."

Jordan said "You only get one chance—blow that and he won't fall for it again. Rowe has to believe you've got a reason to be there, and that means *right* there where he is."

"So you *do* mean you wait for him to…" Colin caught his voice rising, his feet taking an angry step toward the two cops.

He broke off, looked at those grim faces. Jordan glared right back at him, Bea looked down but there was no doubt in her eyes.

Colin stared at them, and scrabbled for a change of subject.

"Terri?" He turned to the gurney. "This is our first chance to test something. Now that I've got more skein than I've ever had—"

He reached one hand over to the other and began loosening the skein on it, peeling it off to pool in his palm and gather around it. His exposed flesh felt bare and awkward without its strength over him.

He went on "Eric was always sure that getting enough of it would heal you."

Terri closed her eyes. "You know that won't help."

"We don't *know* anything. Right now we've got you here, and we've got the skein. This is our chance to peek at what we can do after we're done with Eric." Colin stared at her, wishing she'd at least look back at him. "I think I need to see some of that right now."

"Worth a try," Jordan added, with a thin smile.

*God! I'm offering Terri healing in front of a man who's been para-lyzed for weeks—he actually makes me* forget *that chair sometimes.*

Terri's eyes opened then. "Won't help, because my body's giving out. Organs failing, they say."

*"What?"* Bea stared at Terri, at Colin. He hadn't told her that one, that one horror behind it all.

"Worn out," Terri said. "It's been years, and then he ripped out the skein that sustained me. Then Nurse Setter drugged me too... no sur-prise that..." Her whisper faded away.

"So you won't even try?" Colin's voice swelled, pushing back the silence as his gaze caught at hers. "We can look for medications, treatments, everything else out there. All that and the skein helped hold you together once. Here!"

He set his green armload on the gurney, on the improvised cushion where it rested against Terri's side. He started the rest of his skein flowing up off his clothes and gathering to join it.

"Just show me we can try something," he said. "For the life after we win."

The mound of skein lay still. Colin shivered, waiting. Was Terri just going to leave it there?

Then it moved. Terri's eyes narrowed, and she brought the skein flowing up onto her side, her leg, settling over her body and molding around it.

A tremor stirred across her face.

Her body began to rise.

For an instant she could have been *floating*—but no, that was only his shock to see her simply, impossibly pulling herself upright, the skein mimicking the movements her body should have made. Her features trembled again, as if a moment's dizziness had struck her. She sat up.

"See?" he laughed.

One of Terri's legs reached down, down, like testing the bottom at the edge of a swimming pool. With shaky movements and her hands braced on the gurney's edge, she lowered herself to the floor.

Terri was standing, *standing,* leaning there against the gurney.

Bea chuckled "You've been holding out on us."

"No. This doesn't *heal* any—" Terri broke off, clenched her teeth. Then she added "I lived wrapped up in this for years. He never told me what it could do." Another wince crossed her face. "If I move my body, pieces all through me grind and break... But if I..."

Blades sprang out. One from the skein on her shoulder, one on her upper arm, her hand—a whole inch long and more, all there in an instant, as a grimace flickered on her lips and faded.

Cold shock pooled inside Colin. He stared at what she'd done.

At what she meant to do. Her mouth opened.

"Let me trap him for you."

"Are you *out of your mind?*" Colin's shout rang off the walls. He throttled his voice down to a harsh whisper. "You can't even walk!"

"I. Don't. Have. To," Terri said. "And he won't hurt me—"

"Eric ripped that skein you 'lived with' right off you, in just one moment of rage. Of course he can hurt you, he..." *He killed you.*

Terri smiled. "So who else are you sure—*sure*—he'd come to see?"

"No! How, how can you talk like that? We just convinced Eric you were gone! And the way he is today, it's like all the rest is just an excuse for spreading terror anyway." His fist clenched in the air. "Is this some crazy idea that it's your fault? You don't have to..."

A thought smashed through him.

"It's... not guilt? You went along with Zara's trick so you *could* bring yourself 'back from the dead'?"

That strained, sickly face didn't answer.

"I said no! You *can't.*"

His hand was reaching up, ready to shove her frail body back onto her seat—he dragged it back before he humiliated them both, and twisted away from that look on her face. *I did* bring her along once, I tried to leave her at the door when I went after Eric, and now...

Bea's voice cut in. "Are you trying to give him a heart attack? Anyway, Colin's got the experience to face Rowe. He's the one who stood up to him, each time. Terri, I know you want to help but... there are simply too many ways that could go wrong."

Colin looked at Bea, grinned his thanks.

His hand closed around hers. She held it, squeezed it, before she drew it back.

"Heads up," Jordan said. He tapped at his phone. "This could be... no, it looks like an honest accident. No attack of Rowe's yet."

"Yet?" Colin's heart was still pounding. "Yet? You mean there's going to be, while we're waiting around here?"

"No." Jordan's word had a whole lifetime's weight behind it. "I mean it's not as simple as that. He'll do whatever he does, and right now we can't just head him off."

"And Zara? You think she's still safe out of it?"

As soon as the words left his lips, he could feel Terri's gaze digging into him. *So many secrets are coming out here, I lost track of my own.*

"Where's Zara?" she asked.

"She's fine." His answer came too fast, too obvious.

Slowly and clearly, Terri said *"Where* is Zara? What happened?"

Colin's eyes tried to look away, but he forced himself to face that rapidly-cooling gaze. She had him caught, alright.

"When Zara went out?" he began. "Eric attacked her. She's recovering fine, but she's in the hospital, and... Eric went to her there, but he decided not to take it any further then."

*"He* decided?" Terri's voice was a whisper now, and it choked. "Our mother almost died twice, and you didn't tell me."

"I... You never told her." He grabbed at that thought, a moment's bitter reprieve while he could be the one on the attack: "That you're so sure you're dying, and you're giving up. I just blundered into knowing—were you going to hide it from every one of us? Just lie there and wait for it?"

"And what good would that do now?" She shook her head, and her voice went flat, as if she'd squeezed all doubts out of it. "My choice. What I need is to stop Eric."

"What you *need* is to not throw your life away. This is not happening."

"You say no, and that's it?" she snapped.

"That's right." His eyes locked onto hers, probing for any weakness, any way to back her down.

Then she said "I want to talk to Zara."

"What, you want her blessing for sacrificing yourself?" The vicious thought left his mouth before he could catch it.

*"No!* To hear how *she* is."

Terri reached out for Jordan, toward the phone he was still earnestly focused on. Her skein-covered arm moved as quickly as anyone's, but he saw it shake in the air.

Colin sighed. "Here," and he unplugged his own cell.

She pulled it from his grasp and, eyes clenched in concentration, she tapped out the call.

"Terri?"

A hushed tone filtered through the speaker, as Zara whispered to the daughter who was still supposed to be dead.

Jordan turned his chair, a smooth pivot toward the doorway, his eyes discreetly avoiding the da Costas'. Bea stopped him with a light hand on his arm.

"We're right here," Terri answered. "All four. But, I wish you'd told me what you'd been through."

"Ah. I'm sorry for making all of you worry. I... I thought I could slow an exodus out of town. And if the worst happened, I had the spell, and I just might be able to solve all our problems."

Colin leaned toward the speaker as he said "The worst *did* happen, or started to, and we're just lucky you're still with us. You have to know it was too risky." He glared at Terri, and her eyes turned away. "I'm sorry, but you know you weren't ready for that. Not to go out looking for trouble, when Eric had a whole open countryside to come at you from."

"He already took the Vargas House itself. I suppose I thought I could make a stand somewhere, for what's left of the town." Zara gave a rueful laugh.

Terri said "You were attacked. Twice. You didn't even call?" A different kind of pain pulled at her voice, a hollow, helpless sound.

"I thought I'd put off worrying you. One mistake after another, it seems. I never meant to hurt you."

"I know. But..."

Terri swallowed, a motion broad enough to bob her head.

Then she went on "In the hospital? There were reports... worse things about me. In a month I could..." She stopped.

"Please, let's not talk about that now," Zara cut in. "We can deal with that soon. But, Colin? Have you tried that new *treatment* on her again?"

"Of course I have." He smiled at his sister, at the heavy coat of armor she wore. "And I was saying it could combine with every kind of treatment out there, whatever works for her."

Terri said "You're so sure? We show this to the doctors, will they let us keep it? Could we afford my bills, even?"

Her eyes were fixed on the phone now, blind to all of them as she argued with her mother. So determined to make them face the harshest parts of it.

"Not now, please," Zara said. "Let's deal with one problem at a time, shall we? Are they keeping you comfortable?"

"Fine."

Not true. Colin glanced around the room—the house looked as bare as when he'd left it, no way to look after Terri. One more thing they'd put on hold while they flailed around for any chance against Eric.

"Is everyone else alright? Any news on the hunt?"

Jordan said "We're digging through his patterns right now." He gave his phone several taps—he'd been flicking through it for most of the conversation. "The plan's to spot him as soon as he makes his next move."

"You mean when someone dies."

"It's never that simple." Jordan shared a glance with Bea—*was that how they looked when I said the same thing?* "But we mean to find him, and trap him, ASAP."

"Trapping him makes it sound easy, doesn't it? You must have some reason to be that confident." Zara's usual warmth pulsed in her words, the voice that pushed people to forget their doubts.

"Teamwork," Colin said. "Jordan's contacts, then Bea and everything I can do. We're doing everything to make this work."

His voice died away. He'd been trying to say they might not come back—not so different from any other plans they'd tried, but all this strategizing now made it harder to look away from the danger.

"You're going to try and make him attack you, aren't you?" Zara said.

"It'll be the two of us. But, yes."

She blew out a slow sigh. "I wish I could be surprised it came to that. You can't promise you'll be safe, can you?"

*Just for a moment? An obvious lie, a joke, to perk us up for one second?* But he said "No. I wish I could, but no."

"Then, when you're done, will we still have a town here? You won't let Eric wipe us out, or start another panic and empty us? Tell me we'll all have something we can build on at the end."

"Sure we will," and he tried to smile.

She was still asking for *all* of them to be there. As if Eric had no say in that, as if Terri couldn't be slipping away...

"I'll hold you to that," Zara said. "As long as that's clear, I can let you deal with the rest. I love you both."

Colin whispered it back, and Terri joined in. Then Terri hung up, and silence hung over the room.

The next to speak was Bea, soft in the stillness. "She does make someone want to keep that promise. She should never have asked."

"She knows all that," Colin said. "It's just... none of this is easy to face." Except for Bea, maybe; she talked about not flinching like it was her personal code.

Jordan said "Faster is still better." His fingers zipped over his screen now. "We head off Rowe's spree before it runs much further. And we make no mistakes."

"One chance," Bea nodded, turned to Colin. "You have to lure him out, where I can reach him."

"Right—"

*Except I've got too much skein to hide.*

The thought crashed through him. He glanced at Terri, at the great mass of green heaped up around her. Of *course* Zara, Walters, everyone who saw him wearing all of that had noticed the difference, and so would Eric.

So... did *Bea* have to play target, because she *had* no protection? A shiver crept over his skin. He watched her, watched them all, trying to think. Was there some way to hide the extra skein, to still walk out near Eric and look weaker than he was? Or did it have to be her?

Jordan set his phone down. "Nothing solid yet, but Rowe has been busy in the north side. Up there you should be close."

"Ready," Bea said. "You?" She glanced at Colin.

His eyes met hers.

And she *saw*, his fear for her must be etched all over his face—the whole firm set of her features softened. *Is this what she pushes through every time, watching me and the skein go in first?*

His mouth twitched. He *should* say it, he should send her out into the crosshairs, if she was the right one this time. He could grit his way through the worst part, seeing her in danger. If it had to be her.

He glanced at Terri again. And the skein.

*No! Not a chance, she can't throw her life away when she's got so little of it left—*

"Colin?" Bea said. "Something wrong?"

The simple concern in her voice lit a warmth in him. Enough for him to force out the truth:

"Eric's going to keep killing. But if the trap's set, if we stay close to it and we—"

Terri's eyes were on him—

"—we close in fast, think what Terri could add as the bait."

Bea stared at him. "Are you serious?"

"Bait, and pin him there," Terri breathed, as if any louder would break the moment. "Then you and the spell. It's still the same plan with better bait. If you're fast enough."

"If," Jordan said. "If you two position yourselves right."

"Seriously?" Bea was still staring at Colin, her eyes had never left him. "You're going to let her do this?"

"My choice," Terri said. "And I have to."

"She means…" Colin cleared his throat, struggled for words. "She means we've got just one chance that Eric could fall for this. If Terri's the best one to send in there, then this comes down to how many other people we'd be risking—us, or anyone—just to keep her out of it.

"And she has to."

# CHAPTER TWELVE

# WHAT WE FIGHT FOR

They were only partway toward the likeliest blocks when Jordan called in to them.

"Car crash. Multiple victims, sounds like it came close to multiple deaths." His professional words and grim voice pushed the news past tragedy and into a warning. "And the cause is unknown."

Bea brought the car roaring forward.

The sound almost covered Terri's voice from the back seat. "He could be staying to watch. To feed the panic."

"That's our best shot," Bea said. "But he has to buy that we'd pull over for this, in the middle of what looks like sneaking Terri out of town. You picked what to say?"

Colin shook his head. "Guess I'll have to read the crowd first." He still felt half-naked, only a thin layer of skein under his shirt and up under one long sleeve, and over his eyes. That should give him some protection and a stronger punch, and he might even risk using the spell if he had to. But all that would only be backup to Bea, and Terri.

The first sign was the slowing traffic, in a business street at the closest Rayo Hill had to afternoon rush hour.

Then they saw what slowed them: a small white car that sprawled just beyond the corner, its front mashed in against a multicolored mini-van. An ambulance had pulled up beside them, and a handful of people stood around watching. More faces peeked out from the businesses' doors and windows.

Colin swept his gaze around the corners, the roofs, the ways the patches of cover shifted in his view as they pulled up. No glimpse of Eric yet.

They parked in the shade of one two-story shop, and he looked back at his sister. The blanket almost covered her and the skein that braced her along the seat, but a bit of her head peeped out for Eric to catch sight of.

"Ready?"

"Finger on the phone to bring you running," she said. "If he comes, I'll keep him here."

Colin and Bea stepped from the car. Opening the doors brought the sounds to life, from a few muted figures to the mixed murmurs of frightened, angry people. He turned back for one more glance down at Terri, but instead he swung that glance on up the street—too obvious.

"Sure you're ready?" Bea said beside him.

Skein in place, phone ready for the signal... "I draw him out, hope he sees her and makes a move."

She whispered "I mean, if this goes south? Can you stand to lose Terri?"

"Of course not. So I won't let it happen." He made that a chuckle, wishing he felt as casual as that sounded.

Then he darted past her, eyes fixed on the people ahead, trying to look like he'd impulsively pushed ahead of her. As long as his distraction let her slip back and hide where she could back Terri up.

The ambulance was pulling away already, with its siren off—these people were lucky, this time. Of the several men on the street, one looked to be favoring bruises and another leaned against the stricken car.

Colin grabbed one more look around as he ran up. Still no glint of Eric's halo behind one of the sidewalk's bushes, or peeping down from the stores' roofs. But there were too many people peering out windows and doors, thinking they were sheltered from whatever stalked the town, and several more right out on the street.

Then Colin knew what to say.

"Why are you standing around? He could be back!"

"He? What d'you mean *he?*" snapped one man, older and red-faced.

The other said "Told you it wasn't my fault." That overweight man stood right beside the front of the car, blocking Colin's view of the impact.

*"Fault?"* The first man's voice rose. "You slam right into me—I had my daughter with me!"

*Loud is good, in case Eric was just leaving here and it pulls him back.* The phone in Colin's pocket was silent, but it might buzz at any moment.

The second driver began "How many times do I have to say it—"

Colin stepped between them. He raised his voice to shout them both down: "It's not his fault!"

The first man's face went redder still. "Yeah? Where were you, you didn't see what he did!"

"I saw it *before,"* Colin answered. "When a car skidded, crashed, for no reason." He looked at the car, but the plump driver still stood blocking the front wheel—what he could see *looked* slashed, or was that just the impact bending it? "You've all heard of it, hours ago. Outside the hospital."

"The sniper?" An old woman's voice rose. "That maniac, here?"

Someone else babbled "No, no, they said there was no gunman—"

Colin stole another glance around. Something shimmered on the far roof.

*Don't look!* He forced his gaze away from that glimpse. Eric needed to think they'd missed him, so he could look around and spot Terri. If that one glint of light had been Eric at all.

He turned back to the people around the car. "There *was* no gunman. What kind of bullet does that?"

He stepped around the driver and pointed to the damaged wheel. There they were, indentations in the metal and the wheel well around it—too deep to be washed away by the waves of metal crumpling where the cars collided.

Eric's claws, slashing out and spreading fear.

*Don't look up.* His back prickled as he kept it turned to Eric. His phone was still silent, but there were too many people right here that Eric could tear into next.

He looked back at their fear-clenched faces and said "There was no bullet last time either. But think—it happened right here, any of us could be next."

There were the two men by the crashed cars, the woman shaking her head, two more standing by their own cars plus at least half a dozen looking out from doorways... all lined up for Eric.

The old woman said "But the cops said there was no—"

"I've seen it happen!" Colin snapped. "Just like this."

A shriller male voice added "He's right! It was the ghost!"

Voices rippled around the sidewalk, faces turning toward the skinny young man rushing out from the shop's door. Colin stretched his glance a fraction further and stole one look out toward the roof. No glint of Eric.

"The ghost, I saw it!" the man screeched again. "A shape of something in the air when the car rolled by, it about tore the wheel off!"

"Ghost?" "That again?" Voices bubbled around the street. *Too many* of them, still here.

"Of course it's a ghost!" Colin shouted.

Heads turned toward him, but he rushed on.

"You think one sniper and a few accidents can explain everything that's hit this town? Just today, or the last few days? What's the death count at—at least six, just counting the *dead cops?"*

"Shut up, there's no ghost!" The red-faced man started toward Colin and the skinny witness.

Colin stepped to block him. "Then what else could it be?" He glanced at the man behind him. "You're lucky you saw it. Or maybe not—it could come back for you, or any of us—"

"You're scaring my little girl!" Flushing scarlet rage, the first man closed in on him.

Skein pulsed under Colin's shirt, strength ready. "Not scared enough! We've lost six cops, everything from cars to nurses to *buildings* falling—so why are any of you still here?"

"Shut your mouth!"

The man drew back to wind up a punch—slow, obvious, it would be all too easy to block and pin him if he swung.

A police siren blared beside them

Two uniformed cops charged out of the car. The bigger, older one looked straight at the red-faced man. "We going to have a problem here?"

The man stumbled back. "Not me. This crazy, he's yelling about killer ghosts!"

The lead cop gave Colin a long, slow look. Taking in his wispy skein "blindfold," and his scars, as if he recognized them.

"Spreading panic, is that it?" he said at last.

No point in denying it. "Trying to warn them. People have been dying, too many, and *nothing stops it.*" He pushed those words out at the people around him, and as he glanced around he tried another peek up to where Eric had been.

"Leave it alone, da Costa. You and me, we need to talk."

The shorter cop moved in behind Colin. The two of them herded him along the sidewalk, while the murmurings raged on behind them.

Colin glanced back at them, and up at Eric's roof again.

Right where he'd glimpsed that glow, the strut of a drugstore sign caught the sunlight. That one glint of light he'd been afraid to take a full look at, it had never been Eric...

"Alright, da Costa, you get one chance," the lead cop said. "You saying you saw Rowe and his rifle around here?"

*Snipers again. Guess we're both reading this wrong.* "I didn't *see* him, but this has to be his work again. And he could still be around here." On some other side.

"He could, is that it?" The cop folded his arms, his frown deepening. "I heard about you. What is it, your mother tried to stop a panic and Rowe snuck up on her, so now you're out starting riots?"

The cop's arms shifted, flexed, and he took a step closer. The other cop angled toward his other side.

*And my only skein's the layer under my shirt.* He could knock the cops aside, but not outrun them or disappear.

"It's not a riot," he said. "Just trying to get them out of his reach. If you know me, you know I've seen what Eric Rowe can do—"

"Yeah, yeah," the cop growled.

At the corner of Colin's eye, something moved.

He whirled.

But it wasn't Eric, it was Bea striding up. "Problem, Avila?"

Crisp, controlled voice, steady gaze, and her own wisp of skein was gone from across her eyes, leaving her the picture of a proper cop.

Officer "Avila" frowned back at her. "Where'd you get to, Detective? Walters is looking for you too."

But if Bea was here, that left Terri *alone—*

Colin spun toward the car they'd left. The smaller cop stepped in front of him.

*"Easy,"* Bea said. "So Walters is looking for us. As what—he thinks I've gone rogue? Am I the threat now?"

"Like we've got time for that. But he wants you where he can see you."

Colin tensed, edged his balance back, poised to leap forward and around the cops... but he let his legs relax. Still no signal from Terri in his pocket.

Bea nodded to them. "Then we'll go. But, it'll do Walters some good to cool down first, right?" And she turned and began walking, back toward her car, and the motion drew them all along with her.

"Could be. That maniac's running us all over town anyway." The cop turned and aimed a glare at Colin, probably meant to be intimidating. "The last thing we need is someone inciting a panic. Get me?"

"I know." Colin let the regret hum in his voice. Up ahead stood Bea's car, gleaming black and undisturbed.

The cop nodded. "Can't say I never thought of evacuating the town myself. But we'll nail him soon."

"Careful. Eric's slipped away so many times. You do know, he might as well be invisible—"

"Don't push it. I said we'll handle it. I mean... you need to be mourning your sister, not starting panics about a thing that'll be history soon."

They reached the car. That covered mound that was Terri looked undisturbed in the back, with the windows cracked for air. Meant to be noticed.

And the cop took a step *ahead of* Bea, toward the car.

Then he turned... looking right past the car, past Terri, to face Bea.

"Word to the wise, Detective? You want to get to Walters while you can, you and your 'source' here."

Bea simply met their gaze. "Noted."

And the two uniforms walked away.

Colin sagged into the car, muscles suddenly quivering and cold. Bea settled beside him, and they watched the cops for that one more moment to be certain they wouldn't turn back.

He whispered "Terri?"

"There's been nothing," she said.

"I see why," and Bea held up her phone. "Jordan found that a man's vanished out of his home, a few blocks from here. Minutes ago."

Colin's fist slammed down on his knee. "We're too late? We went through all this here, and Eric was already attacking someone else?"

"We knew this wouldn't be easy." She started the car forward.

He watched the figures they rolled past. The angry driver from the van, and the one in the car Eric had hit, the nervous man who'd seen the "ghost" strike... still out on the sidewalk where Eric could have seen them. The danger had already moved on, but these people were still just parading for him...

"We'll get him," Terri said. She couldn't even see where he was looking from back there, but she knew.

"Will we?" he said. "I thought I'd get those people out of the line of fire, but I just wound up ranting. And the plan, the real plan to trap Eric, was always a lot of Ifs."

"Because you start worrying about what you tell the bystanders," Bea said. "We just bring Terri near Eric with any excuse that doesn't scream 'trap,' and focus on being ready. The fact that it's Terri should do the rest."

Terri laughed, a gentle, burbling sound. "So now you believe?"

"I know how Eric Rowe is about you," she said. "It was the other risks that looked shaky."

"Like scaring Colin—"

The car braked for a light, only a light jolt, but Terri lay in the back seat with just the skein bracing her in it. Her teasing words ended in a grunt of pain.

"Not funny," Colin said, as if calling her reaction a joke could make it one. "But really, are you okay back there? I know none of this is easy on you."

"You heard Bea," Terri said. "Got a better way?"

"I guess not." Colin let himself ride that thought for a moment. "It *is* about getting you to Eric and trapping him. And there's just no way to find him now, except how he's tearing the town apart. One victim at a time."

*Unless he goes after Zara again...* Colin shut his eyes, reminded himself Eric had already let her go.

"So, we chase him," he finished.

"Then that's where I am."

He had no answer for that, and instead he glanced over at Bea. She seemed fixed on her driving, as completely as if she'd never heard the last words.

Or heard the risks that they weren't talking about. But she had, and Bea *belonged* here, even as part of dealing with…

"Terri?" he whispered. "Do you believe it? That you've got only a month to live?"

"I'm starting to think I have to."

He closed his eyes, fumbled for an answer.

She added "And that's the reason I'm here. Can't let him win."

*It's not true, it's not true!*

*Or, we just can't know.* The doctors hadn't even had a day to look at her this time, and Dr. Morton put his own spin on it all.

He looked at Bea again. Her eyes were still on the road—but they shifted, he saw her gaze angle to take him in too. Waiting for what he might need from her.

He pulled his gaze away to watch the streets. The next thing.

They pulled up at a chunky apartment building not so much larger than the largest shops—still near downtown, Colin thought, with that downtown sense of how crowded together people could still live in Rayo Hill. Now dozens of people stood out in the parking lot, and two police cars sat in the street.

Colin and Bea stepped out without a word. Bea moved off along the street, looking for another hiding place to cover Terri. Colin glanced around the lot, the crowd, the corners and top of the buildings; no glimmer of Eric hiding among them.

What he did see was strips of pale green trim along the building and the railing to the door, the signature of Gardner Development. Eric might have worked here, known the place.

The crowd buzzed with unease—the number of kids among them reminded Colin that those families might have been in the middle of dinner. One woman stood in the center of the crowd, the heart of the noise, shaking and staring around:

"They'll find him, they'll find him, he has to be there!"

An older man beside her held a brown mutt of a dog in his arms, shifted his grip to keep it calm. "Just, remember about Joe Martin."

Colin stepped up beside them. "Like how Martin went—"

The dog whined and twisted in the man's grip. Smelling his skein.

"—how he went missing?" Colin tried again. *Until I found his body.*

The woman stared at him. "Who? My husband was *right there,* and then he was gone. And the blood…"

Voices rippled around her, sharing the fear.

"The police just cleared us out," she said. "They say they'll find them, but my son, he was out playing and I don't know where…"

The dog whimpered again. Colin's warnings faded on his lips, and he said "I'll see if there's news."

He dodged away through the crowd, past the man's protests that "But the cops said—" and headed for the building's door.

Inside, he saw no police in view. Nobody was in view, just a bright-painted corridor, but its apartments' doors yawned open all down the hall. A long light above it buzzed, flickered.

Stairs on the right led away to the second floor, but he edged past them. He could only go in a short way, a few seconds more if he had to dash back to Bea and Terri.

*Unless I walk in on Eric. Most of my skein's gone—I'd have to let the spell burn us both.*

He edged down to the first door. Some child's song was playing softly there—he leaned in, glanced at the two crowded rooms for a lost child or an invisible killer. He risked moving for the next door, still just a few seconds deeper in.

Footsteps thumped around the corner up ahead. Quick, irregular steps, several people searching. Those would be the police.

Colin paused… but off to his side, something moved beyond the doorway.

The boy couldn't be more than four. He stared back at Colin, clutching a stuffed tiger that matched the cartoon on his shirt.

Colin took a step toward him.

His phone chimed.

*Not a vibration for Terri, not the other numbers I've blocked, but I left one number out—*

He grabbed it out. The screen said *Zara*.

"Hold on," he told her, as he gave the boy a smile.

"Hold on?" Zara's voice demanded. "I hear you're out spreading panic—"

The child pulled back a step. Colin lowered the phone and eyed him—dirty, confused, just the kind of boy that could have wandered off and gotten lost.

And drawing back as Colin watched. *He would, with my scar and even this gauzy blindfold-thing over my face*—Colin pulled the strip of skein away and smiled again.

"Your mom's looking for you."

"Stranger." The boy's voice was softer than Terri's. "Don't go anywhere with a stranger."

"Smart. So don't go *with* me—I'll stay right here and you go on past me and outside. Can you hear all your neighbors out there?"

Footsteps closed in behind Colin.

He looked around. Back at the stairway he'd passed, a tall cop stepped into view, gun drawn and aimed at the floor, so far. "Better show me your hands. We told everyone to clear out, it's not safe here. You know that?"

"I know." Colin kept his hands in view and edged back from the doorway. "I just came looking for a missing friend." He motioned to the doorway.

The boy peeked out.

The cop said "You okay, son? Anyone bothering you?" The kid shook his head. "Get on out of here. You too, da Costa," he added.

So all the cops knew him now? At least it saved him from being a suspect. The boy scurried past him and out the door.

As Colin followed, he remembered the phone in his hand. He brought it back to his ear.

"Hello? What was all that?" Zara said.

"Me trying not to panic anyone. While I can."

"But—"

"Sorry," and he glanced at the cop behind him and lowered the phone.

The lot outside looked a fraction brighter, with the skein off his eyes. He peered around a moment at the frightened crowd; could he still spot Eric's shimmer in all of this?

The boy scampered in among them, and his mother snatched him up in an embrace. Colin moved toward them, the tumult of voices swelling around him after the near-hush of the apartments. The tall cop was still watching him from the entrance.

The mother stared at the cop, then back at Colin. "Did they find my husband? He was right there, and then *gone!*" she shrilled, no thought for what the confused child might hear. No thought of getting him to safety either.

The older man beside her hugged his dog. "He didn't *vanish,* you know that's not what you saw."

*Too many voices, too many people here just waiting for Eric to get them.* Colin said "I wish I could say he didn't—"

The dog whined, squirmed half out of its owner's arms.

Colin pressed on. "Look… when someone's hurt or disappears in plain sight, we have to think about the worst. Nothing we do stops the ghost."

Except enough skein. Or the spell.

"You're wrong, you're wrong!" she said. "He did vanish—it's not some ghost—"

A scream ripped across the lot.

Voices broke out on all sides, trying to swallow the sound and its direction. But the startled, twisting figures of the crowd couldn't block the shape toward the back of the lot: a woman staring over at the tiny playground beside it. Colin raced, dodged around people to reach the edge of the lot.

A uniformed cop waved people back. Back from a big, three-children-wide slide, with the lifeless body of a man stuffed under it.

*A kids' place... and Eric must have wrapped his victim, wrapped a* dead body, *in invisible skein just so he could dump him out here in the midst of everyone...* Colin swept a gaze around at corners, roofs, anywhere that the monster's shimmering might be.

"All you cops—" The woman's voice ripped out behind him, climbing and tearing itself ragged. "Why couldn't you save him?"

The crowd around her took in that shout and broke it up into jagged murmurs, questions, whimpers—but they were still too many of them, still *here.*

"It's not the cops' fault!" Colin yelled.

His shout broke through the confusion. He saw heads swinging towards him, and he flung more words at them.

*"Nobody's* stopped this thing! You can't hide from it, you can't stop it."

Except with five syllables and a touch. And they'd never believe that.

The officer lumbered toward him, hand brushing his gunbelt. "Alright, that's enough."

"Listen, you may never see the ghost coming. But—"

*I* could *tell them the spell, if I took all my skein off first. Then they'd have something, if they ever needed it... all these people...*

The cop growled "I said that's enough."

The phone in Colin's hand *vibrated.*

His fingers locked tight on it, tight around that merciless shock. He stared at it, its pulsing shoving away all the voices around him. Terri's signal.

The cop drew closer.

Colin whirled and bolted down the asphalt. He dodged around two men, a little girl, all those figures looking around in frozen uncertainty as he flew past. Another twist and he was veering around the open side of the lot with a clear line to the street.

What sounds he caught behind him said that the cop had fallen back. Then it all fell away, as he broke free onto the sidewalk.

And up the block, he saw where they'd left Terri.

His first glimpse showed nothing but the simple black car. Then he remembered, the skein for his eyes was still clutched in his hand—he slapped the strip on and willed it to fasten and clear his sight.

The huge spectral form loomed at the car's door.

Eric stared through the window, stared down at Terri... Colin choked down the need to charge right at him. But the killer never glanced toward him, toward anything but Terri. The hands that had just killed hung still as stone.

Eric shimmered into full sight, still motionless. Did he even realize?

Colin crouched down behind the grill of the first car, a handful of cars down from them. His fingers touched heated metal, the car's bumper, and he locked his jaw down against a yelp as he yanked his hands back.

Up beyond Eric—past a blessedly empty stretch of sidewalk—the next house's front door cracked open. That might be where Bea kept watch, it was close enough.

Eric took a slow, awkward step toward Terri's window. Then another, closer.

He stopped, jerked back one long step and halted. He still *guessed,* he must have...

The car's door burst open. Terri stumbled out, unsteady feet on the sidewalk, barbs stretching from her skein as she reached toward him. Eric staggered back, back onto the dirt beyond. Something in his staring, shocked balance failed, and he tumbled backward, gaze still on her.

Terri clambered toward him. The mass of dragonskin around her dwarfed Eric's, and the fierce spines thickened as she moved. The fury on her bare face was her first weapon. Her arm swung—a great needle of skein lanced out and struck into his arm.

Then something else broke across her features. A flash of *pain.*

Her step faltered.

*Pieces of me grind and break*, she'd said...

Terri crumpled, her eyes closed and she collapsed on the sidewalk. She lay still, one bare head slumped in a heap of silver-green power, too close among those spines.

A house's door swung open. Bea ran out, racing straight at Eric as he rose and shuffled toward Terri.

Her movement stripped the shock from Colin—he charged from his shelter at Eric. Four cars between them, three.

Bea closed in at Eric's back. There were sounds, voices, back behind Colin, but all that faded away as Bea's hand stretched toward their enemy. Two cars left.

Eric spun, he lashed claws out at Bea, making her swerve clear, safe but off-balance. Colin saw her eyes lock on himself as he swept in at their target's other side. One car.

Eric turned. Toward Bea.

Colin slammed the punch home with all the strength in his arm's skein—something in his unshielded hand gave way, but he surged in to catch at Eric, hold him, give Bea her chance.

The elbow caught him in the side, driving into his thin armor. He twisted, flailed for a grip.

A flash of movement, something writhing where Terri had stabbed—

Something caught him, swept him up, unstoppable.

One flash of sight—Bea shrinking away behind him.

A flash—a house, cars, flying past him.

*He's carrying me up the block.* The single wobbling thought fell into place, and then the ground slammed up at him.

Cold, creeping numbness had to mean he was bleeding. Muscles wouldn't move. Sounds, shouts, burst around him… sharp commands that had to be a cop.

More sounds. Gunshots.

All he saw were the claws, the wicked barbed claws that Eric raised over him. He watched them as they came down.

It knocked all the breath from his chest, and he felt them dig in. He felt, saw, skein ripped away and sliding up to merge with his attacker, as the claws raked over flesh too…

The masked face over him drew away.

The world still *flashed* in and out, more when he tried to rise and the pain flared. There was Bea rushing at Eric… Eric turning to face her… too many heavy, blind police voices all around. Closing in, surrounding them.

Eric moved. He ran *past* Bea, thank God thank God—

He darted on up the sidewalk, toward Terri.

One glimpse: him bending over her.

Then: the clawed hands folding around her. His skein making hers, both of theirs, blur away from sight.

Both gone.

Sounds flooded in, too many mutterings, footsteps, questions, commands. Colin shoved a palm at the ground to lever himself up. He still felt strands of skein around his arm, but moving sloshed the world around in his skull—

Firm hands held him down. "Easy, easy. He's long gone, and the ambulance will be here soon."

A cop. The tall cop from inside the building, he knew that before the face blurred into focus.

Then, "And, Commissioner Walters is going to get some answers."

The world tossed—a sea of voices, figures, dizziness making them all shake. With the cop's face looming over him he could just make out the sidewalk where Eric and Terri had been.

That gray sidewalk filled the world and dimmed to black.

# CHAPTER THIRTEEN

# WHAT WE LOSE

Floating, drifting, slowly rising upward waiting for the way to move, to remember... waking, he was coming awake, so hard to budge...

His wrists were strapped down.

Colin blinked, fought to force the bright haze over him into a single long light above. Muscles felt weak, numb, even within the straps on his wrists—and legs too. Pale room with medical shelves, familiar rhythms beyond the door... back in the hospital.

No skein moved on him, anywhere.

"Easy." That was a man's voice, young, face blurred by the light behind him. "Do you remember your name, and where you live."

"Colin da Costa, Rayo Hill of course." In spite of all Eric's rampages.

And his victims.

And... *Terri!*

"Why, why am I—" He tugged an arm against the strap, and something twinged all down his chest. He froze.

"You kept thrashing around in your sleep, hurting yourself. Now that you're awake, is there going to be more of that?"

*Is Terri—* But he cut off that yell, forced in a slower breath. Calm. His shirt was gone, replaced by some kind of hospital gown, and he had no skein at all. "I'm okay. But... is Bea alright? Detective Simms?"

"She's fine." The doctor, even younger than he sounded, smiled and reached over to the strap.

Colin let that relief warm him an instant, before he had to ask "And Terri? Did they find Terri?"

The doctor's hand pulled back. His gaze turned to meet Colin's, too slowly.

"Hmm. Mr. da Costa, what's the last thing you remember about your sister?"

*Oh God. He thinks I'm asking after someone who's* dead...

Colin opened his mouth to answer, to "remember" the proper lie. But just thinking of Terri back in Eric's grip made that too true to bear.

"Memory interference," the doctor said. "Possible concussion. And then your other injuries. More reasons to keep you under observation."

"*No*—"

Colin swallowed that moan and held it down. First thing, first thing was to get out of these straps—no, the first thing was to start getting help, from the doctor and everyone else that would listen. To hold still.

"Please," he tried. "How bad is it?"

"Mr. da Costa, you have lacerations down your ribs, along with a range of bruises, old and new, and then contact with some... corrosive. But there's every chance that you'll be fine, if you take it easy. Now if you'll look over here—"

First he tested Colin's eyes with a light, then began the list of questions: any headaches, nausea, more probes about his awareness that never *quite* mentioned Terri again.

Colin held himself quiet and answered each, wrapping himself in calm cooperation. His chest burned, but his muscles twitched and responded as he tested them. He tried not to tilt his head toward the door, even when he heard footsteps outside it that could have been deadly. Those always passed by.

Finally the doctor said "I suppose the rest depends on you."

"Of course it does. I'll try not to run any marathons."

*Like that matters now. I have to think, argue, beg with someone, those are the only ways to save Terri now.*

"Good." And the doctor reached over and unfastened the straps.

This time Colin waited, until all of them were loose.

Then he asked "About visitors..."

The door banged open.

"I told you," the doctor began, "he needed rest—"

Walters growled "Doesn't sound like a concussion to me. And you listen here."

He leaned in, loomed in, over the young doctor. He whispered something too low to catch.

And the doctor turned and slunk out of the room.

Walters moved in. Arms folded, he stood over Colin, close enough to see the barely-contained twitches of the muscles around his eyes.

Colin said "I guess you yell at me now—"

"What did Rowe *do* out there?" Walters's lips pulled back, snarling with the strain of holding his voice down low. "He shook off bullets, and he charged right through my men. And he just comes and goes right in the street, that playground, anywhere he wants!"

*Like I've been* telling *you...* Colin locked that reaction down, clutched for the same stillness and steadiness he'd needed to convince the doctor. The only way to win now might be to reach this man, to keep those eyes calm enough to listen.

"I... I told you," he said. "You wouldn't stop him with any of the usual tactics. You'd need a better edge than that."

"Like this?"

Walters held up a clump of skein.

Eric had missed that? It dangled from the commissioner's hand in strips, like a handful of silver-green cloth. He *shook* it in the air.

"Your big secret, and the doctors took it right off you," he smirked. "I won't be losing it this time. Or did that stop being a problem—who stole this thing from the lockup last time? Was that Rowe, or you the whole time?"

Hoyle, actually.

But Colin could guess what Walters would say to an answer like that. He just said "Not me. Please—"

His hand went out for the skein, too quick, too clumsy. The pain dug into in his chest again.

And Walters yanked his hand back. "I said I want answers. Everything, *now.*" He brought the skein closer again, savoring his bit of torment.

*After I almost crushed his neck.* Colin forced his gaze past the skein, back to the commissioner's glowering face. "Alright. I guess we're overdue for it, aren't we? What do you want to know?"

Walters grinned. "You asked about your sister."

Hope jolted through Colin, wide-eyed fluttering hope—but Walters leaned closer, and his voice tightened to a hiss.

"My men saw her there, before Rowe escaped with her. That girl is alive, and you *lied* to us. You made every one of us look like idiots!"

"That's not why we did it!" And Walters had been the one stripping away Terri's protection—Colin's hand twitched again, and he forced it flat on the bed.

"Oh no? But you still... How'd you even pull that off? Talk a whole floor of *doctors* into lying for you?" Walters waved his hand around the room, toward the building beyond it. "Or did you just fake every step of it yourself?"

"No!" Colin shut his eyes a moment, struggled for a way to soften it, justify it. Looking up again he said "But we needed some way to protect Terri, *and* all the patients and staff that were right in Eric's path." And Dr. Morton and his friends jumped at that chance, mostly because Zara saw that need in them. Not that he had to remind Walters about any of those conspirators yet.

"You mean you stuck your fingers into that too, same as you have this whole case from Day One. You lie, you keep secrets, you bully your way into a crime scene or chase after a suspect, or else you just slam *us* around!" His fingers tightened on the skein.

"I'm sorry! I attacked you, I know. I keep wishing I could go back and stop that from happening. But… ever since this started, all I wanted was to cooperate with all of you. Until—"

"Until we didn't keep falling in line, the way that idiot Simms does?"

Colin clamped his mouth shut. *Don't defend Bea, don't let him make this about her at all, we have to get past this.*

"I was the first one who knew Eric Rowe was your killer, and I told the police. I shared what I knew about him, I helped all of you rescue Terri—" *once, now Eric's got her again, but—* "I was working with Lieutenant Hoyle, every way I could. And then Hoyle sold us out to Josh Gardner and Eric. And you heard him confess to that," he added.

"Oh, you know about that too? Mighty convenient change of heart he had. Did you go out and *encourage* Hoyle too?" and his voice was its fiercest yet. Then his eyes sparked, widened—the answer must be all over Colin's face.

"Yes I did." Colin let the confession pass through him without flinching, anything to move on. "But it was the truth, you know it all fits."

"Truth? How is any of this even possible?" Walters folded his arms. "Rowe's goddamn untouchable. We shoot him and it doesn't stop him."

"No it doesn't." Colin said it slowly, their first moment of agreement. "You've seen that armor at work. Think about it."

Walters glanced at the skein in his hand. Then his eyes bored into Colin again. "Body armor, yes. But that night Simms almost caught him, they say she put a round right *through his bare hand*. And he's still killing us? What kind of trick is that?"

And then Hoyle's rifle had punched through the skein, and so had Terri's blade—so what had that been in Eric's arm—

"Well?" Walters said.

Colin took a slow breath, and met the commissioner's gaze again:

"Think about what you've seen. Eric's armor is tough, but he's also got the strength to shove right through your cops. Or what the doctors were saying about same stuff, what it did to Eric's prisoners. Most of all, Eric keeps slipping through all your defenses, and nobody sees him. Nothing you do has caught him. You know that—"

"Tricks," Walters said. "He's smart, he's sneaky. He's got everyone twisted up in the head. They even heard Simms singing gibberish today—what was it? *Gratsay ko nova?*"

Colin's eyes snapped to the skein in his hand. But Walters only glared at him, the stuff stayed inert—those words were *wrong*, as empty as the nonsense he called them.

Walters went on "Rowe's got his tricks, but you're the one that fell for them worst. You really think he's a ghost now? A killer ghost? That was what you said when you were panicking the crowds, right?"

"Not a ghost. Just, close enough. He goes anywhere because you can't see him. And that chant is for a reason—"

*Don't, don't say it, we didn't even tell Hoyle—*

He rushed on "But it's *gratshay kodo va.* And you don't want to say it while you're holding that skein."

"Crazy."

But Walters eyed the skein, and Colin saw his brow furrow. If he just tried it and it burned him, or else he let him explain…

Walters snorted, looked back down at him.

Colin added "Alright, I can show you—"

"Like I'd trust you now?" Walters snarled.

"I know. But then, why are you *here?* You won't listen to me, you won't let me show you? And I *can* show you, how Eric makes himself invisible—"

His hand tried reaching again, just the start of a motion, but Walters yanked the skein back. He stuffed it away in his pocket.

Then he shot a glance toward the door. "Da Costa, I never thought you were that crazy. You want to try this again sometime, you better make more sense." And he pulled back, stood up, he turned away toward the door.

"But, what about Terri?" Colin called after him. "Are you at least looking for her?"

Walters sneered. "Alive or dead? Right now, the main 'ghost' we're looking for is Rowe."

"But he's got her, your men saw that! And she's already weak—"

"I keep telling you, this is our job. We'll find Rowe."

He pushed out the door, past two doctors in white, not even slowing as they called out for him to stop.

Colin sat up, twisted to start after him—right into the doctors' warning glare. He sank back onto the bed.

One doctor, the young man Walters had chased off before, asked "Was he giving you trouble?"

"We were trying to talk. Or, I thought we were—"

The other one, an older woman with graying hair, eyed the first. "And you let him in? What were you thinking?"

"I told you…" He looked at the floor.

"We apologize for that disruption," she told Colin. "We'll set instructions so that you aren't disturbed again."

"But…" Colin stared at her, at that hard, uncaring resolve. "I *need* to talk to Walters. If he'll listen, if there's anything that can save—"

He choked off the next word. The more he pleaded for his "dead" sister, the longer they'd lock him down as unstable.

"You'll be alright," the man said. "Your body's simply telling us you've been through enough already. Just sit back and rest."

"Alright." Colin mouthed the word, not even guessing if he'd get to keep that promise or not. "Do you have my other things? Where's my phone?"

"You're wearing all of them, except for what's left of your shirt. There was no phone among them."

"You're sure? You're not trying to—"

The doctor's eyes began to darken, and Colin cut off. Asking if they were keeping it from him would only come off as paranoid.

"I guess I lost it," he added. *It was in my hand when I attacked Eric, of course I dropped it. And now it would be the only thing that can reach out past this room and how Eric stuck me here.* "I know where it was," he sighed.

"There you go. It's past sunset in any case, so the best thing you can do is sleep. I'll look in on you later."

Colin nodded. "Thank you. I know you hear that all the time, but, thank you." He smiled and tried to find some honest gratitude to go with it—for a moment, that warmth flickered on inside him.

Then the two doctors walked away.

He stared at the closed door behind them. His chest ached, more than he remembered when he woke. He brushed the layers of bandages, holding his fingers back from poking, from rooting in among them to explore how broken he was.

No skein to compensate for that now.

No way to reach Bea, or anyone. *There's just me, or what's left of me. And knowing Eric has Terri.*

He swung a foot off the bed. The ache flexed in him—still dull, or were those the drugs? Watery weakness dragged at him, but he could only hope there'd be no dizziness. Everything was harder with no skein.

Skein was all Terri had. And it hadn't saved her from Eric.

He stood upright on the floor, without swaying. He started across the small room, his shoes making soft, hollow sounds against the rhythms of the hospital outside. His hands stayed at his sides, away from the bandages.

The wall took four steps to reach, and he made it, but then he slumped against the cream-colored wall to catch his breath.

*Eric could be here any time, to finish me off.*

The thought scorched through him, that and knowing it should have been his first thought on waking up. Eric had to hate him more than ever, for making him believe Terri was dead... except now, Eric could have all his *attention* focused on Terri herself.

Colin stumbled toward the opposite wall, straining to find his strength and watching for that first dizzy shift that would mean his head had betrayed him. Was Eric turning his rage on Terri now, or just doubling down on the same obsession—

One foot tangled against the other. He caught himself on the bed, fought not to lean against it. Outside the door a cart rattled by.

Eric had been terrorizing the town for days. And they'd just thrown jet fuel on the fire.

*I tried everything, I've never stopped him.*

*What was that thing in his arm?*

*Doesn't matter. The way I am now, the skinny, skein-less Eric could kick me all up and down the floor. I tried, we tried, we failed.*

He clenched his fist. No, no, the rule was always to work on the next thing...

Eyelids closed, flashed open again. Still, rest *was* the next thing, wasn't it?

He glared at the bed, the mattress his hand still clung to. *If I lie down on that, will I ever really get up?* But it could be worth it.

He glanced at the door. Damn Walters—barging in shouting for "answers" and then just brushing him off and walking out. That or, all that had been the commissioner's way of pushing him to talk, plus the doctors coming to break it up.

*Or it's how Walters should be, with someone who choked him and stomped all over his case.*

His hand dug into the mattress. Bea could have worked through the case by now if he hadn't let Eric find all that skein—and she'd still have her career.

*But we found Terri.*

*And lost her all over again, and Eric's madder than ever.*

The door creaked.

He looked up, bracing for Walters—for Bea—for anyone.

Zara rolled in.

Of course she was here, even the doctors couldn't keep Zara da Costa out now. For an instant the simple *rightness* of that fact pushed away her hospital wheelchair, the pains, everything.

His gaze met hers.

"I screwed up," he gasped. "I thought I could protect her—she said she had to—"

"Come here."

He staggered to her chair and fell into her hug.

Something burned, something poked or stretched or squeezed somewhere on his wounds, but he held tight. Their hug could be the whole world.

Finally Zara eased him back. "Now, are *you* alright?" she said, and her voice left nowhere to hide.

"I don't know. He slashed my chest, I guess I'm afraid to ask how bad it really is. And I've got no skein left to lean on."

"I see."

"And, we did put Terri out there as bait, and made her part of the trap too. I mean, I know you did everything to help her hide, but... but she said it was the best thing for everyone..." The last of his breath was gone, and the pain twitched and dug deeper in his chest.

"I'm sure it was," and Zara's lips twitched in a smile. "Still, did you have to run around the street telling people to leave town? That Eric is simply unstoppable and they should go?"

*After everything, everything—*

*"That's* what you care about? That they live together here, not that they *live?"*

The pain tore at him when he shouted, he heard it shaking as his voice echoed off the walls, but he was already gasping for an even longer breath.

"Eric's been killing left and right, and always disappearing again. He's trying to feed the panic—all because we hid Terri from him. Your plan put saving Terri above all of that, and what did you *think* he'd do? But then you went standing out there at the town exit begging people to stay and wait for him to cut them down... and now you blame me for trying to keep them alive, for... for..."

The last of the poisonous words had spewed out, leaving only the pain in his chest as he panted for breath.

Zara gaped at him, eyes bright.

"I'm sorry," he fumbled. "It's just..."

She said nothing. He looked at her, saw the shock had smoothed away from her face. *She's waiting for me to finish,* he realized. But he had nothing left, just a dazed stillness inside.

The door swung open.

"Visitors?" The stranger in the white coat frowned. "I thought they weren't allowing those."

"I'm his mother." Zara sounded calm as ever, but he caught a faint tremor in her voice as she went on "I know the rules; I'm recovering here too."

"I suppose you're doing some good here, *hrrm.* Now let's have a look at him."

He stepped past her. There was something familiar about this stocky, determined-looking doctor.

He motioned Colin back to the bed, and when Colin did sit he leaned in to look. But instead of checking Colin's wounds, he squinted down for a close look at his jaw, his cheek. His scars.

This was the doctor who'd looked at Wesley and the other victims, the one more fascinated with the skein than the patients—

"I knew it! It had to be!" The doctor's words came faster every moment. "They said you had the same marks as those three. And Walters thought he could lock that substance away and then make it disappear, hah!"

Colin felt his lips twitching in a smile. Walters had been no part of it then, but right now he really did have their skein all to himself.

*And he has the spell. Now* Walters *could start growing skein out of people, or put the whole world on that track just like Bea kept warning me.* Any time his own hard-headedness let him.

Colin forced his face into calmness and looked back at the doctor. "I'm not sure what you mean."

"You have to! Your scars match those three unfortunates—much less serious, but unmistakably the same. And then there's your sister's condition. In theory the substance that held their flesh together could make a system of bindings that might let her heal imperfectly—"

"My *sister* is *dead,"* and Colin slammed the gates over his fears, just to get the lie out and shame him into silence.

Instead of embarrassment, the doctor's eyes only gleamed brighter. "Her condition matched my theory too well. It's medically impossible—you must explain it, since she can't. Talk to me!"

Colin stared past him, to Zara, horror flowing between them. This "doctor" really was blind to who lived or died as long as it solved his medical riddle.

*Medical... Eric... Hoyle's rifle had shot him right through his armor, and I saw* skein *growing inside a wound.*

And Eric kept saying he could heal Terri.

Colin sucked in a breath that burned along his ribs. He had to get *out* of here, if it wasn't too late already.

He lurched to his feet and made for the door.

The doctor stepped in front of him. One hand blocked Colin, a light touch against his shoulder—nothing he couldn't pull aside, but that would lead to twisting, pushing, when he was still struggling to walk.

"What are you doing?" the doctor barked. "You want to tear those cuts open?"

"But she ..."

Colin steadied his breath, stared hard at the doctor's darting eyes.

"What if, all the skein's secrets were waiting out there?" Colin said. "All of them, and all that was being thrown into a twisted try at healing someone, and to hell with what it does to her?"

Zara's eyes went wide, watching over the doctor's shoulder. Colin pushed his gaze, his words, at the doctor with all the strength he had.

"You want to know what the skein does, right? But you tell me, if someone uses it who doesn't care what it costs—can you stand here and let that happen? Or will you get me out of here and stop it?"

"I..."

Those eyes blinked, darted back and forth—as if, somewhere in his head, the man's fascination with the mystery was smashing against the idea of very real consequences.

Then those eyes closed, and his head shook.

"No. No, you're talking nonsense. You go sit down before I call the nurses."

Colin sagged on his feet, suddenly out of breath.

Zara begged "What is it? I'll try to pass it on to Bea—tell me something!"

"I, I don't know. Terri could be anywhere." He shuffled backward, balance swaying. It was always the same silent wall sealing them in, just *finding* where Eric was.

The doctor closed in, eyes settling on Colin again, hungry. "The *skein's* secrets? So it has a name, then? And what do you mean, how is it being twisted, *hrrrm?* You have to tell me!"

Colin's gaze sank to the floor. "No. I don't."

"Intolerable!" The doctor flung the word at him.

Somewhere deep out in the corridors, a shout broke out.

Shock yanked Colin's head up, had him coiled and straining his ears for another sign. The hospital lay quiet, with all its scattered night movements swallowing up any more distant noise.

"I'm talking to you!" the doctor snapped.

Colin turned to Zara. "You hear that?"

"It could mean anything," she said. "But—"

He lunged for the door. *If Eric is here, what does that mean about Terri—*

The doctor's hand clamped on his arm and pulled him up short, flaring pain down his chest. "What's gotten into you?"

Colin ripped his arm free, swaying on his feet. "You remember the attacks on this hospital? Eric came and *killed* your patients? Think back, you think it can't start again?"

"I told you no!" The pudgy man stepped around to block Colin again. Zara rose from her chair and started towards them.

"Just listen!" Colin said. Still no other shouts down the floor, but that didn't mean much.

"I'll do no such thing," the doctor said. "This is simply—"

"I told you—"

Feet raced through the sounds outside. Closing in, one pair of light feet, that he recognized just before Bea flung the door open.

For an instant he could only stare in relief, watching Bea sweep an urgent glance around them. Her strip of green was back across her eyes again.

"He's here." She turned to look straight at Zara. "Which of you needs that chair more?"

"I think... he does. And I can just duck away to the side, if you're thinking of getting us away from—"

Bea stepped around her and grabbed the back of the wheelchair she'd left.

"I *insist*—" the doctor began, but Bea shoved past him. Colin dropped into the seat, her sheer momentum pushing away the protest at the back of his mind that *I can still walk.* Zara stepped out the doorway, faster than he'd been moving.

Bea rolled them out.

A second corridor crossed theirs just a few doors down—Bea twisted them away from that point, away from Zara, as Colin glanced around. No sounds from that way, no shimmers of stealth, only two nurses walking in the corridor.

Bea bore down on the chair and they began to gather speed. Colin locked his fingers on the hand rests, and twisted around for a look back. Zara was already past the intersection and moving on, at a brisk walk with her shoulders hunched against her own pain.

"Hold on!" The doctor charged up behind them. "Stop there! You, miss, what's that on your face?"

And the nurses turned. Both of them closed in, one of them a man that moved up ahead of them and made Bea slow. The nurse called out "Doctor?"

Another shout rang out behind them, a single startled outcry in what stillness was left in the corridors. Not far, Eric couldn't be far away now.

Then footsteps thundered in front of them. Commissioner Walters charged up, his outraged face and sheer momentum bringing Bea to a halt and driving the nurse aside.

Walters waved toward the sounds and looked at Bea. "Rowe?"

"Yes."

"Get him out of here!" And he pulled out the skein and tossed it in Colin's lap, then stepped aside, crowding the nurse from their path.

The doctor yelped "What are—"

But Bea rolled them forward and away. Colin caught one look of Walters staring the others down—and beyond them, Zara was already out of sight, hopefully safe hidden somewhere. He strained to listen past the nearby smattering of sounds for any sharper noises closing in behind them.

Bea slowed once to wave her badge at another doctor, then barreled them on down the pale corridors until they slowed and finally wrenched around a turn, out of sight from where they'd been.

"He was looking around the registry," Bea said. "He'll be coming for your room."

"Hide?" His mind couldn't settle, just kept swirling thoughts of *Zara's back there* and *we can't fight him.*

Bea shoved them through the nearest door. Inside, a woman started up in bed, sleepy face stirring into shock—

Bea yanked him backward and away without a word.

Colin tried glancing back again, tried to think as they rolled for the next door. *What are we doing? When Eric finds me gone he just might slash through every room here looking for me.*

The next room was empty. They rolled to a stop.

He said "We have to go back."

"What?" Bea's whisper was hoarse with shock.

"We have to face him. Maybe set a trap, something that works better than Terri did—" *Terri, I'm missing something there—* "or else he starts killing everyone here." He set his feet on the floor and pushed himself from the chair.

"What trap, how?" Bea said. "And, all I heard were quick shouts, not screams like someone found bodies. But if we go out there and he sees us, we're dead."

"How about when he finds me missing? Every second could be someone else killed—"

"I'm not losing you!"

She stepped into his path.

Colin glared down at her. He could push past her... no, this was Bea, she *would* knock him down and use every wound he had against him, for as long as she was stuck on stopping him. What was wrong with her? She stared back at him, braced to stop him cold.

Then her face softened.

"Here," she said. "We set the trap here—it's too late to go back any closer, he'll see us. Get that skein on."

Skein?

Colin looked down at his hands. Of course, he was still clutching the clump Walters had thrown in his lap. He rifled his fingers through it; enough for a good solid gauntlet? No, a bit of weight there would make no difference now.

Instead he pressed it under the hospital gown. It stirred to life at his thought—too smoothly, too ready to make it easy and leave him dependent on its help again. It stretched out and wrapped around as a strap over the bandages, to hold his wounds together.

He tried not to think of what might happen if it rooted *inside.*

He tested a step left, right, and swung his arms. Skein on the wound didn't heal it or replace his strength, but it stopped it from tearing open any worse. Now he just had to make himself move.

Bea was still blocking the door. He took a step toward her, not sure if he could get past her now.

She said "Listen."

Around them he heard… soft sounds, the regular rhythms that were the familiar pulse of the hospital corridors at night. No screams, no panic, no dead zones of silence. Eric could be long gone, or moving unseen past everyone.

"You're right," he said. "We set the trap here."

Her face stretched in a single, perfect smile. "That's more like you, just crazy enough. Here."

She pulled off the strip from her eyes and pressed it into his hand—

*Her hand, is that her pulse racing after staring me down, this could be our last minute alive—no time—but she's looking at me too—*

They both pulled away together. Bea stepped back to the side of the door.

The simplest ambush there was. If Eric came through here, she'd have one chance to touch him with the spell, but nothing but her trust in him to target something she could barely see.

Colin took his place facing the closed door. The skein stretched over his eyes—skein was quick to shed heat, but he thought he could feel some of Bea's warmth on this piece.

The hospital lay quiet. Footsteps here, voices low and confident there, all the ordinary sounds it should have now. Eric was somewhere in there, and so were Walters and the doctor, and Zara... He squeezed his fists tight. *Please be safe.*

All they had was *waiting*—no fighting strength, no intricate trap, just betting everything that Eric would walk through a door without looking to the side.

But if it worked... *then all that skein on Eric destroys him, and we have no way left to find what he did with Terri—*

His heart hammered. Each beat came louder, harder, stretching out the stillness between each...

Footsteps flew toward them.

A single motion, sounds louder and landing further apart than any normal-length stride.

They stormed up the corridor, already close, no time for more than a fleeting *don't look at Bea* and to try to stand ready—

Eric shot past the door, in one instant the swelling sound shifted and began to dwindle beyond them.

Colin yanked the door open. Eric was already disappearing down a corner.

He started after him.

# CHAPTER FOURTEEN

# WHAT REMAINS

He ran like running up a mountain, leaning in and feeling every risk of his clumsy feet slipping, afraid to lose momentum even for a step. There was no *staying behind* Eric, only scrambling to get a glimpse of his back while he was still at the far end of the longest corridors. As long as there was any chance of catching him, or finding Terri... but not both, not both...

Bea ran behind him. He raced on, trying to think which of the familiar paths Eric headed down, what shortcuts they could take to catch that fleeting sound again.

When their own footsteps' sound could bring Eric roaring back around to slaughter them.

Blue-clad and white-clad figures popped out along the sleepy corridors, but those fell back, from Bea waving her badge. Eric's flying footsteps faded in the distance ahead.

Colin dragged himself to a stop, leaning against the wall and forcing his brain to work.

"Colin? Please, look at me—" Bea said at his shoulder, voice hollow with concern.

"Eric is... running like he's chasing something, or..." Coldness was creeping over his shaking flesh. "Or he's tired of here and just wants out... he's heading for the south exit." *Why's my voice sound so confident?* "Where's your car?"

"This way."

She pulled him, guided him, dragged him around turns that let him simply go numb and fight to keep up with her relentless pace.

Until the cool night sky stretched above them. Until he tumbled into the car seat and fumbled with the belt...

She was tapping his shoulder, he must have zoned out an instant. "Colin! Where is he?"

He searched the walls' contours, the stretches of paved shadow between the parking lot lights, as she edged the car around the corner with their headlights off. *We're moving toward him again, when we're helpless if he comes this way and sees us.*

Then they rounded the building and he spotted it, the faint aura that was their enemy, striding up the road and away from them. Moving onto the street.

The moment Colin passed the word, Bea tightened her grip on the wheel and reached for the light switch.

"Keep those off," he said. "We need to catch him, or tail him. Have to hope he doesn't know we're here."

"You sure?" But she left the lights off and started them gliding along the side of the street.

Colin watched Eric shrinking away up the block. Bea drove with her gaze boring into the night, watching every direction for any moving car or parked car door or pedestrian that might drift into their lightless vehicle's path.

When Eric got too far ahead, Colin urged her forward to close part of the block's distance. *She needs to see him herself, I should pass the skein back to her.*

The thought came too late. The second time Eric reached the edge of their sight, they lost him.

The headlights flared on and they raced around the block. Buildings flew by as dark shapes and flashes of sight-blurring glows that Colin raked his gaze over. They swept up one street, along the next, anything to just catch a glimpse of the killer again.

Until they halted at the curb, defeated.

"Why the stealth approach?" Bea said.

"He's got Terri." Colin brushed his chest. The seat belt brought out a dull ache from his wound, even with the skein over it. "I thought... following him was our only chance. Selfish, I know."

"No it's not. You really do hate those hard choices, don't you?" A kind of warmth softened her voice as she said it. Then: "Think he's gone?"

"Looks like it. All I know is..."

The tiredness, the blurring creeping into the corners of his vision, dragged at his brain. He forced his mouth to move.

"I mean, he's *got Terri back.* Why would he leave her to come after us, or anything? All I can think is, if it brought him out here it's got to be enough to keep him chasing after... whatever's worth that much to him. That means the night's about to get a lot worse." He glared down the dim street.

"Sounds about right."

Bea scooped up her car radio.

"Simms here. Requesting a full Be On The Lookout for unusual activity—*any* kind, officer's discretion, relayed back to me." Her voice sharpened, using each precise word as a weapon.

At the other end, a woman's voice said "Received. But, Simms..."

Bea said "I'll wait." And that was it.

Colin shifted in his seat toward her. "What was that about?"

Bea opened her mouth to answer—and her phone buzzed.

The moment she brought it up on speaker, Walters's voice blared out "Alright, Simms, are you going to explain that request or not?"

"Rowe is loose on the streets somewhere." There was no deference in her now, only the firm tone of someone beyond being impressed and not afraid if her boss knew it. "I believe his spree's about to escalate."

*"You believe.* Short for you holding out on me again," Walters growled.

"Frankly, sir? I've been right before. And we've got no other leads—"

"Screw this! Put da Costa on."

*What? Why's he want* me?

Bea tapped the phone into mute. "Be careful what you say."

Colin frowned. What was that, more of her secrecy now, when Eric might be running wild?

He took the phone. "I'm here. Is Zara okay?"

"Your mom's fine already. Now tell me you've got this thing off speaker so the two of us can talk for real."

What? *"No.* You want to tell me something, fine, but I'm not cutting Bea out of it. And we're wasting time."

"Goddamn stubborn..." Walters cleared his throat. "Alright then. You've got *one* chance to convince me to authorize an order like that. To tell cops that are already running on fumes that they'll be tearing around the night jumping at shadows."

"Or the shadows jump at *them—*"

He saw Bea's face wince, at the mention of invisibility. He started again:

"Look, after everything you've seen and tried here, you really want to bet there's *anything* Eric Rowe can't do? Think about that.

"But what we do know," he pushed on, "is that he's fixated on Terri. We faked her death to hide her—and he just found her alive after all. And yet he's still out here on a rampage."

"You figure she's dead for real?"

*He actually* said *that?* Colin clutched the phone, sucked in a breath to snarl back—

Bea's hand was on his.

He shut his eyes, shoved the worst of his fears down inside him.

Instead he said "I don't know! But, it has to be something big, right?"

"Something," Walters said. "And that's it? You're a stubborn, interfering pain in the ass, da Costa... and you're talking sense. Don't make me regret this."

"You and me both." He passed the phone back.

When Bea took it, she added "Commissioner?"

"What now?" Walters snapped.

"Thank you."

"Go do your job already." The line went quiet.

The car felt suddenly still. An island of silence in the shifting lights and depths of the street outside.

"Looks like we did it," he said.

"Now we wait, for any signs to narrow it down." She tucked the phone away and gave him a long look. "The truth now: are you alright?"

"I..." He wanted to brush it off, but his chest was still burning under the seatbelt, and those eyes of hers had to be seeing the pain. "You heard Zara. She gave me her chair because she guessed I was torn up worse than her. Now I've got enough skein to shield that spot... all I need is to dredge up the strength to walk."

"And we just got you *out* of the hospital," and she smiled.

She smiled. *Bea* was making jokes now.

They started the car up again, setting a sedate pace through the night that let him peer around at each shape they passed—anything for another chance of finding Eric themselves.

Colin fought to keep his thoughts on that search, not on what chances Terri had left. But what else could drive Eric out here after the maniac had finally taken her back... he gripped the seat, blinked and stared harder. *I say I've figured him out, but it feels like every day of this hunt Eric gets harder to understand.*

The radio crackled now and then: codes that Bea translated as *domestic disturbance* or *mugging,* and answered with a simple acknowledgment and nothing more.

Colin stared harder into the dark. Eric had to be out there—most likely killing again. This time using the skein Colin had gathered to stop him.

And Terri was somewhere, she had to be.

The scattered lights of cars moved around them, past them on the street, each wending out of sight down one more dark turn they had to pass by. More codes chattered, and once Jordan called with a single "Good work. I'll monitor this."

And Bea said only "Copy that," like she didn't need a single word more from someone who knew what she faced.

Colin's fingers tapped on the door's handle, to hold back the cold that crept through him. He stared at Bea's face, for that first hint of which call might be something more—*it could mean Eric's killed again, but at least we'd know.* Headlights moved on behind her.

Then Bea was saying "Here," and holding out his lost phone. When he took it, she looked away. "I can't believe I didn't remember this sooner."

"I'm just glad you did. You found it at the fight?"

"Right. You're shivering."

She noticed that? "Must be the meds, and all the rest of it."

"And that you've got a hospital gown instead of a shirt." She turned a knob on the dashboard, and heat came roaring up around his knees.

He stretched out to soak in that welcome warmth. His eyes began to close, and he clutched the door handle tighter to stay focused.

Strangely, now that she'd mentioned the patient's gown, he couldn't stop feeling the bare patches of his back, and the fuzz of the seat cushion tickling against them...

Another code came through the radio.

Bea caught up the mic. "Simms, responding." She glanced at Colin. "Missing person."

"You think—"

She brought the car surging forward under them.

He braced in the chair, the lull scattered away in the need to *get him*. Each corner and shift of light rushing by was a chance to sharpen his skein-sight and practice picking out where an enemy just might be lurking. One small thought came that *we aren't equipped to face him*, but they raced on down the street.

Each door they passed that *wasn't* the site put Eric that much further away, with that much more of a head start. Block after block passed, still stretching that lead out... then Bea slowed, slowed, and pulled them over at last.

The house was small and dim—in the night, all the street's houses looked oddly alike now, when his eyes should be picking out where each one was different and what that meant. A man and a woman stood out on the walkway in front, their features lost in the shadows.

"Not sure what this is," Bea mused. "Stay in the car and keep watch."

"Got it."

She strode out toward them. The couple turned to face her, and Colin slid the window down to listen as he watched the shadows.

"You called about an abduction?"

The woman's voice reached him in pieces. "...thought my boyfriend was missing... turns out he just *took a walk.*"

Colin peered around the dark edges of the house, the roof, the spidery shadows of the bushes out front. No invisible aura, no lurking figures.

The "boyfriend" glared at the woman. "I don't believe this—you called the cops on me?"

"I thought you were gone!"

"It was a *fight!* I mean, sure I was mad, but it takes more than the ghost to keep me away."

Colin looked around again, for any trace of Eric moving somewhere in the darkness. Nothing.

Bea said "Seems like you're both okay here. Have a good night." She turned to go.

*The ghost. They're talking about Eric, they're laughing at the threat—*

Colin swung the door open and headed toward them. "A word of advice?"

The man eyed him, a nervous look scrunching his face as Colin drew near. "And just who are you?"

"If you want to be safe from the ghost, don't go out at night. No, don't stay in town at all."

"Ghost?" The woman glanced at Bea. "Hold on, did he say there's an actual ghost here?"

"There's a serial killer," Bea said. "You've heard that people have been dying, and it's not safe on the streets tonight. That should be enough to keep in mind."

She waved them back inside the house. When they stepped behind their door, she led Colin back to the car without a word.

*I'm sounding crazy again, like when we were out with Terri trying to get noticed, and now they see me wearing this hospital thing too.* But his warning could have saved their lives.

Bea drove them up to the next block and parked there, and then she settled in her seat and focused on the radio. A car's lights rolled past them, and he realized they were back to simply listening again.

His fingers drummed on the door handle. He glared out along the dark street, trying to picture how far out in the night Eric might be. Just *waiting* for a sign.

"Eric could be anywhere," he muttered. "This could be someone's last moment, right now."

Bea nodded, a slow, considered acknowledgment.

He huddled in his seat, shivering again. One car passed, two, three. A few coded words of a report came, and Bea let it go by.

He added "Or he's already killed somewhere, or gotten whatever he wants. Somewhere we'll never know, until he wants us to."

The words only faded in the car's stillness, not even touching the night outside.

*But we don't know Eric's killing again. He could have stopped...*
Colin's eyes squeezed shut. *If he's giving all his attention to Terri again... or all his motive has faded away because Terri's gone...* No, *no,* they'd already seen how he got when Terri "died" once—

"We *can't* let him kill any more of us." The words burst out of him. "Come on, after so many bodies can't you call for an evacuation?" Or use everything they had to defend the people—nobody knew there was a real, invisible murderer in their midst, they didn't know the spell.

Bea said "We'll get him." Like it was certain, fixed truth.

"We never have!" His hand knotted around on the door handle. "We have to pull out every stop, get everyone on board—"

"Do you ever think..." Something in the *softness* of Bea's words made him stop and listen. "Do you ever think what happens after we take Eric Rowe down?"

"What, if we emptied the town out to somewhere safe? At least they'd be safe."

"I mean, what happens to *you,* after we win. You need to stay alive for... No."

Her head moved, one small degree that aimed her gaze squarely into his.

"No, I was going to say for your family's sake, but I never liked talking around a point. I mean, can you try staying alive for *me?*"

Her hand folded over on his.

She went on "You think I forgot that kiss? You think after this I'm going to walk away and forget the lunatic who drags himself out of a hospital to track down his sister? You and I have some unfinished business—no, we have something we barely started. The next time you throw yourself at that 'ghost,' you try to remember that."

Those eyes were blue suns, shining in the face he knew so well. Her hand gripped his... she could have, should have, held it tight to keep him there, but her grasp was still tentative, while his fingers shifted to hold hers in return.

Her face hung right there, it would be so easy to lean in and start a new kiss... but her touch, his smile, said it was the wrong moment. Holding her hand was just enough to keep the world in balance.

They held that balance, as lights slid by in the street, and rarer figures stirred on the sidewalk. The radio spoke again and again, and she heard each and let each one go, a slow, muted reminder that their enemy was still plotting to destroy that harmony. Still, maybe...

"All units, attack on Location One."

Bea grabbed at the keys, the wheel, wrenched the car from the curb. Her face was white.

"Where is—"

"The police station."

His hands—empty of hers again—clenched, locked on the seat and the door handle as they roared through the night. That was it, Eric had lost his mind... or he'd decided just how far out in the open he'd go to shatter the town.

The cold was back inside him, lodged in his flesh. *All the times we've taken Eric on, and now I have just enough skein to* walk *without bleeding.* But they raced closer, closer.

The long, low shape of the police station was blurred halfway to anonymity in the night—except for the cars with their flashing lights scattered around the street. What might be a dozen people thronged around the entrance, held back by one cop bellowing *keep back* so frantically he must be doing more than to spread panic than calm it.

Bea led Colin right past him, to plunge into the dimness.

Officers crouched around the front space, pressing themselves behind the desk and furniture, from what Colin could make out in the low lighting that had to be an emergency generator. Shouts, cries for help, sparked and clashed around the building beyond his view. He and Bea crept up to the broad shadow of the front desk, with scattered papers turning under his feet.

The uniform crouching there looked straight at Colin. "You get back out of here, now—"

Colin ignored him, staring around the furniture and the corridors leading on into the dimness, where Eric could come at them any moment and they'd never really *see* him.

"He stays," Bea said. "Where's the killer?"

A man's shrill scream spilled out from the dimness ahead. One cop darted into that corridor—Colin wrenched his gaze off him, tried to look around for where the attack could come.

At one desk, a motionless arm lay stretched out in a puddle of blood. The air hung thick with sweat, *fear*.

Gunshots blasted the moment into chaos, to screams and a rush of darkness and movement. Cops scurried forward from desks and corners, scurrying to the next piece of cover. The lights ahead had just been shot away, Colin realized. Eric had a gun.

He scrambled up behind Bea, straining his eyes through the chaos.

Some whimpering sound came from the darkness ahead. Bea nudged Colin back against the corner they crouched behind, and she crept forward, slowly. The faintest movement in that gloom could be Eric.

A figure hobbled around a corner ahead—young, scruffy, leaning on the wall and fighting to keep moving out toward the lights. A cop in black moved out to meet him.

A spectral shape moved around the corner.

"Up ahead, look out!" Colin yelled.

Eric lunged. Just a flash in the dimness, and the man in the uniform slumped over and Eric raced away, leaving the lame bystander shrieking.

Figures stared around, guns darted one way and another in search of their target. But with the lights broken, none of them could have seen more than a flicker. Blood pooled under the fallen cop—too much, he lay too still.

*That corner, is Eric still behind there or somewhere else—*

A cop grabbed at him from the side. "How'd you know? What was that?" His face scowled suspicion in the dimness.

"He blends into the dark. Listen!" Colin strained to hear, but the first victim, the cops' rattle of steps, and the other voices through the halls tore away any footsteps.

The police closed in on the two men, the living and the dead, with Bea leading the way. They all moved together, still disciplined, but he could see that fraying as their heads and guns darted around more and more wildly. Eric's terror games were taking their toll.

Colin reached to help the limping man along, but cops shoved him aside. The officers helped, dragged, both victims back toward the light.

*There at a corner—Eric's head, he'd circled around—*

He hauled in a breath to shout, but Eric dove right at him.

Colin flung himself backward, down, dropping flat as the claws swept in. One tangle of falling and shouts and motions around him— the killer rushed in and *gone*—

The floor hit him, smashed along him and turned the world white...

Standing, he was still dragging himself to his feet again, his torn chest screaming under the skein. Around was a haze of figures, all staring different ways. But one shape beyond them, Bea, gaped at him in what had to be pure relief. *Eric* did *miss.*

"You alright?" barked the nearest cop.

Another said "Why are you still here?"

Colin gritted his teeth, forced his head to look around. Eric had to be behind one of those corners, or circling to come at them again soon. He turned again, his head spun, but there were too many ways—

The nearest cop said "That thing went for you. Why?"

"I told you," Colin gasped. "I saw him in the shadows. He's too fast..."

*He's after* me, *now?* The thought flooded through him: Eric could have come here just to draw out the brother who'd let Terri suffer. Eric had come for him at the hospital...

Colin staggered away, twisting toward the lights at the front. If he got Eric away from them—

Someone moaned. A drawn-out sound up in the corridor, around a turn ahead, and Colin and all of them turned toward it.

Bea snapped two gestures at the cops. They split, a few pulling the two victims back while the others followed her forward. Colin moved with them.

Gunshots boomed out to shatter the enclosed space. Colin joined the cops in dropping flat—he saw Bea with a few others that made it to cover—but the lights over the corridor ahead shattered into darkness.

The echo faded from his hearing, enough for a sound to rush in: a ragged voice up ahead screaming "We're next, we're all dead…"

*"Come on!"* Commissioner Walters's roar smashed through the sounds. "Watch your backs!"

Flashlight beams sprang up, from the branch opposite the screaming. Walters and a handful of cops stepped out and started across the corridor.

Colin swiveled his head, looking from one dim turn to others. Nothing they had could stop Eric unless they grabbed him and used the spell… but the cops couldn't even see him.

Bea stepped forward to Walters's group.

*They need to know they can't see him.*

*I have to show them.*

He reached under the hospital gown. His fingers sank into the waiting skein.

Footsteps hurtled by, a corridor or two away. For one breath a pair of inhumanly far-spaced footsteps broke through the chaos of sounds. Somewhere out there, Eric was circling closer.

Walters led his team up the turn ahead, Bea moving with them.

*No time. No time to show them invisibility or anything, just—*

He wrenched the skein off the bandages, dragged it out.

The halo of Eric's head peeked around a corner.

Cops turned, stared at Colin and the stuff in his hand—but he wasn't forming a weapon, not this time.

Instead he yanked the last bit of skein from around his eyes, and Eric vanished from his sight as both pieces fall from his hands to let him yell *"Gratshay kodo va!* Say it, trust me, if you see anything move near you—*gratshay kodo va!"*

He flung the words at the dazed faces, at the chaos of echoes around them, at the flicker of lights. Around the corner where Eric was, was that a faint blur pulling back from view?

The nearest cop said "Calm down, just breathe—"

Up ahead, Walters slowed, glanced back at him, stared over at Bea. But too many faces stayed turned away, ignoring him, ignoring him as crazy.

*I'm really doing this.* He sucked in breath for another shout.

One footstep, too loud. He looked up, he could just make out the faintest shape charging into the corridor, swinging around the cops in the way and rushing in at him.

That extra instant of delay gave Colin's lips time to move. *"Gratshay-kodo-va—"*

Eric *kicked,* and a chair, a simple plastic chair, hurtled at him. Colin twisted away, something struck his side—

He swam through pain to drag in a breath, fighting to get the spell out again—

The hand slammed down over his mouth. Iron-hard, part of it came flowing against his flesh into a suffocating grip. Something else reached under his stomach, scooped him up in a wave of pain, and the shocked faces around him blurred away.

He wheezed against that clutching force, anything to push the syllables out again, but that monstrous strength smothered them all. Agony battered at his throat, his thoughts.

Bea ran toward him—he caught one hazy glimpse backward at her as Eric swept him away, feet first and quicker than any human pace could match. His fists thrashed, like beating on a statue and only making his own wounds ache.

The building's echoes broke open into the wide street. They darted past the crowd, away.

Then the darkness pressed in closer. Something folded around Colin's midsection, gathered his legs in, then his arms. The hand still held his jaw and forced his face away from seeing it, but... Eric was wrapping him, *cocooning* him, in skein so they could both disappear. Like all the victims he found a reason to carry off.

The skein closed over his face.

# CHAPTER FIFTEEN

# WHAT WE CHOOSE

He gasped at any wisps of air he could reach, fighting against the grayness that lapped at his mind like the wrappings swallowed his sight. Every bounding step Eric took was a drumbeat of pain.

Somewhere *outside* the skein was a babble of distant voices—crowded, scared, the people gathered outside the police station. Those were already dwindling, gone, fallen away from the seething mass around him.

He squirmed where he could still move. *I couldn't save them, stop him, anything*—the hand clamped over his mouth crushed out any scream of outrage. Or the five syllables that could end the fight.

And kill them both, with them swimming in this much skein. *Am I really thinking of that?* But just striking back at all would feel better than the air he couldn't get.

If he could just…

The truth shot through him: this was *skein* he was sealed in, Eric had trapped him inside a weapon.

If… if he could take control of the layers around his head just enough to force that hand back and release the words. Or wrench his body free.

*Focus.* He tried to draw his will together, to feel the need and the familiar cool substance around him, and not the lurching, shuddering pain in his chest. Just one surge of strength, the only way to see Zara, see Terri. He held Bea's face before his mind, and their "unfinished business."

*Or else Eric's taking me to Terri.*

The images tumbled, tangled. This was still Terri's only chance, only Eric knew where she was... saying the words would kill her as surely as him and Eric... if she wasn't already...

*I know what she'd want.* The fraying fingers of will steadied, and he sunk them deep into the skein.

Every jolting step burned his wounds, harsh and unstoppable as Eric's grip on the skein that moved them. *But I know what it really is, dragon-skin, and I say let go!*

The prison only squeezed tighter.

He flailed his will, his body, his need against the stuff, but it gripped and flexed and swept him on as if his command never touched it.

*So many times, Eric has seized my skein, but I've never taken control of his—*

He forced that thought down and flung everything against the skein.

*Open.*

*Do it.*

*For all of us.*

*Open, open, open...*

A ripple stirred across the smothering world. Something moved.

Then the hand crushed down against his mouth. The grip under his body *shook* him in a wave of pain. The world lurched *down,* slammed up again with what had to be Eric's feet landing from a sudden high leap, battering at his focus. The next step jolted him forward, then two more together, not even keeping a rhythm of shocks he could try to brace against.

*Eric took me alive, but he sure doesn't care much if I live through this.* Colin clutched at strength and tried *not* to think of a grape in a pinball machine. Just one more fraction of space and a decent breath—

The jolting steps had slowed, he realized, slowed and begun picking their way along something different from the open streets. He had to do it *now*.

They lurched to a stop—and Eric tossed him away, sent him spilling from all the skein and tumbling, rolling, over unforgiving ground.

He lay limp and aching on the rocks. Eyes closed, certain something had broken... some of the rough ground wedged or stuck in his arm, something shifted in his chest. His lips tasted blood.

But the sounds...

That exact balance of far-off voices, movements on one side and another, just peeping through the night breeze, he knew those before he opened his eyes.

Seeing was a more twisted recognition. The wan starlight on that splintered table, the toppled bookcase—and the broken wall behind them that was the jagged bones of the Vargas House.

*He took me* here? *The center of Zara's and my work with the Hillside, the first place I found skein and Eric came hunting for it.* The place Eric had eagerly brought down with his own claws. A fragment of lemony furniture oil reached Colin through the dust, from the pieces under him that he'd taken for stones.

A hand slammed over his mouth—*again.* Eric loomed over him and blotted out the starlight, wrenching him to sit up.

The other hand caught at his ankle, snapped the cold of a handcuff onto it and then the other ankle. Then Eric shoved him down and darted out of reach, before his whirling mind remembered to try the spell.

The vicious bastard didn't bother chaining his hands.

Eric sat hunched on top of a section of fallen masonry, like his destruction had made it some kind of throne. In the shadows, the mass of skein bulked him up bigger than any bodybuilder.

"You could yell." Eric's voice was so low, he might not even mean to be overheard. "See who comes."

A hundred yards away, the sound of a car moved through the night.

Colin forced down the spinning in his head. "Then you kill them too?" Dust clung to the blood on his lips, and he spat them away. "For what—for the crime of living near the heart of the town that hurt Terri?"

"Good one. Or were you thinking of stalling and hoping someone will track you?"

He held up a small, flat fragment of something. Colin squinted in the night… it had to be remains from his phone. He hadn't thought of that either, or felt the moment Eric tore it off him. *Bea gave me that.*

But Eric had turned away, staring somewhere into the rubble beyond Colin's back. Colin tested his fingers, tried to think. Weakness tugged at his limbs, from what had to be a dozen tears and bruises. Something tickled in his chest.

Turning his head hurt—and what he saw of the wall behind Eric still screened them from outside.

At last Colin broke the stillness. "What is it you want now?"

"To talk. Don't you see her?"

Eric motioned to the rubble, a thin patch of shadows… no, that figure was *human.* A sprawling scarecrow-form with all its skein stripped away. Her head lay limp on the debris, but that dark strip had to be a gag around Terri's mouth.

Colin twisted up, crawled, tottered on his shackled feet toward her.

Something blurred above … Eric plummeted down to land ahead of him, skein muscle leaping and catching his weight with only a low thump on the rubble. Claws sprouted from his fingers in warning.

The spell rushed to Colin's lips, but where Eric crouched was more than ten feet away—a world to cross with the chain shackling his steps. Colin halted, wished for even a scrap of skein to cut himself free.

Something, at that thought, something on him stirred.

Eric shifted where he crouched, watching his enemy but sharing his gaze with Terri, and his voice went soft. "You let him hurt you again. But I'm ready to heal you."

Colin heard himself saying "Skein can only hold us together, it doesn't repair—"

"Quiet!" Eric only spun toward him a moment, then turned back to keep them both in view. "Ignore him. I told you, I can heal all of it now. I know it."

Terri still didn't raise her head—whatever she was playing at, it held Eric's attention.

Colin kept every muscle still. He *had* felt a bit of skein reacting on him—but so small, where was it? He strained for the fragment to move again.

Eric said "Nothing to fear now. I've found the answer, I can fix everything." He held up his arm.

The gnarled mass of skein slid away from his flesh. Under it, a patch of his forearm glinted, and he turned it to catch the starlight.

Scabbing over the flesh—where Hoyle had shot him.

And Bea had done worse to his other hand.

Colin stared as Eric raised that hand higher. There within the wound was more skein, growing into his flesh, tendrils weaving in among the shattered bones, weaving and twining and merging...

Eric flexed the fingers—they didn't even move like human fingers now.

"It's so simple," Eric said. "You know you can do it. You *know!*"

A ragged edge crept into his voice. As if she wasn't...

Terri hadn't stirred. As if she'd been still, for so long...

Colin's mouth went numb. *Don't say it, don't poke at it,* but he whispered "She hasn't been answering, has she?"

Eric glanced over, and his skein settled back around his arms. "She's been stubborn. But I brought you all here to show her: it can work."

"Maybe she *can't* answer—"

Eric was already looking back at Terri. "It's so easy. I see now, all this time you've been rejecting the skein instead of letting it take root. But that can't go on, so you start healing or I'll split your brother in half."

The words droned out without one change in his tone.

Terri lay still.

Eric spun around toward Colin, claws forming again. "You hear me, Terri? You think it's a *bluff?"*

Colin couldn't move. The great mass of ruthless power reared over him... and he still had to whisper:

"I think... she can't hear—"

*"Shut up!"*

Eric's claws spread, his arms yanked back poised to strike. Colin gasped at the spell and his voice choked.

Eric halted, wrenched himself away. His head turned to look around, and he shuffled back a step.

He spun away. With one rattle of debris he darted away, toward a broken space in the wall, and shimmered from sight in mid-leap.

Colin caught his breath, listened into the night—his heart was still pounding. But somewhere among the far-off sounds of the streets, he caught a racing footfall, and another further away. A breeze shifted over the broken rims of the wall. Some faint sound, some animal, rummaged through the ruins, a broken room or two away.

He shuffled a step with his chained feet, leaning out for a look past the gap in the outer wall. Eric had actually stopped himself, he'd been so close to cutting him down...

A cough came from where Terri lay.

He spun toward her, one fear inside him crumbling away as he limped and staggered over the scattered debris. He reached her, gripped the strip of cloth around her mouth—it took all the strength his fingers had to wrench the knots open and let her spit out the larger wadding underneath that kept her gagged.

"Tried to stall," she said. "Sorry."

"You're okay? *Please* be okay."

With his fingers on her face, he felt her nodding more than he saw it. He stared around, shifting his feet against the chain that kept them, him, helpless.

"You have any skein, anything?" he asked.

"No. You?"

"Not sure. How about... try this." He gripped the outer piece of the gag again. "If it gets him close, you've got him."

She nodded, and he wrapped that strip around her mouth again and tied it to leave a bit of slack over her lips, invisible in the night.

"Hope it works," she said. The outer gag barely muffled her at all.

Colin twisted back toward the wall, hands and feet dragging him over the broken, cluttered ground. Eric was out there somewhere.

The closer he came to the wall's gap, the more he saw the familiar lines of the street and houses in the night—as if this were some new *window* in the side of the Vargas House. Far down on the sidewalk, two dark figures were walking. Were they who Eric was after?

*That was skein I felt on me, it has to be.* He stretched his arms and willed the stuff to move again, if he could just pick that motion out from the mass of pains and gashes that twisted all down him. It could be some fragment that came loose when Eric dropped him, it had to be *somewhere.*

Those two outlines on the street, passing under a streetlight now, those were cops.

He gathered a shout, caught himself—it might just make Eric strike sooner. And before he tried—

He clamped his eyes shut and pictured the bit of skein moving again, wherever it was, praying this scrap would be enough to cut the chain. The breeze whispered over the shattered walls; at least that animal and its rooting around had gone silent.

No skein stirred on him. He looked up.

The two cops down the block were gone.

He stared out at the sidewalk. They could have stepped in among the houses, or Eric could have... *I'm losing time.*

Just a tiny bit of skein, but he'd felt it before. Somewhere under the ragged hospital gown, maybe, somewhere, if he could just find it.

Eric slammed down in front of him, reappearing as he landed shockingly close—Colin tumbled back away from the sight. He tried to roll, dragged himself up ready to curse Eric's vicious joke.

Eric clutched a cocoon of green, and the wrappings were already peeling away and merging back into his armor to spill a scrawny, moon-faced police officer onto the rubble. The cop stared up, and his hands fumbled at his belt—for weapons, tools, that Eric must have snatched away.

"Where's Izzy? What'd you do?" the man coughed.

"He won't be reporting in, no." Eric turned his back on the prisoner, facing Colin. *"This* is your town? You keep ripping yourself to pieces to save it, and they still don't believe you. I could fly right down the street and they wouldn't even see!"

The cop grunted "Now listen to me—"

Eric whirled back. One hand streaked out to latch around the cop's mouth, and hoisted him into the air. The prisoner wheezed and spluttered for breath, his fists flailing helplessly.

"Stop it!" Colin snapped. "Just... just stop, are you out to kill *everything?"*

"No, no." Eric turned to face Terri. "You hear me?"

"She can't—"

"More lies." He stepped toward where she lay. "No more playing possum, no more stalling me. We're fixing you *now."*

Terri moaned. A soft, weak sound against the cop's thrashing.

*To lure Eric into reach.* Colin knew it, and he forced his eyes and mouth to stretch out in horror as he held their one hope off of his face.

"A trick," Eric said. "You tried that before, Terri." Instead of moving, he gave the choking cop a shake, not even glancing at him. "Stop fighting me, girl. It's all so simple."

Colin pulled his chained feet in under him, even knowing Eric was still too far to leap at.

And Eric drew back still another step out of reach. "Watch. It's as simple as this."

He stretched out a finger into a claw inches long. The cop's face went pale.

Colin yelled "Stop, don't—"

The point sank into the officer's chest, silver-green piercing into black cloth and on through it. The man gave a smothered sound of pain, and his face twisted under the grip on his mouth.

Colin leaped, a single headlong lunge with his hands straining out for the enemy—

Three whole paces beyond his reach. He crashed to the ground with the spell only half spoken.

"Stop *defending* them!" Eric said. "They made their choice, every one of them that dragged you down—" he spun toward Terri— "now you have to open your eyes and see you can be free again. See?"

He drew his hand back from his victim... but the claw stretched and flowed between them, reached out to form a tendril into the wound. Eric's hand moved as he worked it deeper in.

"Then you simply... mold it."

He rippled his other fingers like a sign of how he must be shaping the one strand, twisting and probing under the skin. The cop's breathing slowed, steadied.

Eric laughed. "It's easy. See?" He held the man up higher for Terri to view.

Terri's face stared up from the shadows. The starlight caught the wide horror filling her eyes.

"Easy," Eric said again. "Just control the skein, that's all. But... you should all see this..."

He turned and set the cop on the ground, suddenly gentle. He drew his finger back, and Colin could just make out a bit of green breaking off and lingering in the man's chest.

Eric leaned over him. "Now you show her. Just try to feel it in you, and make it hold you together—"

He stepped away, back toward where Terri lay. Close to her.

"*Gratshay kodo va!*" Terri's foot kicked out at him. But the kick fell short, her leg couldn't reach, and Eric dodged clear.

"*Ungrateful—*"

"*Gratshay kodo va!*"

The cop's voice was a perfect mimic of Terri's tone, as he lunged at Eric with a fist lashing out.

The cop stumbled. He faltered, hands clutched at his chest, his mouth moved in a soundless shriek. He toppled, hands thrashing over his wound, at what was inside it.

"*Make* it stop!" Colin screamed at the cop. "You take control, you can do it, or it'll eat you—"

"So *stupid!*" Eric roared. "Why couldn't you listen?" A long claw flicked out from his hand.

He slashed it down, down, through the officer's neck, and the body went limp.

Eric *kicked* that shape over onto its back. He leaned down, stabbed into the chest and drew his claw—and the rest of his skein—back with a single sucking sound.

Colin could only lie in the dirt, staring, as the smell of blood tainted the air. Far, far away a car rumbled along a road. Back deeper in the ruins, that animal was rattling the rubble in blissful ignorance...

Eric's head twisted toward that sound. "Huh. You made me forget again—"

He sprang away into the wreckage... disappearing into one thing he'd destroyed and turning his back on another kill. On *two* of them, this cop had lost a partner out there.

Colin looked at the officer, at the severed meat and the lifeless eyes. He saw Terri watching too, saw the guilt in her eyes that she'd shown him the spell.

Eric's footsteps bounded deeper away, sending rubble clattering as they passed.

Colin locked his fingers on the cuffs. Even a sliver of skein could break those, if he traced where it was on himself...

The footsteps started back.

He looked up, *willed* the skein to show itself—

Eric loped into view, with a bound and gagged Zara over his shoulder.

Colin's breath caught. *He... he had Zara here all the time, that was no animal rustling around, but he was holding her in waiting until...* He looked from the butchered cop to his helpless mother, and cold dread wracked through him.

Eric set Zara on the floor, just clear of the spreading blood. With one sudden motion he snipped her gag away and darted out of reach.

"You ready to tell your daughter to live?" he snarled. "Not throw her chance away because she's scared of me, or some grudge over the town?" The last words could have been any petty thing, the way he said them.

Zara looked right past him. "Terri! Colin! What's he done to you?"

Terri said "Nothing, to us."

*So far.* Colin added "Careful..." *But, careful about what? Eric could do anything, any moment—he said he* forgot *he had Zara—*

Colin wrenched his eyes shut. He still had one bit of skein, somewhere, if he could wall out the world and find it.

"Take it!" Eric was saying. "It's the town or you—I'm saving you!"

"This is *saving?*" Terri hissed back.

Zara added "Damn you, damn you, how many people do you want dead? Is that all you want, more bodies—"

The skein stirred. Colin felt it move.

Inside his chest. A trace of it shifted, against his rib, worked in under the bandage and trapped within his flesh—

"Take it!" Eric said. "All the rest of them, Terri, they're killing you. Gardner used you, he bought Hoyle and he had Setter *poison* you just to scare me. You look back at this town: Vargas, the Stricklands, the Gardners, all killers…"

*The skein's in my wound. Like the cop it was killing, like Eric.* His stomach lurched.

"You take it now!" Eric roared at Terri. "Or—no, these people are still holding you back—"

He advanced on Zara.

Colin stared, his fingers dug against the broken floor, helpless and out of reach. His mouth opened ready to scream that all of this was wasted, that Terri was dying anyway—no, that would just drive Eric harder.

Eric stretched out his claws, taking whole heartbeats just to draw their length out.

Zara glared up at him. "And you think this is going to get Terri back?" her voice cracked back. "You lost her when you started killing for her. If you care about *her* at all—"

The strike smashed into her.

She spasmed, jerked again as Eric ripped the blades free. She slumped where she sat, but *how bad, how far was she still sitting up—*

Those eyes still glared at the enemy, that defiance keeping her presence there in her face. It wavered, already struggling.

Colin locked his will around the fragment of skein inside him. But that scrap would never patch anything, and inside Eric the stuff was…

Eric spun back toward Terri. "We get rid of them, all of them, and you'll be free. You know we—"

Colin cut in "The skein won't fix her. Even if it could heal her, just look at yourself. You've had it inside you for what, days now? And it's messing with your mind."

*"What?"*

Eric turned away from Terri and Zara, and began walking toward him.

Colin went on "Maybe it got into your bloodstream, or your nerves, or something. You were ruthless once, but you had a purpose: keep Terri, get more skein for her. You tried making deals with Gardner, then you begged me to cut out the complications and bring this back to just us and healing Terri. But now?"

He motioned up at the huge, skein-wrapped figure approaching.

"Now you're nothing but rage. You torment people just for crossing your path. How was Zara holding anyone back? No, the skein's making you crazy."

"What do *you* know?" And he glanced back at Zara—

"I know the skein comes from a dragon's body. Dragon-skin."

His words made Eric freeze, look back at him.

Colin locked his eyes on where Eric's would be, under the layers of green. "Look at yourself. Look at what you've done, to Terri—"

"Police! Who's in there?"

The shout ripped through the night, from somewhere out on the street. Colin twisted to look back, but the remains of the wall blocked them off.

"She's been stabbed!" he yelled at them. "Help her—*please!*"

And he looked at Eric again, begging him to back down.

Another police voice shouted "Stabbed? Is *he* still there?"

Eric growled "Quiet, you—"

"*You're* the one who was making noise," Colin said. "You brought them here. Or you thought killing a couple of cops wouldn't bring more of them around? See, you're losing control, none of this is what you want." He looked at Zara—was she still moving? "Please. It's Terri's mother."

Eric's hands jerked to fling out his claws. He twisted away, leaped up to the top of the broken wall, and winked out of sight.

"Look out!" Colin yelled into the darkness. "The cop-killer, you'll never see him coming!"

Then he hopped, crawled, hobbled his way across the shattered room toward Zara.

Somewhere beyond the wall, shouts were breaking out and gun-shots blasted. He pushed Eric's savagery from his mind: Zara lay in front of him, bleeding, twitching, and her staring face looked *wrong* in the faint light.

Terri croaked "She alright? She alright?"

His mother's face, so weak, fighting to hold on...

*Stop it!*

He yanked his hospital shirt off. Scrabbling fingertips searched the dark stains on that form—*just a form, don't think*—for tears through the cloth, for the sources of the bleeding. There, and there—he wrapped the shirt around the damage, pressed it down, hard, anything to hold it all closed for another instant.

*Could skein hold it together?* The thought tore at him as he strained to tie the wrapping down. *Not the tiny bit in me. And Eric's shown what that leads to.*

There'd been more shouts, screams, out beyond the house. Eric had to be *playing* with his prey.

He wrenched the last knot tight and felt her flinch. That had to be enough.

Then he dug, tore, at the bandage over his chest, ripping through the spasms. Right *there*—beside that rib, it had to be.

Pain spiked. His focus shattered to fragments, but he stabbed the fingers deeper and willed the thing to come worming out—

A moan, he stifled a moan to turn all that need into focus—*how can it be so small, it's all tearing loose*—the world went gray—

Tumbling away, he was tumbling aside clenching his fingers and knowing he had to hit the ground hard.

*Blank, blurring, ringing and ringing that went through every-thing...*

The ringing faded when he shook his head.

He looked up, saw the blur in his eyes settle. That huge shadow-gray, green figure must be the one that knocked him flying.

"Eric?" Terri, that was Terri's voice. "Killing more cops—and now it's my brother?"

"They're holding you back!" Eric said. Then the skein-covered face turned to fix on Colin. "Dragon? What did you say, you mean this is dragon-skin?"

*At least he's listening to that.*

Colin heaved himself up to a crouch, with his hand clutching the sliver of skein he'd torn free. He glared back at the looming enemy.

"I said you're losing yourself. You keep the 'skein' too close and it twists up your blood, your mind, something! Look—you just killed more cops, right here where you're 'hiding'!"

"They shot at me!" Eric snapped. "And it could be two of them, twenty, none of them take more than a second. Nothing's getting in my way, nothing!"

"Won't help!" Terri's shrill words cut through his. "I'm already dying."

Eric stared, moaned, he sprang away to rush toward her.

Colin reached down to the chain at his feet.

"You can't!" he heard Eric saying. "I'll stop that, I'll *make* you live—"

The scrap of skein, smaller than a fingernail, slid inside the hand-cuffs' lock. He pinched it tighter, concentrated.

Rising behind his will came Terri's words: "Better dead than turn out like you. Or with you."

The skein burst outward in a ruin of metal. The lock cracked open.

He shoved it clear and looked up—

Terri launched herself, from curled on the ground into a clumsy leap at Eric. Eric dove back, hurtling out of reach.

She toppled across the ground.

Colin bellowed and charged, dropping the skein and slamming his unbound feet into the floor to hurl him at the enemy, calling the spell as he stretched out.

Eric leaped clear, crashing off a wall and tumbling on backward, shimmering from sight.

Sirens screamed in the distance.

Eric's head jerked around—the sudden move pinpointed where his blur stood, even in the night. The broken remains of the walls and rubble hemmed him in, *how far can he run before I land that touch...*

Colin forced down the seductive rage and stepped back, back to beside Zara. Terri didn't move.

"Listen to me!" he shouted at Eric. "Whatever it's doing to you, it's speeding up! The first cops that came here, you tried to lead away, right? Now you're just tearing through them like they won't bring backup here! Where does it end? Listen—"

"You're *dead,*" Eric screamed. "You're all dead, every one of you. But... I'll save her."

A voice from outside blared "You give it up, Rowe!" The tinny sound of a megaphone couldn't hide Bea's voice.

Colin edged sideways, stared for the gap in the wall. Two uniforms stalked past it, with Bea keeping close behind them—in place to slam the spell onto Eric if he went after one of them. And there had to be more cops out there, many more...

Footsteps clattered inside, Eric's feet kicking through the rubble as he landed at Terri's side. Crouched to reach toward her.

Terri's fingers twitched, Colin *saw* them move against the ground.

Then he was flinging himself at Eric's back, gasping out *"Gratshay-ko—"*

The fist flashed into him.

—Still, lying still and letting the world spin, holding onto the ground against all the tipping, dust and splinters in the fingers...

*Like when Eric lifted Terri up, that time I remember. But it's wrong, why's he got his hand blocking her mouth... this time he's wrapping his skein out around her...*

This time.

*No, not again*—Colin forced himself to his feet, shook the dizziness away.

Eric lifted the helpless shape of Terri into his arms, one hand still reaching through the forming wrappings to cover her mouth. Skein flowed and shimmered over them, and they disappeared.

Footsteps closed in through the corridor. That was Bea, too late.

One flicker of movement darted up. A thump came from the high rim of the broken wall, then another sound beyond it.

The gap in the wall, then—that was the fastest way after them. Colin stumbled toward it.

Bea stepped to block his path, fists rising.

# CHAPTER SIXTEEN

# WHAT WE BECOME

His eyes locked on Bea, standing in front of the wall's gap braced for a fight. Eric's fleeing footsteps had already been swallowed up.

Swallowed up by other sounds—he saw cops advancing through the ruins, but more than any of that, two EMTs in white rushing to where Zara lay.

"You can't chase him," Bea said.

His gaze filled with the medics, with the short, sharp commands that shot between them as they fought for Zara's life. They *were* fighting, he heard no desperation in those words. She shuddered on the ground.

"...you need to stop," Bea was finishing.

*Stop?*

Colin pushed toward the opening. Bea's hand blocked him, shoved back and brought him to a halt.

"Let me go! Eric's out of his mind—he's got Terri..."

Bea only sidestepped to block off the rest of the gap.

"So you're going to kill yourself out there?" Her face twisted in frustration. The hand on his shoulder drew back, to a tentative, lingering touch. "What if it's too late for catching them?"

*"No!* I think..." The words tumbled from his mouth. "I think if Terri gets the chance she's ready to kill them both! It'd just take a few words, the way they're wrapped up now."

He leaned around to peep out through that broken wall, at the street outside. Every second they must be getting further away.

"You can't catch them," she said. "And he could still come back, after Zara."

He looked over at his mother, at the EMTs. The checks and prods and patches they did over her blurred in his mind—but the *pace,* the firm, unpanicked rhythm they took was built on hope.

Bea said "You just keep an eye out here, in case he sneaks back." She held up a handful of skein. The stuff he'd dropped at the police station.

He snatched it from her hand and twisted past her, on past the stunned gasp she made, and leaped out through the hole.

The pavement slammed up against his feet. Under the clouded sky, the street looked barely any brighter than in the ruins' shadows. It looked ghostlike, far too empty even for this late, with only a few stark figures in police black pressing in from the right—

He twisted left, hoping Eric would have been evading those too.

Bits of debris clattered under his feet, and he stumbled to the sidewalk. *Or Eric could have dashed clear across the street and through the block.* Cold waves lapped at his flesh when he slowed. He'd left his shirt with Zara.

One cop glanced down the street at him, looked away. They had to be fixated on catching Eric, then.

*But I've got* blood *on me, Zara's and mine, I can't stay and be spotted.* He crouched down, used the skein in his palm to snip off the handcuff trailing from his other ankle. Then he separated the skein, enough to cover each of his knees with a flimsy brace. One last scrap went across his eyes as he broke into a run.

A swaying, staggering gait, somehow keeping his balance over the legs that the skein kept bending to drive him on. And the street he'd known all his life, it blurred into a haze of houses, fences, cars, bushes, none the same but all too *empty.*

A motorcycle moved, somewhere beyond what could have been whole blocks of silence. Somewhere behind him, a shout came from where the cops had been.

A figure stepped onto the sidewalk, away from unlocking his car—some man, face blurred in the dark. Warm concern filled his voice: "Are you alright—"

"Did you see my sister?" came the reckless words, knowing nobody around could *see* them.

"I, maybe, I heard something down there—" The neighbor's arm waved.

Colin stammered thanks and rushed in, in along the space between two houses. The brick wall between them forced him in against the house's shadow, dimming the light under his footing.

*I can't be keeping up with them, by now Terri could have destroyed them both. Or I do catch them and I've got nothing left to stop Eric.*

The back wall twisted across his path, five feet of brick that brought him up short. He glanced around, lost in the blur between houses' shadows, brush, abandoned things, with no sign which way was what.

He pulled in all the breath he had, felt the fire lodged in his side, and flung it all out in a scream of *"Terri!"*

The echoes faded in the silent street.

A light moved up ahead, a car on the street beyond. A black and white police car, moving on past and gone.

Colin cleared the wall in a haze of climbing and rolling, and swayed on down the next sidewalk. *I'm not losing her again, I'm not!*

A tree formed out of the darkness ahead, branches spreading over the sidewalk. Lights shone in a window, one home still full and playing music like an oasis of peace.

Another sound *rattled* from the house beyond that.

There beside the wrought-iron fence, an outline crouched. Eric crouched there and tugged against the fence, where cords of his skein wrapped around the bars. Stuck.

Hazes of exhaustion scattered and Colin rushed at them.

Eric slashed a hand out to tear away the bars he was fastened to. His other arm held the cocooned Terri under it, and that hand still covered her mouth.

Skein from Eric's feet crept together, merged, and he stumbled against the fence. *That's Terri, she's fighting him for control!*

Colin slowed to take in the sight. Eric glared at his feet, pulled them free. His free hand lifted above Terri in a fist before he yanked it back and stared at it in shock.

*They're both wrapped up in the same skein, so no spells, but then how can I stop him—before she uses the spell herself?* He reached down and grabbed the skein from both of his knees.

Then he charged. His hands clapped together, the skein merged and settled on his fist into a heavy-knuckled glove, and he slammed his punch into their enemy.

Eric half-turned—more a confused swaying than hurt—and then the skein at his legs flowed and twisted at his balance.

As Eric stared down, Colin sank his fingers into his arm. The massive skein clung there, then it rippled... Colin peeled a strip of it away with a roar of joy.

He lurched back a step, another, out of Eric's reach. The still-huge figure swayed, fighting Terri's influence—the same battle for control that had left his skein loose. Colin pressed his prize to his wrist and flowed it out along his arm.

Eric's feet settled under him. One sharp footfall was all the warning Colin had as Eric dove at him. The punch crashed against his arm, still overwhelming power that his thin-armored block barely turned aside.

Eric's leg moved—Colin jumped back before some kick could shatter his unprotected leg. His balance teetered, but Eric hung back—

Eric's other hand reached up from its grip under Terri, pointed at him, and a lance of skein burst out from it. Colin twisted, blocked, felt something slice through his forearm. He tumbled backward.

Eric lifted his free hand and formed claws.

Sprawled on the grass, Colin began dragging himself up, watching his enemy and struggling for balance. Eric advanced—and the skein on those feet tangled again.

Eric raised his hand and rapped the knuckles down on Terri.

Then he froze. He stared, at his fist, at his captive... a thin moan slipped from his skein-covered face. So there it was again, after all Eric's talk about his "devotion" to her, being so sure that was stronger than his temper or the skein's influence or *anything*. He still turned on her.

The cocoon shivered, pulled back from around Terri's face.

*"Gratshay. Kodo."*

*Don't, don't, you can't, it'll devour you both—*

Terri stopped. She smiled.

A bluff. The truth of that flung Colin to his feet as Eric stared down at her. A lunge and a stronger, skein-armed punch staggered Eric back.

Colin raked his hand down and caught a whole section of the green over Eric's chest. It shook, writhed, and came free, and his other fist struck at the thin-coated space under it, drawing a groan.

Blades jabbed out at his bare fingers as he pulled back, but they twisted and shrank away—Terri again. And more skein was flowing off of Eric's arm to swell the cocoon around her, more every second. Colin caught at Eric again to rip away another piece himself.

Something moved out at the front yard. Even a glimpse of that measured stride pegged it as Bea.

Eric flung him away. Colin's legs gave way again and spilled him backward, but this time he rolled clear and to his feet. Terri had dropped *away* from Eric's grasp, and the half-armored killer looked around... even with those bare patches he had more skein, more power, but he was alone.

Colin circled around toward the fence, cutting Eric off from fleeing on into the yard—and Eric twisted toward him a moment late, and pulled up, blocked. He spun away toward the street, and froze as Bea closed in there.

Eric fell back, staring around. Terri lay still, ten feet and more away from him... and her cocoon began to split apart.

Bea stepped slowly closer, arms spread wide ready to catch any dodge around her.

Eric crouched. Where his back hunched, the skein on his back billowed out, stretching and spreading into the beginnings of wings as he tensed for a spring upward.

A shape stabbed into him from across the yard, thrusting out from where Terri lay, catching his rising wing.

Terri had peeled her skein away, drawing it all into a lump around her hand and the long "finger" she'd sent out to her target—her mouth opened—

*"Gratshay kodo va."*

The scream came from them both. It ripped out from their depths, as the weapons they carried began to feed. Colin watched Eric's broken juggernaut flail and stumble, as Terri whimpered and fixed her gaze on her hand... and her single piece of skein fell away.

Eric's screams raged on, as Colin crept in with his eyes on Terri. Her hand looked pale in the night, and he heard her moan.

Eric roared to blast the screams away.

His head flew back, the roar stretched out, and the skein trembled and slid back from his face as his spasms of agony stilled. Back under his control.

Colin circled to guard Terri as the roar faded. Eric loomed over them, silent, covered in patchy armor that looked thicker than ever after feeding. The ragged remains of the wings trailed from his back as he turned.

His hand moved. The skein twisted into a blade.

He spun away, toward Bea, and lunged.

The massive figure slumped in midstride, toppled, as the boom of the gunshot split the night.

Then silence. Only the dimness around, and the still, limp figure sprawled before them.

Colin edged toward that shape. Where there had been a face, a head poking above the armor, Bea's shot had left... next to nothing.

Terri stared at the body, eyes wide enough to swallow the night. Her face began to tremble.

A voice out in the darkness called out, then another, and the silence peeled back. *They heard it too.*

He glanced over at Bea, where she stood keeping her gun on the remains of their enemy.

Suddenly she looked up at him. "You *had* to go after him. *Every time,* you just can't stop yourself."

"He had Terri—"

"Stop it," she snapped. "Don't pretend you care what your excuse is..."

Out around the blocks, the sounds gathered. So few, when so many more neighbors must be staying down behind cover, but slowly the voices multiplied. A car engine drew closer.

Bea shook her head. "Just get the skein out of here."

Colin reached down and... drew the skein off of Eric's body. It slid free without even a quiver—like pulling it up from any other patch of the ground.

The shape that had worn it really was just remains.

Then the cool touch of invisibility slid around Colin. He backed away and let the police cars surround the location, let the whole site push him away into the night.

# CHAPTER SEVENTEEN

# WHAT WE KEEP

Too many notes were crowded onto the second-hand laptop screen. Colin flipped it shut and stepped away from Zara's bedside, to let Clarence take his place there.

Jessie hung further back, by the jungle of flowers crowded onto the table. None of them spoke loudly, not with Terri's condition still hanging over them. Or just the chance that the doctors would notice how many visitors Zara had now.

Clarence began "I think you've got another family that's taking in roommates, and another who needs it for a while. Thanks to the blog."

A week in bed did nothing to weaken the warmth in Zara's voice. "I never thought that mention would help. It's good to be wrong."

"And, I heard another kid joking that we'd get more tourists if 'the ghost' were still haunting us."

The door rattled—Colin's head jerked toward it, but it was only some ordinary, unfamiliar woman slipping inside.

Jessie grumbled "Yeah, I'm sure that's why Colin tried calling him that before the end." She gave Colin a rueful grin.

He had to look away. But, Jessie meant well, and she had her own horrors to laugh off from before they rescued her.

Zara looked over at her. "And what's the latest on you leaving?"

"It'll still be a few days. Depending on things."

Silence settled around them. *Depending* on if Terri went into recovery, or even woke up again.

Colin said "We appreciate you being here, believe me."

Then the woman in the back said "You always say the next steps in rebuilding the town would be easy. I think I see why." Her hair had fallen over the edges of her eyes, but those eyes peered right through it at them all.

"Oh?" Zara said. "And why is that?"

From the careful way Zara watched this woman—and the way *she* eyed Colin—he placed her now. She had to be one of the reporters that kept poking around.

"Since you've got Colin here." Her hands were empty, but her fingers twitched as if she should have been taking notes. "He's the one who saw the whole crusade against Eric Rowe, and he got you through it all."

"Hey, all of that was just… happening, everywhere," Colin smiled. "We were all in the middle of it, so there was nobody who saw that much."

The word *saw* turned his mouth bitter. No, all those cops and victims never saw Eric coming.

"But you found your sister, after all these years. Yes, the famous Detective Simms did that, but wasn't it your work too?"

Jessie cut in "The tip came from a co-worker of Eric's, a man who later died for it—"

"Dennis Fields, I know."

She stepped closer to Colin, eyes searching him in a way that made him glad there wasn't one scrap of skein on him.

"But," she added, "you're trying to find the good in this, aren't you? You're sure Terri will wake up, and Rayo Hill will recover again—"

Zara said "If you're hoping for an interview, you should ask for one." Her smile was a soft warning.

"Yes, I've *heard* those statements. So much evasion about how Rowe just seemed like he was everywhere. But the man was so obsessed with Terri that you tried faking her death—how'd you get the hospital to go along with that?"

"With the cops' help," Colin said. At least Walters had agreed to cover that much up; Dr. Morton might still hang onto his position here.

One more person who'd be paying the price... Colin looked down, felt his hands trembling.

"But, you were part of the whole manhunt, weren't you?" she went on. "You volunteered to trap Rowe at that diner, and even made it out alive. So did you really just miss the time when Simms finally saved your sister for good?"

"Sounds like you should talk to Bea, then," he said. "If you can— she's been too busy for anyone—"

He heard his voice rising at that, louder than he wanted. When the door opened, he almost expected the attention.

"I'm sorry," the doctor warned, shifting his glasses as he stared at the five of them. "That's enough excitement for Zara now—let's give her a rest."

With a flurry of quick wishes for her, they filtered from the room.

Out in the corridor, Sergeant Jordan came wheeling toward them. Colin could feel the reporter's eyes tracking them all.

Clarence said "I should get back to my shop—"

The reporter stepped in front of Colin. "The truth now: was Eric Rowe really *everywhere?*"

He faced down that hungry gaze. "It seemed like it at the time."

"They talk about him having some unstoppable, bulletproof body armor—that nobody can identify, or find. Or are the police just that incompetent?"

"There's no need for accusations. A killer like Eric... who could have known?"

Then he had to turn away, to hide what had to be on his face. *We knew, we let him keep his secrets and kill so many of us...*

"Nothing, I guess," she snapped. "Is that why our 'hero' here ended up chanting broken prayers and telling everyone it *was* a ghost?"

From the corner of his eye he saw Jessie glaring at them both. At least Jordan was keeping quiet.

She went on "I guess that happens when you see so much death you can't count—"

*"Andy Anderson.*

*"Leo Tozer.*

*"Officers Alan Ling and Frank Stone.*

*"Officers Jane Walton and Sebastian Rosa.*

"You have to get them right, if you want to even try reporting this," Colin added through his teeth. "Who was next, do you know that one? *Do you?"*

"Uh..." She flushed, looked at the ground. "I'm sorry. I'm... trying to do you all a favor, your town could use..." Her voice died away.

Colin bit back the name *Joe Martin Senior,* and tried to ease his ragged, angry breathing back to normal.

Then a voice came in behind him. A bright, free sound buoyed up by its own good news:

"Terri's awake again. You wanted to see her?" The nurse's smile could have lit the whole corridor.

Jessie laughed *"Do* we? Zara—" She and Clarence rushed for Zara's door, and the reporter slipped along behind them.

Something rose up in Colin's chest, a great flood of *too much,* everything they'd won and lost and how the whole world just changed again...

He staggered away, away toward the exit.

Jordan rolled up behind him. "Not surprised either, are you? Go on, you go get some air."

Colin tried to answer, but Jordan was already spinning his chair around, and the words wouldn't come. Instead he scrambled away.

* * *

The walk led him on and on, until he felt sweat soaking into his bandages, until he felt Terri's recovery shaking down from faith into solid fact inside him. Until he reached the ruin of the Vargas House.

The street was still too quiet, from behind its remaining walls—he caught more bird voices than human ones. He picked his way over the wood and dust and fragments strewn over the floor.

A scattering of books lay among them, and he gathered those out of the rest, setting them aside in a stack. Just a bit of order in the confusion here, when nobody had come to start on really cleaning this up.

Or almost nobody. He looked at the yellow markers and lines of string lying around it—the first look of the inspectors that had broken down the damage here. *Could we rebuild it? How much* should *we, when it's not the historical Matt Vargas House anymore?*

There was no way to rebuild the *lives.*

He squeezed his eyes shut and felt the trembling rise in him again. How many of those deaths were because *they* kept silent about what was killing them—

Colin forced himself forward to a walk. Do the next thing, right.

Deep into a pile of wreckage he reached, and brought out a flood of skein. He looked around, saw two of the original pillars Eric had split, lying together under chunks of ceiling, in a heap behind the inspectors' sign: "Hazard – Unstable."

One skein-powered kick sent the timbers flying, had them crashing against the wall and let the rubble grumble and settle.

The birds went silent. He drew back his fist, reined in the urge to smash more, more.

"You're not with Terri."

Bea stood behind him, watching him. Her face was more still than he'd ever seen it, unreadable.

"No, but we talked with her all week. I knew she'd pull through...
No, I *had* to believe it..."

He stared at her, searched her face as if those eyes could make
sense of the whirling inside him.

"I mean, we could have done so much more for her with the
skein—there must be *some* uses that are safe. Or ways we could have
kept more people alive, if we'd shown them about invisibility and all
the rest. But instead we..."

"If we told anyone," she said, "we could end up with more people
captured and fed into making more skein. And that's just one way the
death toll could have been so much higher. We made our choices toward bringing this to a clean end, and sure enough Terri's
recovering."

He glared at her. Of course Bea was *so sure* she was right... *and
now she's the town hero who finally took Eric down...*

But that vicious little thought faded, and he saw pain flickering in
her eyes too.

He said "It's just *so many* dead. Because you kept the secret—" He
stopped, tried again. "No, because I trusted you, even when I tried
something else and it all blew up, I always came back to trusting you,
I still do... We stopped Eric because of Terri, Zara, the police, Hoyle,
but you always, I'll always believe in you... but still, Leo and...
and..." His voice crumbled in a sob.

Then her arms were around him. As a survivor, a friend, and then
closer. Until the pain had passed.

*****

*Keep reading for a look at the Spellkeeper Flight series in:*

The High Road

# from THE HIGH ROAD

This time it couldn't be hide-and-seek.

Nine-year-old Mark Petrie trotted across the grass when he saw Angie break from the trees and run toward the park's edge. The way her father had dragged her out of the park that afternoon, he'd thought he'd never see her there again.

So he went straight after her. He barely gave a glance back to the picnic table where his uncle was arguing about that "politics" stuff with his grumbling friends, their dinner still not unpacked.

When the grass changed to hard street-side sidewalk under their feet, Angie glanced back at him, her face just level with his. "I'm not stopping. I'm not waiting for him to catch me."

"Your dad? But we were only—"

She rushed on up the street, dodging between the scattered people in her path. Mark followed her red hair in the deepening twilight, still trying to work out why Mr. Dennard—a cop, as much a hero as any of Angie's other relatives she talked about—would have turned so angry at their playing with some of the family's old coats and belts.

Mark twisted around an old couple and their yapping dog, trying to keep Angie in sight. He passed sizzling burgers at the food stand, and his stomach clenched, reminding him the day was late and his uncle had been putting off their dinner. He tried to hold the emptiness down by thinking of the fun they'd had that afternoon—

Playing *Defend Sha Ta Ruath*—wherever that was—and letting their make-believe tell him *anything* could be about to happen—

But he was just hungry, and confused.

They reached the street corner at the edge of Rosewood Park's huge block, before Angie slowed and looked around.

"Where're you going? What happened?" he asked as he reached her side.

"I have something to ask my mom." She started across the street.

The word froze Mark a moment and he had to scramble to catch up again. Angie was going to her mother, after... how had she said it once, that mothers could run out on you? He still remembered the pain in her voice then, like Angie was better off with her gone.

She glanced over at him and added, "This is the way? If we keep going it's easy to hit Heat Street?"

"You mean Heath Avenue? The rich place? I think so."

She only moved faster now, with the sidewalk clear of park-goers and only the thinner evening crowds to weave through. Streetlights glowed along their way, just starting to stand out as night deepened, drawing the line between them and the stream of cars on their left.

By the second block, the sidewalk was even clearer. Now and then Mark passed people wrapped in scattered conversations, wreathed in cigarette smoke that added to the stench of car exhausts. Even some of the summer laughter he'd been hearing around the park seemed to thin away, while the air cooled and his feet hurt. Again and again, he saw the people Angie raced past turning to look at her flight.

Mark had lost count of the blocks they'd traveled before he managed to catch her arm. "It's getting dark. You can't just—"

"He said," and she spat the words at him like a weapon, "Dad said Grandpa died in a crazy-house! But he was my *mom's* father, Dad must be wrong, he has to be lying about him—"

She stopped, looked around the street. She must have seen something behind Mark, because she slipped from his slack grip and
twisted away, heading up a side street, out of sight of the main road.

Mark scrambled after her, his thoughts pounding harder than his
feet. The way Angie always talked, all her games about her family and
its exploration of Sha Ta Ruath, and its soldiers and leaders and all the
rest, and now her father said the things she *lived* for only ended in
something awful?

*At least he's not in jail like* my *dad,* came an even darker thought.
*And her mother's alive.*

The air felt colder now. They trotted past a construction barrier in
the street and on through the shadow of a tall brick shape, and their
feet sounded louder as the noise of cars fell away behind them.

The buildings pressed closer here, but a block ahead Mark could
see the skeleton of a half-finished building silhouetted against the
night. His nose itched at the construction dust in the air.

"Mark—" Suddenly Angie was turning back, toward him, past
him.

He couldn't see what she had, only lines of darker brick pooling
shadows into the slightly-paler street ahead. But that dimness, and the
street traffic sounds so faded away behind them, brought a new shiver
to his skin as he followed. Her footfalls were slower than they'd been
all night. Hushed.

Then—

"You just keep going."

Growling right in front of them, appearing from around a corner, a
huge man with some kind of black cap and a snarl of teeth flashing—

Angie, stumbling a step to put herself between Mark and the
stranger they were backing away from—

Dim streets, alone, but the cars droning by not so far away, *peo-*
*ple—*

The man took a step toward them. His arm reached out.

"HELP!" Mark yelled, with all the power his lungs had.

The next second, the big man had an ugly, blocky tunnel of a *gun* barrel pointed at them.

"Now you done it," he grated. "Wrong night for that. So you keep your holes shut or..."

*Don't look at the gun,* Mark told himself, feeling his heart stampeding, trying to tear his chest apart. If he looked to the side he could see Angie staring around, and another man—with the same kind of black cap over his scalp—moving up from where they had been headed, with a knife in his hand. Dust, so much dry, dead dust filling the air.

The gun tilted upward, relaxing the threat for a moment, and the man behind it grinned at their helplessness and lumbered toward them.

Then the gun swung higher as something yanked that arm toward the sky and a shape that had closed in behind the gunman's back twisted, spun, and sent the big man slamming to the pavement.

The gun clattered away. The man with the knife swore and broke into a run toward them, only to duck away inside a door as their rescuer reached inside his coat.

Angie gasped "Dad—" and there was awe in her voice.

Detective Dennard roared, "Just *go!*"

His tone, there was something wrong, like it was too fierce to fit inside his throat. And his hand drew back from his gun holster and brushed the belt at his waist...

In the next heartbeat, Angie's hand had locked onto Mark's arm and she pulled him into a run. His feet flung him along the pavement with her, toward the open streets. But he still stole a glance back, for a glimpse at her father chasing after the other thug.

Except Mr. Dennard was gone.

They ran. Ran through the night, forcing already-aching legs to carry them, with nerves on fire from the danger they'd brushed up against. In the rush of his heaving lungs, Mark at first missed the booming sound far, far behind them, until he realized it had spread and cascaded into a wild chorus of gunshots.

Blocks later they met a police car screaming toward the sound, and their shouts brought the cops over and let Mark gasp out a few words of what they'd seen. As he did, he realized Angie's father was closing in on them, as if he'd been only a few steps behind.

Angie flung herself into her father's arms without a word, or a single sob. Mark could only stand back, struggling for breath and watching them.

"*Listen* to that!" one of the uniforms said, raising his voice over the gunfire. "There ain't enough backup in the city to get me in there. That's got to be more than one gang killing each other—and you almost walked in right when something set them off?"

*Almost* walked in? Right, Mark thought, the three of them must have been blocks away from where the shots had sounded like they'd started. They had to have been.

Then Detective Dennard said "I… don't think I can be a cop anymore."

He kept his face bent over his daughter as he said those words. But Mark heard something in his voice, something that sounded too bitter to be the fury he'd shown before. Was that—shame?

Mark felt the two pieces in his head, refusing to go together. Angie's father had been running with them while the gangs started shooting far behind them… but that voice now… he couldn't make them fit.

No matter how he tried.

*   *   *<br/>*   *   *<br/>*   *   *

*Dammit, Angie…*

Mark threw his weight on the pedals, legs pumping, fighting for any extra distance he could get from the gang closing in behind him. Through the rasp of his breathing, the Blades' pounding feet sounded like only inches from his heels. All because even on his first day of work he'd *had* to stop for her call.

The alley's end loomed up ahead, and he squeezed the back brake to slow and skid around the poster-covered brick corner. He heard one shrill "So what's in the box?" before he swung out into the Anchor Street crowd, safe.

Easy as that.

Swerving narrowly around two lumbering dockworker types, Mark lurched to a stop to answer their shouts with a breathless, "Sorry, sorry," before walking the bike on. His breathing settled as he worked through the crowd, maneuvering along a sidewalk full of people, probably some afternoon shift letting out—one of the thickest crowds in Lavine city. Darkening clouds thinned the light around them, and his sweat swam in the air, making him shiver in the growing cold.

Tired, but safe. "Beats telling Gene my new phone got me killed," he muttered.

But what was the point of him learning every street in town if he couldn't use the time he saved on a message run to stop in at Angie's—or when she wasn't home, pull over to take her call? That bit of slack in his day was supposed to be the good thing about this job, he'd figured on that benefit ever since his junk Chevy had died and started him thinking of options besides waiting tables.

Didn't matter; the danger was over. Just because it was the Blades again, or they'd been near Angie's, didn't mean the gang had any reason to keep after either of them.

He glanced back again, and his knuckles tightened on the handlebars. The punks were still behind him.

They were just strolling along, some twenty feet back. Two silent figures with their leathers and black do-rags, already drawing uneasy glances from the workers they passed.

*Still on me? But only two of them, where'd* Rafe *go?* Mark stared up and down the street, trying to think if they'd really bother staying with him much longer. Or, he could put his knowledge of the street routes to use again and lose them, if he could find one gap in the crowd.

At that moment a car pulled out from its parking space, leaving a hole at the edge of traffic, and Mark leaped forward. A woman shouted as he twisted his bike past her, and he barely swerved clear of a wrought-iron lamppost, but he broke through onto the street. Free.

Once his tires dropped off the curb he hopped onto the saddle and began pedaling, finally able to move. *Faster, faster, I'm lightning, I'm a bullet train, I'm the damn Sha Ta Ruath Express if it has one...* He swept down the narrow space between the honking rush of traffic and the parked cars, eyes alert for any door that might pick just that moment to swing open into his path.

The light ahead turned red, but instead of slowing he only banked for the corner and angled onto the cross-street's sidewalk to rush along the new angle. But just as he turned he saw the black-capped rider away to his left, roaring down at the intersection on his Harley.

The crowds wouldn't last... that motorcycle would get closer by the second... so, he could stop while he still had some witnesses and hope he could brazen it out without the Blades remembering his face later. Unless the gang really had been lurking near Angie's because after all these years—

Besides, he *knew* the streets. Another twist of the handlebars brought him up a side street, with a parting glance back that showed he'd have a few moments out of the biker's view. The way ahead was just as empty and riddled with alleys as he remembered, and he arced to the side and ducked into one.

With a van parked squarely in its middle. A battered red barricade.

"Of *course,*" he spat, and jumped down, trotting with the bike toward the narrow gap even as he heard an engine thundering in behind him. He heaved the front wheel up, twisting the handlebars to make as narrow an angle as he could, and pressed in... a tip just catching and scraping on the graffiti... then his heart restarted as it squeezed free.

The low box bungeed over his back tire wobbled and almost came loose, but it didn't matter. Now he had only open space ahead.

The Harley's roar rattled off the buildings behind him, dropping to a lower growl as it crept up the alley like a prowling beast. Mark leaned back out of sight, against the van's rear, listening for any pause in that motor... but it only crawled slowly by and finally gathered force and roared away.

He drew in a deep breath and let it seep out. Even in the thick stormy air, he could smell exhaust from the van, still *fresh*—would the alley have been clear just a minute earlier? He reached down to tighten the bungees around his box. At least his old green Raleigh could wriggle past where their motors couldn't, and foot soldiers wouldn't bother chasing him for long. Just as he'd thought, he'd ridden rings around them.

"Mark?"

The voice from around the van was low, worse than a shout: the calmness itself told him who it had to be.

Rafe went on "Still running errands for small bills? I always said you need someone who's got your back."

Mark's fists clenched. *We're a year out of high school, and he still thinks he can make me one of his thugs?*

*I can't let him rattle me.* Rafe couldn't have seen him duck back here; he had to be bluffing, calling blindly up each corner to see if he'd get an answer.

Then Rafe spoke again. "*This* time, the best place you can be is away from Joe Dennard. This won't stop until it comes out the far side of ugly."

Dennard. The night of the gang war. Suddenly that was all Mark could think of—even after ten years, after most of the Blades who'd lived through it must be dead or in prison. What could Rafe and the rest of them know, or *care,* about what might have happened back then?

But if they did—Mark found he couldn't breathe. If the gang was after Dennard—and they'd spotted Mark for being outside Angie's—were they already closing in on the father and the daughter too?

Then he heard a footstep, then another, the sound receding as Rafe walked away, up the pavement, to be swallowed up by the sounds of the city. He hadn't seen Mark after all.

Mark stayed flattened against the van for five more long, controlled breaths. Then he crouched down to look under it—he hadn't been so well-hidden, after all, not if anyone stopped to look for his feet—but saw nobody lingering out there.

His hands were trembling as he started the bike up the alley. At least his tires were silent as they built up speed, not like running feet would be. But he had to go faster, faster, get some space to stop and call the Dennards.

*"Bastard!"*

The sudden yell twisted his head back, to see the other two Blades charging up the alley at him. He flung himself forward.

Then the handlebar lurched and tipped, and he wrenched it blindly to keep it clear of the wall, clinging for balance, still looking back at the Blades... seeing the bungeed-down box working loose from the rack...

*It's dangling over to foul the wheel—*

Somehow, somehow, he kept the bike steady as he leaned forward and kicked back wildly, then felt the box break free. He scrabbled for the pedals again, fighting to build speed and hoping the gang would duck away from the falling box—or even stop to tear it open to discover the sample suit coat some designer had been so damn eager to have delivered.

*Push!* The street ahead still looked empty, no barriers to him, but also no witnesses if they caught him. Still, the thought of racing blindly into the lane made him twist, sweeping around the corner onto the sidewalk past a flash of red hair that had to be—

He heard the curses first, so fierce he had to steal a glance back. In that one instant he saw two recycling bins falling by the corner in a mess of green and blue and strewn metal. And a door, closing. Angie must have already ducked through it after knocking the bins into the Blades' path.

Mark had to imagine the rest as he powered up the street: how the first Blade might twist around the bins, but maybe the other would slip on some of the scattered cans… his mind kept supplying the sound of bowling pins crashing down together, but of course what mattered were the seconds Angie had bought him to get up to speed at last. And that she had spotted the bins and the open door in the one split instant he'd raced past her. Of course.

He rushed past block after block, keeping to the clearer side streets and zigzagging between them when he could. As he worked on picturing the evening streets' layout he remembered his new cell's GPS tracker app; of course, when he had broken off his call with her to run from the Blades, Angie could have used her own cell to find him. That could have given her some little warning that he was doubling back here, enough to set her trap.

With that guess in mind, it was only a matter of time before he settled onto the bike lane on Garcetti, and looked back to see a motorcyclist wearing a familiar denim jacket and red helmet moving up from behind him.

The old relief at seeing her was colored with an odd stain of envy, now that Angie's nimble Kawasaki had held up while his Chevy's breakdown had sent him back to pedaling. *Not that that matters, if the gang is hunting her father.* He pulled over to wait.

As his feet touched the pavement he felt his head spin, tension suddenly squirming up and down his muscles and turning them to water. The Blades had almost… and Rafe had…

A sudden thought made him burst out laughing, sagging against the handlebars.

Angie pulled up beside him, frowning at him as he fought to get a full breath. "Mark? Did I miss something?" Concern softened her voice more than usual.

"Just realized," he gasped out, trying to show her he hadn't lost his mind. "Even without your help, they... they lost that chase years— years!—before they met us..."

Her eyes narrowed suspiciously. "And why is that?"

He hauled in some air, and tried to say it properly. "When the first punks started their 'club.' Motorcycles couldn't squeeze through where I did, and runners couldn't keep up... but e-e-ever since they named themselves the Blades..." The laughs broke through again and he collapsed over the bike.

A moment later he heard her finish "...they wouldn't dare chase you on skates!" and break out laughing herself.

When they both had their breath back, Mark drew himself up, his lanky frame looming over her compact one. The one friend he'd kept by him, the girl who'd gone from severe pneumonia to winning track records. The girl who still held on to even bigger dreams, if she could get away safe from what he'd just learned.

He made himself meet her eyes. "Except... it was Rafe Martinez himself. And when they spotted me, I think it was because they were watching your place, and... he said they're after your father. I mean, if they finally found out he was there, and he really did know something about how the gang war started—"

"He threatened Dad—and you think it's for *this* thing again?" Her simple features tightened in frustration. "For the last time, give it a rest." She spun away, glaring up at the blackening clouds. "And it's been ten years. What could Rafe 'find out' that can have dug all of that up?"

"I don't know. I don't even know why he warned me; I've already turned down enough of his damn *offers*. But what I *think*—"

Mark stopped and bit back the flare of anger; he should have known arguing this with her wouldn't be easy. He met her gaze and settled his voice to its gentlest, steadiest tone.

"I think *something* had them waiting around your place, when I rode by it, and they even knew me, all of them. And that means they'll be back for you again, if you stay around here." He stopped there; no need to say again how he still couldn't forget the fury Dennard's face had held that night—or the shame after, then and when he turned in his badge, after weeks of bloody inter-gang warfare.

But Angie must have guessed where his doubts led, because she sighed "But years back—while he was saving our lives!—he was a block away when the 66s opened up on the Blades, and yet somehow it's *his* fault? No, this has to be about what he is now. If they can control the park's guard, they control the park, control the drugs and God-knows-what else they can do there. And they want me as a way to get at him."

She glanced around the sidewalk traffic, as if the gang might already be creeping through the crowd toward them. In just moments, Angie had it all figured out—without blaming the man they both wanted to trust. And he had to admit, her answer did make more sense.

A car honked on the street beside them.

"Mark?" She was looking back toward him.

"Yeah," he sighed. "Look, maybe it doesn't matter what they want from him. If they were at your place, they want to use you against him, but you're leaving the city anyway—and you still are, right? Staying isn't supporting him, it just gives him more he has to watch out for. And don't think about putting your plans on hold, that's one more way the gang wins."

"I... oh of *course* I'm leaving, I know that. I should like it more when you're right." Her head sank, then straightened a second later. "But you both have to keep yourselves safe, too, or I'll just be right back here." And she grinned.

"Sure, *anything* to keep that from happening." The joke came as a reflex, while his thoughts scrambled to catch up to how she'd be safe again, free, gone. He added, "If they're watching your place, I can round up some reinforcements to help while you pick up a few things—"

"No, I should just call Dad and go, and work the rest out later. Besides, *you* still have to explain to your boss about that package. And aren't you seeing Grace tonight?" she added as she started her engine.

*That's over; it's Lucy now.* But he didn't say that, only smiled back and dug out his phone as he pulled onto the sidewalk. He only had to keep the smile up a few more seconds, and then she was gone.

*She's gone off to learn to fly planes, and when I'm trying to show her I'm the fastest courier on a bike, I get shot down.* "Nice going," he muttered as he dialed.

# ABOUT THE AUTHOR

*"Whispered spells for breathless suspense."*

Ken Hughes dreams of dark alleys and the twenty-seven ways people with different psychic gifts might maneuver around each corner. He grew up on comics and adventures before discovering Stephen King and Joss Whedon, and he's written for Mars mission proposals and medical devices, making him an honorary rocket scientist and brain surgeon. Ken is a Global Ebook Award-nominated urban fantasy novelist, creator of the Shadowed Steps series, the Spellkeeper Flight, the Mirrorman, and many more series of supernatural thrills.

Don't get him started on puns.

Find more books and join the Overview newsletter at:

KenHughesAuthor.com.

www.ingramcontent.com/pod-product-compliance
Lightning Source LLC
Chambersburg PA
CBHW021341250626
47155CB00002B/731